CARVED
IN BONE

A Henry Rios Novel

MICHAEL NAVA

Carved in Bone
A Henry Rios Novel
Copyright © 2019 by Michael Nava. All rights reserved.
First Edition 2019

Hardcover ISBN-13: 978-1-7336091-0-4
Paperback ISBN-13: 978-1-7336091-1-1
Ebook ISBN-13: 978-1-7336091-2-8

Published by Persigo Press
584 Castro Street, #203
San Francisco, California, 94114
www.persigopress.com

For my husband, George

*"In your cheek
One day, appeared the true
shape of your bone,
No longer padded."*

—Thom Gunn, *Lament*

*"There's a dance pavilion in the rain
All shuttered down... "*

—Johnny Mercer, *Early Autumn*

*"There is a secret tie between
the wound and the weapon."*

—Carl Jung

My special thanks to my friend,
Matt Coles, who gave me the
plot to this book forty years ago.
Better late than never, Matt.

1.

Eden Plain, Illinois, June 1971

MARCO CAUGHT HIS BREATH AND grunted, "Is that all you got?"

Bill lunged at the other boy, pile driving him onto the bed beneath a poster of a shirtless Jim Morrison in leather pants. Flailing wildly as Bill scrambled to pin him, Marco's hand smacked the wall and grabbed at the poster, ripping off a bit of Morrison's leg.

"Shit!"

Bill released him. Marco showed him the crinkled paper.

"Dude! I can't believe you did that."

The poster was Bill's pride and joy but his father, when he had first seen it, had looked at it for a long time, and then at Bill. He said nothing but a hardness in his eyes demanded an explanation. Bill mumbled, "He's a rock and roll singer, Dad." His father replied, "You sure you want to keep that up there, son? People might get the wrong idea." Bill burned with shame but repeated, "He's just a singer." His father frowned and left. They hadn't spoken of it since but whenever Mr. Ryan entered his bedroom, the first thing he did was to pointedly glance at the poster, letting Bill know his explanation had not been convincing.

"It's your fault, squirt," Marco was saying. "You fight dirty."

"Don't call me squirt."

Bill was sensitive to the difference in their height, a gap that opened when they hit puberty and had only widened since then, so that he was now four inches shorter and twenty pounds lighter than his six foot, two-hundred-pound football playing friend. Marco looked old enough to buy beer without being carded. Bill was still a boy, kid brother cute, open-eyed, guileless and slender. Both his older brothers had played first string football at the high school they had all attended, but Bill was too small for the sport. He had earned his varsity jacket playing shortstop. At home games, he would scan the bleachers to see if his father had come, but more often than not, it was his mother, sitting alone, who waved at him. In Joe Ryan's opinion, baseball was, at best, a way to kill time until football season began. Football, his dad liked to say, that's a man's sport. Full stop.

Marco sneered, "Suck my dick."

Marco perched on the edge of Bill's bed, still holding Morrison's leg in his big hand. Bill was

2

standing, his back to the window. It framed a freshly mowed backyard in a new housing tract at the edge of a small town that was becoming a suburb of Chicago's suburbs.

Shirtless and sweaty, they smelled like teenage boys whose hygienic practices, casual at the best of times, steeply declined in the summer. They had been wrestling like this since they were seven years old. They were eighteen now, recent high school graduates, spending a final boyhood summer together before the autumn took them their separate ways. Marco was bound west to play football for a second-tier team at a state university in a neighboring state. Bill was headed to the University of Illinois at Springfield to study business. Bill felt their coming separation like a constant, faint ache in his chest and Marco, too, sometimes seemed to be touched by the same sadness. But, having no vocabulary except the roughhouse language of American boys, they never spoke of this feeling of impending loss.

Suck my dick.

They had first flung the taunt back and forth when their penises were little pink worms with no minds of their own and the words were nothing more than another insult they had picked up from Bill's older brothers, like *retard* and *spaz*. But, while those words remained in their vocabulary of abuse—now supplemented by *asshole* and *shithead*—they rarely hurled *suck my dick* at each other and when they did, like

3

now, the words seemed to have been infiltrated by the faintest note of questioning.

Since that morning two years earlier when Bill had awakened with semen-saturated BVDs and fading images of a naked Marco in his head, his feelings for Marco had sailed past best friendship into a swamp of confusion, desire and shame. On double dates—always arranged by Marco and his girlfriend of the moment because Bill was officially "shy" around girls—he struggled to keep his attention on Patti or Nancy or Suzy, but always it returned to Marco, to the hollow at the base of his throat, to his surprisingly slender fingers and the heavy curl of black hair that no matter how often he pushed it back, flopped to the center of his forehead. To Marco's eyes, so dark they seemed black but were, upon closer examination, a dark warm brown and lit from a depth that seemed to be the source of the mystery of Marco Ferreira.

That there could be any mystery at all about the boy he had known all his life confounded Bill. The casual horseplay they had engaged in forever had become freighted with meaning for Bill. The briefest brush of skin against skin when they wrestled was like the striking of a match that flared into yearnings in his chest and belly both exciting and terrifying. At night, the image of Marco showering formed in his head—his thickly muscled legs and chest brushed with dark hair, heavy cock bobbing in the bushy pubic patch, and the high, round butt—and Bill's hand groped for his cock. He jerked himself off quickly before self-loathing overcame his arousal but then lay there, his hand coated with semen, hating himself for what he wanted, but helpless against the want.

And this, more than wet dreams or jerking off to Marco's image, was how Billy Ryan knew he was a queer. Sometime after his pubic hairs sprouted and his father had haltingly given him the talk about sex, Marco had become mysterious to him in the same way he understood girls to be mysterious to other boys. It wasn't the mystery of sex—that had been reduced to crude talk about blowjobs and hand jobs and fucking pussy and who would or would not put out. Something more than sex held the boys in thralldom to the girls. It was as if the girls held the answer to a question the boys had not even been aware existed until puberty when the scales fell from their eyes and they saw that without a girl they were and would remain fundamentally incomplete. The question for them was: who am I? And the answer, blasted through speakers in the gym at school dances or wafting through tinny car radios or on hi-fis in teenage bedrooms all over Eden Plains, Illinois, in the pop songs they all listened to, was: I am no one without you.

When Bill Ryan looked into Marco Ferriera's eyes, his heart lurched and he knew he was no one without Marco. The feeling sickened him. No one had had to say it, but to be a queer was so far beyond the pale of Eden Plains, he was sure it would be better to be dead than to be that thing. More than once, he had considered steering his car into a tree or going off into the woods around the lake house with his dad's shotgun and blowing his head off. But he hadn't because apparently, he was a coward as well as a queer. Instead, Bill had tried to solve his problem by pushing Marco away when he grabbed him but Marco would not be deterred and, with his greater strength, he invariably pulled Bill into a roughhouse embrace. Only—and this is what really confused Bill—those embraces often seemed more like hugs than assaults, more affectionate than aggressive. It seemed to Bill, or was he only imagining it, that when they wrestled now, Marco pressed his body against Bill's a moment longer than he needed to and Marco's breath glanced his neck like a kiss. And once, when Bill dared to return the pressure of the embrace and look into Marco's eyes, he thought he saw an answering tenderness.

He thought he saw that tenderness now as he met Marco's eyes. The taunt— *Suck my dick*— which maybe wasn't a taunt after all, hung in the air between them, waiting for Bill to give the ritual reply, *You'd like that wouldn't you, fag?* But Bill had lost the power of speech as he gazed helplessly at Marco's olive-colored chest and his red gym shorts and his hairy legs and big, smelly feet. *Say something!* he told himself, his heart pounding in his chest, the air in the room suddenly thick and close. Then, as if in a dream, Bill took a tentative step closer to the bed, then another, until he was standing between Marco's splayed legs, so close to the other boy, he could feel the heat radiating from his skin. He dropped his gaze from Marco's eyes and waited for Marco to push him away but instead Marco closed his thighs around Bill's legs, skin against skin.

Bill met Marco's eyes. He saw fear and hope, heard Marco's anxious, stuttering breath, felt his warm flesh pressing his legs.

Then Marco whispered, "Go on Billy, do it. Suck my dick. Please."

It was the *please*, gentle, almost pleading, that convinced Bill Marco was serious. Still, he hesitated until Marco raised his hand, brushed it against Bill's arm and said, "It's okay, Billy. Don't be afraid. I won't tell anyone."

Marco parted his legs, hooked his fingers into the waistband of his shorts, lifted his butt off the bed and tugged the shorts to his feet, springing his thick, hard cock loose from its nest of wiry black hair. Bill had seen Marco's cock hundreds of times before in the gym showers but always with a furtive glance and never when it was hard. Now he studied Marco's cock and saw that the smooth head and veiny shaft and fuzzy balls were, like the rest of Marco's body, beautiful.

Nervously, Marco said, "Let me see yours."

The request startled him but then he

understood. Marco had exposed more than his cock, he had exposed his desire for another boy, and he needed assurance that it was what Bill wanted, too. Bill pushed down his shorts and briefs to his ankles and stood naked before his friend. The room, so familiar that Bill no longer even saw the objects that furnished it, seemed suddenly different, strange, as if it belonged to another boy. A boy who collected baseball cards and pretty rocks, who was pictured with his dad in a framed photograph holding up his catch after a day's fishing at the lake, who slept beneath a plaid coverlet and kept his baseball bats in an imitation elephant's foot umbrella stand. Not a boy who now sank to his knees, wrapped his fingers loosely around his best friend's cock and opened a mouth that had, until that moment, been used only for eating and speaking.

The slightly rancid smell of sweat and moist cotton and Marco drove him closer to the beautiful flesh, but then he hesitated. While he had often imagined himself in this very situation, about to take Marco's cock in his mouth, he assumed he would have to steel himself to the task to overcome what he had been taught was the inherent nastiness of everything "down there" male and female. Taught by his parents and the nuns and priests who had guided his education from kindergarten to graduation, taught with words and gestures and expressions in a thousand ways that the openings and appendages that lay below

8

the waist were disgusting and gross, the cause of man's fall and the occasion for sin, and to be used only for excretion or, out of sad necessity, for the making of babies.

Marco's fingers gently threaded his hair. Bill looked up and saw the uncertain grin and the soft, affectionate eyes.

"I want to do it to you too," Marco whispered in a thick voice.

Bill closed his eyes and took Marco's cock in his mouth. The taste was meaty, a little sour and salty, but it was not, as he had feared, disgusting. Rather, after the first shock of sensation, it seemed he tasted Marco not only with his mouth but his entire body and then not only with his body but his emotions as a wild excitement flushed his chest and turned his cock into steel. At that moment, all the proscriptions went out of his head. This is what he had wanted and, by some miracle, Marco had wanted it too, and now it was happening. He began to move his tongue and mouth around the steely thickness of Marco's flesh.

"Teeth," Marco warned softly.

Bill looked up and nodded, then returned to the licking and sucking. Marco gripped Bill's shoulders and stood up. He began to move his cock in and out of Bill's mouth and murmured, "That feels so good, Billy."

Bill struggled to breathe and once or twice pulled away with a cough and a gasp but then again took the other boy in his mouth, even as he blinked tears of exertion and spit dribbled from the corners of his mouth. Marco's pubic hair was surprisingly soft against Bill's face. He cupped his hands around Marco's butt and felt the flex of his glutes as Marco drove his cock into Bill's mouth. He experimentally let a finger trail into the crack of Marco's butt and lightly pressed it against his hole. Marco gasped and wiggled his butt and Bill's finger slipped into the dry heat of Marco's innards.

"Jesus, yeah," he mumbled. "Finger me."

His mouth stuffed with Marco's cock, his finger jammed into Marco's butt, Marco murmuring "feels so good baby, feels so good," Bill trembled with joy. Something half-thought and half-emotion passed through his mind, fragmentary and fleeting. He wasn't giving Marco a blowjob; he was making love to him with his mouth and his hands, expressing with his body everything in his heart. And he suddenly understood this feeling of love for Marco as he gave him pleasure was exactly what his father had told him sex was supposed to be like.

"Billy, I'm gonna..." was as far as Marco got before Bill felt the hot gush of semen fill his mouth. He swallowed convulsively as Marco stroked his hair and moaned his name.

Bill sat back on his haunches, wiped his mouth on the back of his hand and saw his father standing in the doorway.

"Dad—" he gasped.

His father's eyes were dark and terrible. As if blindly, his father grabbed a bat from the umbrella stand and strode across the room. In a moment, he was upon them. Bill's last glimpse of Marco was of the boy pulling up his shorts and running out of the room. Bill stumbled to his feet. His father swung the bat at him, catching him on the left side of his torso, slamming him to the floor. He lifted the bat over his head, his eyes still blank with fury.

"Daddy," Bill pleaded. "Daddy."

His father dropped the bat, hauled Bill to his feet and shoved him backwards against the window with such force the glass cracked.

"You do this shit in my house!" his father screamed. "Under my roof."

Bill, slumped beneath the window, his side bursting with pain, sobbed, "I'm sorry... I'm sorry."

His father, too, was crying, but, Bill thought much later, one of the many times he replayed the scene, had he had touched his father's tears, they would have burned his fingers.

"I don't know what you are," he father said hoarsely, "but you're not my son."

The window glass had cut him and he was bleeding. His side shrieked with pain. He saw his father grab the Morrison poster above his bed and rip it down. He stomped out of the room. Clutching his side, Bill staggered to his feet, took a few steps, collapsed on his bed and sank into darkness.

Every Saturday, the night nurse played Casey Kasem's Top 10 countdown on her transistor radio at the nurse's station. When he had first come to, after surgery, he heard Carole King singing *I hear the earth move under my feet...* This week she had been knocked off as number one by a song about Indians: *Cherokee people, Cherokee tribe, So proud to live, so proud to die.* Five weeks. That's how long he had been in the ward, long enough that the other six beds had turned over once, twice, three times. The broken ribs had begun to heal, the cuts to his back and shoulders from the glass had closed and the incision that marked where his spleen had been removed had gone from fiery red to pinched pink.

After the surgeon had inspected his handiwork, he asked a nurse, "Why is he still here? He can recover at home." The nurse murmured a long response of which Bill heard clearly only the words "family problems." The surgeon had cast a glance his way that Bill imagined was filled with revulsion. But then, he imagined that everyone who came near him knew all about the unspeakable thing he had done and was disgusted at having to breathe the same air as he did.

When he been returned to his bed after surgery and his mind was still scrambled by anesthesia, he had opened his eyes to see his father, wearing his work clothes, standing at the foot of the bed. Later, Bill thought he must have taken time off work to come to the hospital. He stood there for a long time, not speaking, not moving, his hands in fists at his side. His eyes were distant, as if he did not recognize the figure on the bed at whom he was staring. After a few minutes, he bowed his head, a gesture at once helpless and dismissive.

"Dad," Bill croaked. "I'm sorry."

His father turned and walked away.

No one else in his family came to see him. Not his mother or his two older brothers. Not even his grandmother who called him her treasure. Certainly not his tobacco chewing, woodworking grandfather. No one from his class. Not Marco. Not anyone except Father O'Neill from St. Philomena's, a short, stocky, bald man with hairy knuckles that Marco used to joke proved priests jacked off.

The priest pulled up a chair, touched Bill's arm and asked, not unkindly, "How are you doing there, Bill?"

Bill, who had known only the detached touch of doctors and nurses, burst into sobs he could not control.

The priest let him cry, murmuring, "It's okay. Everything's going to be okay."

"No," Bill said. "It won't be okay. My mom won't even come to see me."

"You put your family through a lot. People

know what happened." He sighed. "I've been talking to your folks. Trying to get them to take you back."

For an instant, his heart stopped; for, in his panic and terror, he had never actually imagined that his family would not, somehow, find a way to bring him home.

"What do you mean, Father?"

"Listen to me, Bill," the priest was saying. "This is a small town and the people here, they have ideas about things, about what's right and wrong, that they aren't going to change." His voice dropped to a whisper. "So, let me ask you, are you a homosexual?"

It was a question, not an accusation, and asked neutrally, but the word scalded him.

When intrusive thoughts of a naked Marco had first begun to trouble Bill's sleep, he had gone to the city library, a place he rarely visited. He furtively searched the card catalog for the subject headings *Homosexual* and *Homosexuality* and then the cross-references to *Deviance* and *Abnormal Psychology*. Too fearful even to write down the call number of the half dozen books he had found, he instead committed them to memory. He went into the stacks and pulled the books off the shelves, one at a time. He hid them in other sections so that if anyone approached while he was reading, he could shove the book back on the shelf and pretend to be looking for works on baseball or gardening. The books told him homosexuals were mentally ill creatures who preyed upon boys or haunted public toilets where they tried to force themselves on unsuspecting men. They were easily recognized by their physically weak and hairless bodies and lisping speech. Some wore makeup or even, in extreme cases, paraded around in women's clothes. They were deceitful, cowardly and, while oversexed, incapable of love. Emotionally stunted if not deformed, they could be found working in female occupations such as hairdressers or interior decorators because, fundamentally, they were not men at all, but women in men's bodies, freaks of nature.

Although Bill failed to recognize himself in these descriptions, he could not deny that he shared the one defining characteristic of these creatures: a sexual attraction to other men. And if that was true then, even if all the other particulars did not match up, was he not also, unavoidably, homosexual?

"Yes," he whispered to the priest. "I'm sorry."

The priest sighed. "I'm sorry too, Bill. I had hoped this was just a mistake."

"I don't want to be this way," Bill said. "Can you help me?"

The priest shook his head. "I've met other men like you," he said. "What you have is a mental illness, like being retarded or schizophrenic. There's no cure."

Bill reached back into the memory of his

confirmation classes to ask, "Can't you absolve me?"

"I can absolve your actions," the priest said, "but I can't change who you are. All you can do is abstain from that kind of behavior."

"I swear I'll never do anything like that again."

"That's good," the priest said, "but it's too late for you here, Bill. Everyone knows."

"I'm going away, to college."

The priest looked away for a moment. "Your folks aren't going to pay for your college now."

"What?" Bill asked, despairingly.

"You're eighteen now, legally an adult. Your folks aren't responsible for you anymore. Maybe it would be best if you just left."

"Leave?" he asked, panicked. "Where would I go?"

"There are places where you'd find other people like you. The big cities. Chicago, New York. There are a lot of you in San Francisco."

Then he understood why the priest had come. "My parents sent you."

"Your mother," O'Neill said. "Your dad's not going to let you back into the house. Your grandma wanted to take you in, but your grandfather said no."

"But my dad, he visited me."

"I know. He came to confession because he knows it was wrong to hit you. I told him as a penance he had to come and tell you he was sorry.

He tried, but he couldn't. Your dad's a good man, but he has his limits."

"But he's my dad," Bill said, helplessly.

"He's a man, first, and what you've done..."

The words trailed off and they sat in silence for a minute.

"What happened to Marco?"

The priest frowned. "That should be the last thing on your mind, Bill Ryan."

"Where is he?" Bill insisted.

"He has family in Massachusetts," O'Neill replied. "That's all I'm going to tell you. Don't even think about looking for him. You've done enough harm to him."

"I didn't mean to. I..." He shut his eyes against the words he heard himself speak. "I love him."

The priest said quietly, but with complete conviction, "If you loved him, you wouldn't have perverted him."

"But he wanted—"

"Enough," the priest snapped. "I didn't come here to argue with you."

The kindliness was gone from the priest's face, replaced by a mask of coldness that did not conceal the fear in his eyes. Bill realized the priest was afraid of him, as if he were the bearer of a loathsome, contagious disease. A wave of nausea choked him. He wanted to shout, *You know me, Father! I'm Billy Ryan, Joe and Margaret's youngest, Tom and Matt's brother. I took first*

17

communion from you. I served you at the eight o'clock Mass. You coached me in Little League.

"What should I do, Father?"

"Leave," the priest said crisply. "You should leave."

He signed out of the hospital in borrowed clothes because he had been brought there in shorts and socks soaked with blood. The pants were too long and the shoes pinched, but the discomfort they caused was nothing compared to the skin-crawling misery he felt when he stepped out into the bright morning and saw his mother sitting in the Buick. She glanced at him when he got in and, without a word, began to drive.

Usually when it was just the two of them in the car, they playfully argued over whether to turn the radio dial to his rock station or her easy listening one. It was one of the many jokes they shared that confirmed his status not only as her baby but her favorite. Now, the radio was off. On the backseat was a suitcase and his varsity letter jacket. She drove down Main Street, past the two- and three-story nineteenth-century buildings that housed everything from the Elks Club and the Woolworth's to the head shop where he had bought the Jim Morrison poster. She turned left on Cedar where the trees thinned, the sidewalks got grittier and the only businesses were bars and pawn shops. She pulled up in front of the bus station and parked.

"Mom. I'm sorry."

She turned sharply to face him and said, "Everyone knows, Bill. We'll never live this down."

The hot tears rolled down his face. "I'm sorry, I'm sorry."

In a softer voice, she said, "I know. I don't know what else to do, Billy. I can't bring you home. Your father would..."

"Kill me? I wish he had."

"Oh, Bill," she said, with a sad shake of her head that could have meant yes or no. She dug into her purse and pulled out an envelope. "Take this."

There was money inside. "Mom," he said brokenly.

She was crying now too. "Go on, Bill," she said softly.

After that, there was nothing to do but climb out of the car, grab his jacket and the suitcase and head into the station.

2.

San Francisco, November 1984

SPRINTED UP A DIRT PATH covered with pine
needles and brown leaves to one of the paved
roads crisscrossing Buena Vista Park. Edging
one side of the road was a stone, retaining wall.
In the gutter between wall and road were chunks
of marble and granite, some bearing part of
a date or a name. These were shards of grave
stones salvaged from the cemeteries emptied at
the end of the last century when the city had
claimed their space for its growing population.
I veered off the road onto another dirt path and
galloped up wooden steps that led to the summit.
On wobbly legs, I walked around a circle of grass
where two couples—male and female and male
and male—glanced at me for a moment before
returning their attention to the view.

Veteran's Day, 1984. Ronald Reagan, just
reelected president, said it was morning in
America, but in San Francisco where I shared the
sidewalks with men who looked like the unburied

dead, the mourning was altogether different. As for me, still shaky three months out of rehab after nearly drinking myself to death, I often couldn't tell which moment my life had struck, morning or midnight.

Through a break in the thick surrounding woods, the city unfurled itself below me. Low-lying gray, dun, and pearl-white buildings covered undulating hills beneath the achingly blue autumn sky. Just beyond the hilly neighborhoods, a single red-orange tower pierced a heavy veil of incoming fog: the Golden Gate. A bird keened in the oaks above me, a fog horn moaned in the bay, the low swoosh of traffic drifted up from the streets. Wild roses splattered red blossoms on the hillside. The air was fragrant with the scent of leaves and earth and ocean.

San Francisco at its most beguiling; the kind of view that either broke or mended hearts. As for me, suicidal drinking followed by bare-knuckled sobriety had shattered my emotional gauges. I knew if I stood there one moment longer I would burst into tears, so I jogged to another clearing where the woods blocked out the city.

From there, I detected a few faint trails in the brush. The park was a famous cruising ground for San Francisco's gay men. It was they who had made these trails as they stalked each other. On a beautiful, sunny afternoon like today, the park should have been buzzing with covert activity but the woods were empty and still. Something else was stalking the city's gay men, a virus that bludgeoned them with grotesque diseases, leaving them blind, demented and emaciated before it killed them. It passed from body to body in the naked intimacy of sex, so that, while all of us were at risk, none of us knew for certain whether or not he carried it.

I had never played in the park—the police sometimes raided the woods and I wasn't about to risk my law license for an outdoor blowjob—but I'd had sex in bathhouses and bedrooms all across the city. I assumed I was infected. Every morning I woke up and wondered whether this would be the day the virus struck. That anxiety lasted only until I called Larry Ross, ten minutes after I opened my eyes, as he had ordered me to do when he became my AA sponsor five months earlier.

He invariably opened our conversations with, "Have you prayed yet?"

I don't believe in God, I told him the first time he asked me this question. No, he replied, well then who rescued you from your apartment when you banged your head on the coffee table and were lying on the floor drunk and bleeding out? That was my sister, I said. The sister you hadn't seen in three years who just happened to turn up that day? The apartment manager called her, she was my emergency contact. And why, Larry persisted, did the apartment manager choose that day to call her? It was a coincidence, I said, but he seized upon the trace of doubt in my voice. You're not sure of that. You think it may not have been a coincidence and that doubt, Henry, that tiny shred of doubt, that fragile belief that maybe something in the universe gives a fuck about your life and well-being? Let's call that God and you can pray to it. What am I supposed to say, I replied, as sullen as a teenager. How about, help me and thank you. Fine, I said. And that had become my daily prayer. Help me and thank you.

"Yes," I replied that morning as I did every morning. "I said the thing."

I could sense the smirk on the other end of the line. "Good boy. What are you grateful for today?"

This was the other part of our ritual. Every morning, I was required to list three things I was grateful for.

"It's a beautiful day. I have enough money coming in this month to pay my rent and feed myself. I woke up without a hangover."

"It's a beautiful day down here too," he said from Los Angeles where he lived and practiced law. "What are your plans for the next twenty-four hours?"

"I'm going out for a long run. After that I'll head to the office to work on a suppression motion I have to file by Friday. Then I'll go to a six p.m. Big Book study and then dinner with some of the guys from the meeting."

"That's a good plan. Nice and simple."

"Yeah, well, life is simple when there's not a lot of work coming in."

"Have you given any more thought to the job with Western States?"

"I don't know. Working for an insurance company? It doesn't sit right."

Larry was considerably higher up on the legal food chain than I was. In our last conversation, he had told me a friend of his, an insurance executive in L.A., had mentioned his company was hiring investigators on a contract basis to help clear their backlog. He had pitched me to the executive who told Larry he was interested in talking to me and to pass along his number. I still hadn't called. I had been—was, was trying again to be—a criminal defense lawyer but picking up the pieces of my practice after my crack-up was slow going. Still, as much as I needed the work, the idea of investigating insurance claims and potentially denying someone payment of a claim rankled me. I again explained this to Larry.

"I understand," he said impatiently. "Henry Rios for the defense, sticking up for the little guy, can't bring himself to work for the big bad corporation. You think every insurance claim is legitimate, Henry?"

"I wouldn't know," I sniffed.

"Answer the question," Larry said in a cross-examination voice. "Are all insurance claims legitimate?"

"Of course not. Whenever there's money to be made, there's going to be some fraud."

"That's right, and do you know what happens when an insurance company pays out a fraudulent claim? It passes the loss on to its other policy holders. Their premiums get jacked up because someone gamed the system. In other words, the little guy gets screwed."

"So now you're pitching this job as consumer advocacy?" I asked sarcastically.

"I'm not going to tell you you'd be doing God's work by helping Western States avoid paying out claims, but you wouldn't be in league with the devil, either. Why don't you ditch the black-and-white thinking and try living in the gray zone with the rest of us. I know you're barely scraping by and could use the income. Take a case from Western States, see how it feels, and if it doesn't feel right, you can always walk away."

"I don't know, Larry..."

"Henry," he said, adopting the rich baritone he undoubtedly used to cajole reluctant clients. "Wouldn't you rather have someone with an open mind like you investigating an insurance claim than a hack looking for a way to deny it before he even begins?"

Grudgingly I replied, "Yeah, I can see that. Okay, I'll call the guy this afternoon."

"Good. Talk to you tomorrow morning?"

"Yes, and uh, thank you."

"You're welcome," he said and then signed off as he always did with a gruff, "I love you, Henry."

I sat on the log, breathed in the silty, fragrant air and glimpsed through a narrow opening in the latticework of branch and bush a shard of cityscape. Not far from here was the hundred-year-old Victorian mansion, converted to a recovery house for male alcoholics, where I had lived until three months ago. A requirement of residency was attendance at a nightly AA meeting in the double parlor. One Tuesday night I was sitting on a threadbare couch waiting for the meeting to begin when Larry strode into the room. His appearance alone—six-five and rapier-thin—would have made him hard to miss, but what really set him apart in our shabby crew was his immaculate navy blue, three-piece, pin-striped suit, starched white shirt, red silk tie and gold cufflinks. His head was shaved and buffed to a high shine. He stood at the archway, looked around, saw me staring at him, came over and seated himself beside me. Beneath the pink dome of his pate, he had the face of a crafty infant. I was utterly intimidated.

"Larry," he said, extending a delicate-looking hand that concealed a powerful grip.

"Henry," I replied, shaking his hand.

"You a resident here?"

"Yes."

"How much time do you have, Henry?" he asked, the standard AA ice-breaker.

"Thirty-one days," I said, my voice involuntarily shaking.

His features shifted, became gentler, and I saw the kindness in his bright blue eyes. "How are you doing on day thirty-one?"

For thirty-one days I had done everything I had been told to do; attended therapy and meetings, read the Big Book of AA, kept a journal, sat down to communal meals with my fellow drunks and addicts and "shared" my feelings. I did these things out of a desperation so deep that, when I allowed myself to peer into it, I could not see bottom. But no matter how hard I tried, how sincerely I wanted to "work the program," I was constantly aware of standing at the rim of that abyss and the ground seemed to be slipping away beneath my feet. The urge to drink was never far from my mind, swooping in like a bird of prey, threatening to carry away my resolve and plunge me back into the nightmare of drinking and dying.

I had been afraid to admit this to anyone, terrified even, to let the thought fully form in my mind but beneath Larry's compassionate gaze I blurted out, "I don't think I'm going to make it."

He reached for my hand and held it, firmly. "You will."

There was such conviction in his voice and certainty in his eyes that I wanted to believe him.

"How?"

"After the meeting, we'll go out for coffee and talk. Okay?"

I shook my head because my eyes had filled with tears and I was afraid if I tried to speak my voice would break.

We went to a diner where, over plates of eggs and bacon, he told me his story. Larry was a name partner at an entertainment law firm based in Beverly Hills. He was gay but, until seven years earlier, had been deep in the closet. Once a month he flew to San Francisco for what he called his "lost weekends." He hit the bars and bathhouses, alternating booze and cocaine, and having as much sex as he could to get him through the next month of enforced celibacy. Eventually, as the alcohol and drugs took over, he began to slip and started haunting the bars and bathhouses in L.A. where, one night, he met a young man and took him home. The kid figured out Larry's situation and blackmailed him.

"The worst part wasn't the shame or the guilt or the terror that he might expose me, but my complete lack of control. Here I was, with my Yale law degree, my house in the Hollywood Hills, a client list that included Oscar winners, and this twenty-three-year-old punk had me by the balls. Naturally my drinking and using accelerated. Then one morning I woke up with the hangover from hell and a bloody nose from snorting coke and I had a revelation."

"What was it?"

"If I wanted to be free of this little *pisher*, all I had to do was tell the truth. All I had to do was come out." He looked at me over the rim of his coffee cup and smiled. "All I had to do was jump off the cliff." He sipped his coffee. "I'm not brave, but I knew at that moment it was either come out or kill myself because I could not live another day the way I had been going. I went into the office and called my partners into the conference room and told them I was a queer. You know what they said?"

I shook my head.

"They said, that's fine, Larry, now what are you going to do about the drugs and drinking because that's the real problem." He put his cup down. "Can you believe I was offended! Then they told me, one by one, how my drinking and using had affected them. Turns out they'd been waiting for the opportunity to stage an intervention and my coming out gave it to them. By the time they were done with me, my denial was in shreds. Being gay wasn't a problem, it was who I was. Addiction, that was the problem. Two days later, I went off to Hazelden. That was seven years ago. Been clean and sober since. Now, tell me why you don't think you're going to make it."

Recalling the last weeks of my drinking when I had holed myself up in my apartment and drank until I passed out, then came to and drank some more, I took a deep breath. There wasn't a scintilla of pleasure left when I poured another drink down my throat. After a certain point, I couldn't even get drunk anymore. There was no thought, there was scarcely even a flicker of consciousness. I was no longer myself. I was a stranger sitting in his underwear in a dark apartment drinking himself to death.

"It's like what you said. The loss of control. I didn't want to drink, but I couldn't stop myself, even when I knew I was dying."

"But you did stop," he reminded me. "Thirty-one days ago."

I nodded. Yes, I had stopped drinking but—I stared at the muddy residue at the bottom of my coffee cup, looking for words to express the pervasive fear and anxiety that clouded my mind in my waking hours and seeped into my dreams; the unsettling feeling that I was fundamentally unfixable; defective.

Addressing the coffee cup, I said, "I feel like my entire existence is a mistake and when I feel that way, I really need a drink."

"It's just a feeling," Larry replied, calmly. "If you don't obsess it over it, it will pass."

"What about the urge to drink?"

"Give it time. That will pass too."

"But—"

"No buts," he said firmly. "Here's where you have to stop thinking and trust what other drunks like me are telling you about the process of getting and staying sober."

"Thinking is what I do. It's how I make—well, made—my living. You know, I'm a lawyer too. Criminal defense."

"And I'm sure you're a very capable one," Larry said. "No doubt you have a brilliant mind you use to analyze complex legal issues and strategize defenses. But that fine brain of yours can be your enemy in this situation."

"Meaning what?"

"Meaning, your mind turns your feelings into problems and tries to solve them the same way it solves legal issues, by analyzing them and considering all of their facets and possible outcomes. But feelings aren't meant to be solved, they're meant to be felt and released. Your real problem isn't what you feel but that you don't know how to feel."

"Come on, everyone has feelings," I said, resentfully.

"But when your feelings troubled you, you drowned them with booze. That's not an option anymore. So, when a painful emotion or memory comes up, you're going to have to learn to sit with it until it passes or talk it out with someone who's dealt with the same feeling and gotten through it sober. That's what the fellowship is all about. One drunk talking to another. Do you have a sponsor?"

I shook my head. "No, not yet."

"You do now."

"You? You live in L.A."

"You've never heard of the telephone? You'll call me every morning, ten minutes after you wake up, before your head starts spinning. Plus, when we need a face to face, I can run up here or you can come down to L.A."

"I hate L.A.," I said, automatically.

He grinned. "Spoken like a true San Franciscan. We start tomorrow, okay?"

I nodded. "Thank you."

"Throwing out the lifeline is what we do, and it works both ways. By helping you stay sober, I also help myself."

As I lay in bed that night, listening to my roommates snore and fart in their sleep, something shifted inside of me. The clouds of fear and anxiety parted just a bit and I was warmed for a moment by what felt very much like hope.

I worked out of an office on the second floor of a converted Edwardian on Market Street, halfway between the Castro and Hayes Valley. Mine was the smallest in a suite of offices I shared with three other lawyers. I paid more rent on the office than I did on my basement apartment. Between the two rents and my share of our secretary's salary and the utilities at both places, I was eating at a lot of dives and greasy spoons. I looked good though. I had a closet filled with bespoke suits, custom made shirts, handmade shoes and gorgeous ties that had belonged to a friend of Larry's whom AIDS had killed just as I was leaving the halfway house. They were the nicest clothes I had ever owned but I'd been reluctant to accept them.

It's either you or Goodwill, Larry had told me, adding with a smirk, Robbie would have loved to get into your pants, so I'm sure he wouldn't mind you getting into his. When I still demurred, he said, You can't catch AIDS by wearing the guy's suits. I almost asked, How can you be sure? but instead I accepted the gift. Still, even though Larry assured me the clothes had been cleaned after Robbie's death, I'd spent money I didn't have getting them laundered and dry cleaned before I wore them.

Most mornings I'd put on one of these beautiful suits and head to the criminal court building on Brannan where I was on the 987 panel. The numbers referred to a section of the Penal Code that authorized the appointment of a state-paid lawyer for indigent defendants when the Public Defender had a conflict of interest and couldn't take the case. I'd check in with the clerk and sit there, hoping for an appointment. Like everything else in San Francisco, though, 987 appointments were doled out based on who you knew. I didn't know anyone. Until I'd gone into rehab in the city, I'd lived and practiced in a small university town thirty miles south of the city where my drinking had left my reputation in tatters. So, in San Francisco, I wasn't part of the old boys' network and, to the extent people recognized my name, what they knew about me wasn't positive. Most days I went back to my office from arraignments empty-handed. The phone didn't ring much either. I knew I needed to join the local bar association and put myself out there, but lawyers' gatherings invariably involved drinking, sometimes, a lot of drinking, and I wasn't ready to face that yet. Financially, each month was a juggling act and more often than not I dropped a ball. Larry was right, I needed work. Any work.

I got to my tiny office and searched my desk for the slip of paper where I had written the name and number of his insurance pal: Myles Landon. I picked up the phone and punched in the number before my second thoughts got the better of me. A secretary answered, took my information and put me on hold. An insipid version of *California Dreamin'* was well into the second chorus before a male voice came on the line.

"Myles Landon," he announced confidently.

"Mr. Landon, I'm Henry Rios. I think our mutual friend Larry Ross talked to you about me for a claims investigator job?"

"Oh, Henry, yes, of course. Larry spoke very highly of you. Sold me on you, in fact. The job's yours if you want it."

I was taken aback, having expected an interview and an, okay, thanks we'll let you know.

"Uh, you don't want to ask me about my experience?"

He chuckled. "What experience? According to Larry you're a criminal defense lawyer looking to moonlight for some extra cash. That right?"

"That's about the size of it. I don't know the first thing about insurance except that my malpractice premium is too damn high."

He laughed again. "You should insure with us. Look, what I need is someone who asks tough questions, is a good judge of credibility and can deliver a succinct report of his findings. That's what trial lawyers do, right?"

"Yeah, I can do those things, but don't you want my résumé or to meet me?"

"Are you trying to talk yourself out the job?" he asked, jovially.

"No, but this isn't like any other job interview I've ever had."

He dropped the salesman's mirth and said, "Larry tells me you're six months sober."

"Larry told you that," I said sharply.

"Don't be upset. He didn't break your anonymity. I've got seventeen years myself."

"Oh. Well, uh, congratulations."

"Thanks," he said, the smile returning to his voice. "The point is, you need a hand and I'm in a position to help you. As for your qualifications, Larry vouches for you and I trust Larry's judgment." He cut off my stammered thanks. "Ruth Fleming runs our office up there. I'll have her call you in the next couple of days to work out the details of your contract and give you your first assignment. She can fill you in on what the job involves. Okay?"

"Yes, that's fine. Thank you."

"Look me up next time you're in L.A. Goodbye, Henry."

I sat there for a moment after he hung up with the phone still pressed to my ear.

Everyone has a picture of himself that he carries around in his head, Larry told me in one of our morning conversations. You know what yours is? No, but I think I'm about to find out. Yes, you are, he said. Your story is that you're completely self-sufficient. You don't ask for help, you don't want help, you don't need help because you've got it all under control. Am I right? If you say so, I sniffed. He laughed. Don't get your feelings hurt. You're not special, there are lots of guys like you. Me, for instance, at least at work. I can't show weakness or doubt. That's the mask we have to wear out there in the world, but don't confuse the mask with who you are. So, who am I, then, according to you? I asked. Just a person, he said. A good person, but human like everyone else. You're crawling out of a deep hole, and your instinct will be to do it yourself, but you can't and if you try, you'll only dig yourself in deeper. It's probably too much to expect you to be gracious, but at least promise me you won't push away the hands that reach down to help you. Can you promise me that?

"Done," I said and put the phone down.

3.

BILL STOOD ON THE SIDEWALK, suitcase in hand, outside the Greyhound terminal. Behind him, the loudspeaker announced arrivals and departures. San Francisco was shockingly cold after the long ride through the torrid summer of a half-dozen states. His body ached from the cramped seat and he was still dazed by his sudden transformation from son and brother to banished pervert. More than once on the journey, sudden tears like an unexpected storm scalded his face. He was wept out and exhausted and felt more dead than alive as he stood on the dirty sidewalk and tried to get his bearings in the frigid, foggy city.

He had not been the only young person on the bus. There had been a German couple, blond and high spirited, traveling the country on the ninety-nine-dollar special summer fare. A young soldier got on the bus in Cedar Rapids and rode as far as Reno. A long-haired boy who smelled of male musk and patchouli oil boarded at Salt Lake City and flashed a warm smile as he made his way past Bill. They approached him at rest stops, recognizing him as a member of the tribe of the young, but he deflected them with his single-word answers to their questions and his air of misery. Only the hippie boy persisted—his name, he said, was Stuart. Bill sensed from him a special, particular interest that both attracted and repelled him. *He's like me,* Bill thought when Stuart, standing beside him at a trough urinal at a rest stop in Nevada, casually glanced at Bill's dick and smiled. Bill had fled, but not before looking down quickly as Stuart shook the last drops of piss from own long, thin dick. After that, Bill avoided him.

The bus terminal occupied an entire block on Seventh Street between two busy thoroughfares, Mission Street behind him and Market Street ahead of him. An imposing skyline rose beyond Market Street while, behind Mission, he saw only flat roofs and warehouses. He tried to remember what he knew of this city but all that came to him was a jumble of images from the car chase scene in *Bullitt* and the chorus of the Scott McKenzie song—*If you're going to San Francisco be sure you wear flowers in your hair.*

"Hey, man, this your first time in Frisco?"

Bill spun around to encounter Stuart's smiling face.

"Yeah," Bill said.

"That's cool. You have a place to crash?"

Too tired to lie, Bill said, "No."

"You know anyone here?" Stuart asked.

"No," Bill said.

In a kind voice, Stuart said, "All on your own?"

"Yeah," Bill said, roughly.

Stuart touched his shoulder lightly and said, "I have some friends in the Haight. You could stay with us."

"You don't even know me."

Stuart shrugged. "I can tell you're cool. What's your name?"

"Bill."

"You're gay too, right?"

Bill had never heard the word gay used in conversation before but he knew what it meant. He bristled. "I'm no queer."

Stuart smiled. "Whatever, Billy. You're in Frisco now. No one here cares if you make it with boys or girls."

Bill barked, "I said I'm not a queer."

Stuart's smile faded and he looked sad.

"Okay man, have it your way, but listen to me, the place you want to go is Polk Street. That's where the gays are. Just be careful, okay?" And then, before Bill could react, the other boy leaned in and kissed him on the mouth. "You're cute, Billy. Hope I see you around."

Stuart disappeared into the crowd. Bill had never been kissed by another boy. He looked around wildly to see if people had been watching but if they had, they didn't care. He gathered his things and moved on.

Polk Street, Polk Street. Bill committed the name to memory as he stood on the sidewalk beneath a web of low-lying electrical wires over streetcars ferrying passengers up and down an immense boulevard just as they did in the Rice-a-Roni commercials. He peered up a street called Powell and saw in the distance a cable car chugging up a steep incline and heard in his head: *And the little cable cars climb halfway to the stars.* For a moment, his anxiety fell away and he was charmed. If only, he thought, it wasn't so frigging cold.

The envelope his mother had given him had two hundred dollars in it. He spent fifty on the bus fare, another ten on food – potato chips, candy bars and Cokes – leaving him with one hundred and forty dollars. He left fifty in the suitcase he stowed in a locker at the bus station. The remaining ninety was his stake, to pay for food and a place to stay. He saw a little diner on a narrow street off Powell and ducked into it as evening began to settle in the sky and the streets lamps flickered on.

The diner was furnished with ratty booths and tables on a grimy tiled floor no amount of mopping would ever get clean. Beneath harsh florescent lights, the air was thick with grease and cigarette smoke and curses from the cooks in the kitchen behind the counter. A Chinaman brought him a fly-specked menu from which he ordered a hamburger, fries and a Coke. As he had wandered around the city, he had pondered how to find Polk Street. He was afraid to ask anyone because it would expose him as a queer but he didn't care what the Chinaman thought so, when he returned with Bill's food, Bill said, "My friend lives on Polk Street. Do you know where that is?"

"Polk? When you leave, take a left and keep walking until you see City Hall. Polk Street runs in front of it. You want anything else?"

Amazed by the Chinaman's fluency in English, Bill said, "No, thank you. Wait, what does City Hall look like?"

"Like a big wedding cake. You can't miss it."

The waiter was right: even in the fading light, City Hall looked like an immense, domed cake. He was standing in front of it, on Polk Street, but while he had found the street, he didn't know in which direction to go to find *the queers,* he thought. *I'm looking for the queers because*, but, before he could complete the sentence in his head, someone said, "I'm a queer." The sound startled him. He looked around to see who had spoken but he was quite alone. And then he realized it was his own voice he had heard. His own voice saying aloud the words it had said in his head a thousand times but which, until that moment, had never passed his lips.

"I'm a queer," he said, again. He waited for the ground to open up beneath him and tumble him into Hell, or a bolt of lightning to incinerate him, but all he heard was the traffic noises and the rustle of the wind.

Then, once more, softly but with utter conviction, he said, "I'm a queer."

For a moment, it seemed to him, the world stopped. The cars and buses froze in place, the men in suits exiting city hall were suspended in mid-step. Even the wisps of pink and orange and lavender in the evening sky paused in their unfurling. All he heard was his heart beating in his ears, all he felt was the heft of his own flesh as the magnitude of the revelation—*I'm a queer*—settled into the very cells that composed him. Because he was a queer and that changed everything.

"I'm a—" He stopped himself. *Queer* was an epithet of contempt and loathing and it would no longer do. What had the hippie boy called him?

"I'm a gay," Bill said. That sounded not quite right, so he tried again. "I'm gay."

The world spun back into place.

It was nearly midnight. Bill had discovered the part of Polk Street where, among shoe repair shops and newsstands, were bars which seemed patronized entirely by men. Some of the men matched the descriptions he had read in the abnormal psychology textbooks of his hometown library; willowy, swishy figures in feminine clothes with elaborately styled bouffants giggling and mincing. They were as repulsive to him in the flesh as they had been in print but their presence, like neon lights, signaled to him that he was in the right place.

Had it not been for these creatures, he might not have been sure, because the other men going in and out of the bars looked normal to Bill. Some were in business suits while others wore Levi's and leather jackets or polyester pants and Hawaiian shirts or tie-dyed tees and bell bottoms. He saw slender hippie boys and old white-haired, potbellied grandpas and middle-aged men who looked like they mowed the lawn on Saturday afternoon and then settled in front of the TV with a six-pack to watch the game, like his dad.

At first, he found it hard to believe these ordinary-looking men were gay. After observing them for a few, cold hours, however, he noticed, even among the most normal looking of them, small, delicate mannerisms as they walked by—the twist of a hand, the toss of a head—or heard in their otherwise ordinary voices the faintest sibilance. These gestures and inflections signaled to him that these men were not, after all, like his father or his brothers. They moved differently in their bodies than the men of Eden Plains, more loosely, more softly. Their maleness was undeniable but it was also less insistent. And here and there, among them, strode a few men more beautiful than any males he had ever seen outside the pages of magazine ads or the movie screen.

The beauties were, in their way, as distinctive as the swishes and like the swishes they carried themselves as if they knew they were on display. They seemed to Bill like actors, their every step and gesture more controlled and a little more emphatic than in ordinary life, as if in response to the commands of an unseen director. His heart broke a dozen times that night as he followed them with dazed and dazzled eyes, they were so magnificent and so utterly inaccessible.

More than a few men slowed when they saw him propped against a wall next to a pet store and gave him long, lingering looks, their eyes making a slow, shameless appraisal of his face and his body from the top of his head to the cuffs of his Levi's. The attention excited and embarrassed him, forcing his eyes to the ground where he shuffled his feet on the dirty sidewalk, hoping that someone would speak to him. But no one did. Finally, cold and tired, but electric with arousal, he screwed up his courage and pushed through the doors of a bar he had already passed half a dozen times. Mounted above the padded, double doors was a neon mask and, also spelled out in neon, the words The Hide 'n Seek.

He was overwhelmed by warm air scented with cigarette smoke, beer and cologne. In the dim, reddish light he made out a long bar where clusters of men gathered around stools talking and laughing. There was a scattering of tables on the main floor and a long shelf against the back wall where other men stood, mostly in silence, beers in hand, scanning the room purposefully. Rod Stewart sang *Maggie May* on the flashing Wurlitzer jukebox. Apart from the absence of women, the bar seemed not much different than the college bar his brother Matt had snuck him into when Bill had visited him in Urbana.

He had only taken a step toward the bar when a big hand pressed his chest, stopping him and a deep voice rumbled, "Let's see some ID, kid."

The man was broad-shouldered and muscular in a tight, black T-shirt and jeans, but his bearded face was not unfriendly.

"Um, I just got here from Chicago," Bill said, hoping that name dropping another big city would get him past the bouncer.

"Yeah, well, welcome to California, but I still need to see that ID. Drinking age here is twenty-one."

Bill pulled his wallet out of his pocket and handed the man his driver's license, still hoping for a break.

The man sighed, "You know I can't let you in, Bill. Cops are always looking for a reason to shut us down. Can't have any underage drinking."

"What if I just get a Coke?" Bill said, encouraged that the man had called him by his name.

"No minors on the premises. That's the law. You can hang out with me for a few minutes to warm up, then you have to leave." He returned Bill's license to him. "So," he continued, conversationally, "how long have you been in the city?"

"This afternoon."

The man did a double-take. "Wow, fresh meat. Stay here and don't move. Oh, I'm Pete."

Pete went to the bar and talked briefly to a handsome bartender who glanced at Bill, nodded and smiled. He reached down to the bar, got a glass and filled it, then handed it to Pete who returned to his station.

"Have a Coke on the house, kid," Pete said, handing him the cold glass. "What brings here out here? School?"

Bill thanked him for the Coke and considered how much to tell him. "Yeah, school," he said, uncertainly.

Bill replied with a skeptical, "Uh-huh. Where you staying?"

"Um, I don't know yet. Are there any cheap motels around here?"

Pete frowned. "Are you a runaway, kid?"

The question dissolved his fragile confidence and sudden tears burned his eyes. In an unsteady voice, he said, "Um, my family... I had to leave because—" He got no further and started to cry.

Pete took the glass from his hand, set it down and bear-hugged him. "Hey, Bill, it's going to be okay."

Sheltered by Pete's hard, warm, male flesh, Bill

felt safe for the first time that day. Reluctantly, he freed himself of Pete's embrace, wiped his face on his sleeve, and said, "I'm sorry."

"Your folks found out you're gay and threw you out? Is that what happened?"

Not trusting himself to speak, Bill nodded.

"That is fucked up. You don't have a place to stay tonight, right?"

"No," Bill said, wondering whether Pete was about to offer him a bed. The thought was frightening and exciting.

"Okay, wait here. I know someone who can help you."

Slightly let down, he watched Pete disappear into the crowd while he sipped his Coke. A moment later, the bouncer emerged followed by another man—a boy, really, who did not seem much older than Bill. The boy was tall and stick-thin. His trousers were spray-painted tight and he wore a long-sleeved blouse-like white shirt, buttons undone to reveal a pale, hairless chest. He sashayed behind Pete, stopping to greet friends with a flip of his wrists. His flame red hair came to a brittle point above his forehead. As he approached, Bill saw traces of mascara ringing the boy's bright blue eyes and smelled a gardenia-scented perfume. He was dismayed.

"Here's our stray," Pete said to the boy when they reached Bill. "Bill, this is Waldo. He said you could crash at his place tonight."

"Well, hello, Bill," Waldo trilled, his voice

surprisingly deep. "You *are* fresh off the farm, aren't you?"

"Hi," Bill mumbled.

"I'm gonna leave you two boys to talk," Pete said, stepping back to his post.

Waldo smiled and looked Bill over. Although there was nothing carnal in Waldo's appraisal, Bill felt more exposed under the other boy's bright gaze than he had under the stares of the men on the street.

"Are you afraid I want to get into your pants?" Waldo asked. "Because, hon, let me tell you right off the bat, I'm not into twinks, at all. Pete says you need a place to crash and that's what I got, plus some soup if you're hungry. It's late and Mama's tired and I have to work tomorrow, so are you coming?"

"Um, I don't know."

"Suit yourself, hon," Waldo said, kindly. "You can come with me or hit the street but I gotta tell you, things get pretty ugly out there after last call. Your choice."

The weight of the long day and all of its strangeness and anxieties, sights and sounds came crashing down on Bill. Exhausted and despairing, he said to the swishy boy, "Okay. I'll go with you."

"Smart boy. Let me get my wrap and we'll be off."

Waldo lived in a three-story brick tenement in

a garbage strewn alley street off Polk. He unlocked first an iron gate and then a glass door to let them into a tiny foyer with a dirty black-and-white checkerboard floor. On one wall were mailbox slots and on the others were signs warning the residents against this or that violation of building rules: No Pets! Lock all doors! No drugs on the premises! The air reeked of mildew and stale food smells. A doorway opened from the foyer to a long, dark hall. "This way," Waldo said, plunging into the darkness. "Watch your step, the fucking light's been out forever." He led Bill to a door with a crudely painted "9" on it, fumbled with his keys in the darkness, unlocked the door and then stepped aside to let Bill pass.

"This is home, Bill," Waldo said, flicking on an overhead light.

Streetlight drizzled into the room through a pair of dust-streaked windows. In an alcove half-concealed by a curtain was an unmade bed. He glimpsed a toilet in a tiny bathroom off the short entrance hall. A couch covered with a pink chenille bedspread, a little vinyl-topped kitchen table with two chairs, a scattering of orange crates stuffed with books and albums and an old hi-fi completed the décor of the main room which was no bigger than Bill's Eden Plains bedroom. Cockroaches scampered across the counter of the galley kitchen at their approach. The sink was crammed with dirty pots, dishes, cups and glasses. The air smelled of perfume and garbage.

"Are you hungry?" Waldo asked.

"Yeah."

"Sit down, I made some chicken dumpling soup. I'll grab you a bowl."

The soup, served in a chipped bowl, was the best thing Bill had eaten since before he'd gone to the hospital. The broth was rich and the dumplings fluffy. Waldo watched him eat, a glass of wine in front of him.

"So, where you from?"

"Illinois. A little town."

"I'm from Nebraska myself," Waldo said, conversationally. "Bet my town was littler. So, Pete said you had to leave cuz the folks figured out you were gay."

Bill mumbled an embarrassed, "Yeah."

"Honey, you're not the first. This city is filled with boys like you and me."

Bill lifted his eyes from the bowl. "You too?"

Waldo nodded. "Yeah, me too. My sophomore year, bunch of boys got me behind the bleachers, made me suck their dicks and then beat the shit out of me." He grinned. "Well, I didn't mind sucking the dicks but I didn't like how they rearranged my pretty face. When I told my folks what happened, they said it was my fault for being a faggot and threw me out." He studied Bill. "You're not a queen, like me. How did your folks find out?"

"My dad caught me with my friend."

Waldo asked, drolly, "Was your dick in his mouth or his in yours?"

Lightheaded with fatigue, Bill laughed and Waldo laughed with him. They laughed until tears came and then they wiped them away and Bill asked if he could have another bowl of soup.

As Waldo served him, he said, "You know, we're the lucky ones. We made it out alive. Not all of us do."

Waldo had begun to come into focus for Bill as a real person. He no longer merely saw the bouffant hair and mascara, the limp wrists and tight clothes, which, in any event, Waldo had exchanged for a silk kimono. Out of those affectations, a boy had emerged with kind eyes and a smirk of a smile. Bill relaxed.

"I was giving Marco a blowjob when my dad found us," he said. "He beat me up bad. When I got out of the hospital my mom drove me to the bus station."

"With nothing but the clothes on your back! Those fuckers!"

"I left my suitcase at the bus station. I have a little money."

"You can get your suitcase tomorrow and bring it here."

Bill gulped down a sob and managed a strangled, "Thank you." He wiped his eyes. "I don't know what I'm going to do."

Waldo smiled. "You're going to finish your

soup and then we'll make up the couch and you'll get some sleep."

A key turned and the door opened. An older black man in a rumpled uniform came yawning into the room. He smiled sleepily at the two boys at the table.

"We doing a three-way?" he asked Waldo.

"Bill's just crashing here. Hey, Bill, this is my lover, Eddie."

"Um, hello," Bill said, adding a respectful, "sir."

Eddie laughed. "Sir? How old you think I am, boy? I'm gonna shower, baby boy, then I'm going to bed."

"Sure thing, doll," Waldo replied. "I'll be waiting for you."

When the shower went on, Bill asked Waldo, "Um, does Eddie live here too?"

Waldo smirked. "No, hon, Eddie lives with his wife and his kids over in the Fillmore. A couple of times a week he tells her he's pulling overtime and he comes by to fuck me senseless."

Bill, not knowing how else to respond, said, "Okay."

Waldo said, "You looked at him like you never seen a black guy before."

"There aren't too many in Eden Plains."

"You prejudiced against them?"

"Um, my dad doesn't like them."

Waldo nodded. "Bet he calls them niggers just

like my dad. Well let me tell you something, Bill, you're one of them now."

"One of what?" he asked, confused.

"A nigger, hon. We're all the same. Queers, niggers, spics, chinks. All in the same boat cuz the same people hate all of us. So, we gotta stick together, okay?"

Bill, still uncomprehending, nodded.

"Let's make up your bed. Just toss the bowl in the sink with the other shit. The maid will take care of it."

"You have a maid?"

Waldo laughed. "Child, you are a stitch."

Later, Bill lay sleepless on the lumpy couch trying not to hear the muffled sex sounds drifting into the room from behind the curtained alcove. It wasn't so much the whispered "Oh yeah fuck me, daddy, fuck me" that kept him awake as the low rumble of Eddie's laughter and Waldo's happy squeals. Fun. They were having fun. Fun, he realized, had never entered into his fantasies of Marco.

4.

FRAMED BY A MILLION-DOLLAR VIEW of the Bay Bridge in the window of her eighteenth-floor office on California Street, Ruth Fleming regarded me skeptically. The large, gleaming desk that served as a buffer between us held an in and out box and a complicated, many-buttoned phone but not a single personal item; no framed family photographs or fancy paperweights for her. Her desk proclaimed she was all business, as did the woman herself. Her makeup had been painstakingly applied to project attractiveness without a trace of sensuality just as the silk burgundy shawl that draped the padded shoulders of her jacket seemed calculated to soften her authority. The nameplate on her desk identified her as a vice president. The only other women I had seen when she led me from the foyer to her office were secretaries. Larry Ross's words may have been good enough for her boss, Myles Landon, in L.A., but Fleming tapped with doubtful fingertips the résumé she had asked me to bring her.

"I have to say, Mr. Rios, you don't seem to have any relevant qualifications for this job," she observed in a firm but modulated voice.

"That's what I told Myles Landon," I replied. "He seemed to think my experience as a litigator would be sufficient. You don't agree?"

She frowned. "No, I don't, but Myles is the boss, so here we are."

Clearly, having an unqualified man foisted on her was a reminder that the old boys network was alive and well. I sympathized but was hardly in a position to concur. I needed the work.

"Look, Ms. Fleming—"

"Mrs. Fleming," she said, automatically.

"Mrs. Fleming, give me a chance and if you think I'm not up to the job, I'll quit and tell Landon it was my decision."

She seemed a fraction less annoyed with me. "I'll hold you to that, Mr. Rios." She picked up a folder from her in box and slipped it across the desk. "This case involves a claim of accidental death which would require us to pay double the policy amount."

"How much?"

"A hundred thousand dollars. A lot of money, obviously, but not in and of itself the reason for us to investigate. The cause of death is accidental asphyxiation—apparently, there was a gas leak in the insured's apartment. His, uh, male companion was also in the apartment but he survived. The companion is also the beneficiary.

The claim was filed on his behalf a few days after the accident, but we haven't been able to reach him since."

"Who filed the claim?"

"The agent who wrote up the policy. Not one of our agents. We bought the policy from Confederation Insurance."

"You bought a policy from another insurance company? Is that a common practice?"

"Yes. It's called reinsurance. The selling company wants to spread the risk of loss by carrying fewer policies and the buying company wants the business. It works out for everyone. Anyway, we called the Confederation agent and he said he can't find the claimant either. Obviously, we're not going to take any action on the claim until we have a beneficiary."

"That's all you want me to do? Find the beneficiary?"

She allowed herself a tight little smile. "Well, to start. After that, I expect you to do the standard investigation."

"Which involves?"

She swiveled her chair away from me and reached for a fat binder on the credenza behind her. "This is our operations manual. You'll find a chapter on investigating death claims."

I took the binder and the manila folder. "May I call you if I have a question?"

"I'm vice president in charge of operations," she said. "Perhaps you could call Myles."

I crammed the operations manual and the case file into my briefcase and lugged it into the Gold Mountain Café, a Chinese-American restaurant near Civic Center. The restaurant was close by the county law library and within walking distance of both the civil and criminal courthouses. I was drawn by its cheap prices, decent food and the willingness of its elderly owners, the Chus, to let me camp out at a back booth for a couple of hours and work when it was inconvenient to walk back to my office. If I was being entirely truthful, Gold Mountain held one other big attraction for me: Adam, the Chus' twenty-three-year-old grandson. Adam was their jack-of-all-trades who cooked, waited tables, ran the cash register and even, I saw, passing the place late one night, mopped the floors after closing time.

The Gold Mountain was never crowded and often almost empty. The menu featured both American diner food, burgers and Denver omelets, and standard Chinese food, wonton soup and beef with broccoli, and hadn't been changed in years; new prices had simply been taped over the old ones. Unlike the retro fifties diners springing up elsewhere in the city, Gold Mountain's long, Formica counter, checkerboard linoleum floor and red vinyl booths appeared to actually date to the second Eisenhower Administration. Cracks in the vinyl were covered with duct tape and

Adam's best efforts could not lift the decades of scuff marks on the floor.

Adam was a fresh and vivid presence in the dim, shabby, somnolent restaurant. He towered over his diminutive grandparents and he was massively muscled, his big thighs and powerful chest straining the seams of his black trousers and white dress shirt waiter's uniform. His square-jawed, big featured, broad face, topped with a close-cropped bush of inky hair, had a warrior's fierceness in repose but when he smiled, which he did frequently, dimples and a natural sweetness emerged. Our brief conversations about the fate of the Giants took a turn toward friendship when I asked him about the photographs that inconspicuously lined the walls of the restaurant; old black-and-white images of Chinatown. The one that hung above the booth where I usually sat depicted a counter restaurant filled with Chinese laborers, some in Western clothes, some in Chinese garb, their hair in queues, plainly taken in the late nineteenth-century.

"That was our first restaurant," he explained. "On Grant Street. There's only a counter because back then most of the Chinese were guys without families so they'd come in, sit down, eat and leave. You can still find a few of those old counter restaurants in Chinatown."

"What happened to their families?"

"The guys came over to work and make money

to send home. The women and kids stayed behind in China. Then the exclusion act kept them out."

"How many restaurants has your family owned?"

"Gold Mountain is number four. The one in the picture was destroyed in the earthquake. We opened another one in North Beach but the Italians burned it down."

"They *what*?"

His good-natured expression soured a little. "The Italians didn't want any Chinese in their neighborhood so they torched the place. The third one opened in Chinatown. Then my granddad opened this one in the sixties. The Chinatown place got sold, so Gold Mountain is the end of our little empire."

"Are you going to take it over?"

Adam laughed. "No, this isn't the life for me." He glanced toward his grandparents who were having an animated conversation in Cantonese at the cash register. "A couple of years ago, he had a stroke and she told him it was time for them to retire, but this place is more to him than a business. This is what his dad and granddad handed down to him and he was ready to die at the grill. She asked me to talk to him because," he said with a grin, "I've always been his favorite grandkid. I'm the only one who listened to his stories. We made a bargain. I'd come and work for him and he'll retire next year, after New Year's. Chinese New Year's."

"None of their children want the place?"

He laughed again. "My dad and his brothers and sisters had to work here when they were kids. They hated it."

"So, basically, you're putting your life on hold to work here until your grandfather's ready to retire?"

"Sure," he said with a quizzical grin as if my question puzzled him. "It's for my family."

After that, he'd linger at my table and talk after he took my order or, if he was in the kitchen, he'd come out and take his break with me. I quickly realized there were two Adams. One was the easygoing, all-American boy with the quick smile who loved sports and joked about being too tired from his twelve-hour days to look for a girlfriend. The other was the serious young man who had learned from his grandfather the difficult history of the Chinese in San Francisco and who, when he spoke of it, showed flashes of the warrior I had first taken him for.

Once when we were talking, I mentioned *Yick Wo versus Hopkins*, an 1886 Supreme Court decision I had studied in my constitutional law class. In *Yick Wo*, the court ruled that a San Francisco ordinance requiring permits for laundries violated the equal protection clause because it was administered in a way that denied almost all Chinese applicants. Adam knew all about *Yick Wo* and its aftermath.

"That was just one law," he said. "There

were lots of them to keep us in our place and when they didn't work, the mobs did things like burning down my family's restaurant. The city's always been a tough place for us."

"Even now?"

He frowned. "You ever really looked at Chinatown? I mean, past the tourist joints? It's a slum." The easy smile reappeared. "But there's good and there's bad, right? You know why my granddad named this place Golden Mountain Café?"

"No, and I was curious since there aren't any mountains around."

"In Cantonese, Gold Mountain is *gam saan*. That's what the Chinese immigrants called San Francisco, before they got here. They thought they'd come over and get rich."

"Find streets paved with gold?"

"Yeah," he said. "They didn't find that but a lot of our families found a home. Hey, is that all you're going to eat?"

"Are you trying to fatten me up for a reason?"

He grinned. He'd made it clear he thought I was too thin and often piled my plate with more food than I could possibly eat, then packaged the leftovers.

Larry had warned me not to get romantically involved my first year of recovery but I figured even he wouldn't object to my discreet infatuation with this smiling straight boy. Because clearly,

Adam *was* a straight guy, cluelessly friendly and open and at ease in his big body as only straight guys can be. A gay guy who looked like him would have carried himself with the slightest bit of theatricality to show off the gym-built muscles, and the eyes of gay men in the city at that moment were all touched with a drop of anxiety, like a tiny tear that never fell. Adam's eyes were clear.

I felt Adam's meaty fingers digging into my shoulders and briefly massaging me. "Hey, what you got there?"

The operations manual was open on the table before me. I explained to him what it was and the job I had taken on.

"I thought you did criminal law," he said, positioning himself in front of me, order pad in hand.

"Business is slow and a man's gotta eat," I said.

He smiled. "Speaking of eating, what'll you have today?"

"Surprise me?" I ventured.

"Tuna melt and tomato soup."

"I have that most days. What's the surprise?"

"Side of salmonella," he said. "Kidding!"

He went off and I stared appreciatively at his broad back and big, tight glutes, and then, with a sigh, turned my attention to my work.

Compared to the opaque legal documents I was accustomed to, the operations manual was refreshingly to the point. Thus far I had learned that every life insurance policy contained a contestability clause that allowed the insurer to challenge the validity of the policy within two years of the death claim. Whether the company exercised that option depended on the results of a preliminary inquiry called a death confirmation investigation. This investigation centered on three areas: whether the insured's information on the original application—name, age, gender, address—contained any material misstatements that would void the policy; confirmation of the insured's identity to make sure the insured and decedent were the same person; and verification of cause of death. If those three things checked out, the claim was paid.

I opened the file on William Ryan, the man whose death I was investigating. There wasn't much there: a copy of the application, the policy itself, and the death claim. At the time he applied for the life insurance policy, a year and a half earlier, Ryan was thirty-two years old, lived on Eureka Street and listed his occupation as businessman. Under intended beneficiary was the name Nick Trejo, a twenty-two-year-old who lived at the same Eureka Street address. Beneath the space for "beneficiary's relationship to insured" was the word "roommate." Reading between the lines—two unrelated men, one older than the other, living together in the heart of the city's gay neighborhood—it was obvious Trejo was Ryan's lover and the older man had taken out the policy to provide for the younger one in the event of his death.

"Roommate," "companion," "friend," "lover," "partner." I thought about all those words, some innocuous, some salacious, and always pronounced with a slight, mocking hesitation that simultaneously acknowledged and dismissed the bond, the way Ruth Fleming had paused before describing Nick Trejo as William Ryan's "male companion." A man joined to a woman was a love story. A man joined to a man was a smutty joke. Well, at least the company wasn't trying to withhold payment because Trejo was Ryan's lover as it might have in an earlier time. That was progress, I guess.

I called Brendan Scott, the insurance agent who had issued Ryan's policy, from the restaurant payphone and made an appointment to see him at three. That gave me an hour to kill. What could I learn about William Ryan in that hour? It occurred to me I could look up his obituary at the nearby city library.

Mrs. Chu was working the cash register. She took my money and made change and I went back to the booth and left a five for Adam who was back in the kitchen.

"Will you tell Adam I said goodbye?" I asked Mrs. Chu on my way out. She smiled and nodded.

The last of the city's Indian summer had been washed away in a violent storm over the weekend. The damp streets were filled with small tree branches and the gutters were clogged with leaves. The gray sky cast a funereal pall across the city where everything and everyone, cars, buses, streetcars, pedestrians, seemed to move in slow motion. I pushed open the doors to the gloomy library building with cold fingers. A reference librarian directed me to the fourth floor reading room where back issues of magazines and newspapers were piled on wooden shelves.

Ryan had died three weeks earlier. I pulled a month's worth of issues of the city's gay newspaper and flipped through the first one to the obituaries. They took up two pages, ranging in length from a full column to a couple of paragraphs, all illustrated with thumbnail black and white photographs of the eulogized men— they were all men—some no more than blurred snapshots, others studio portraits.

I scanned the names and didn't find William Ryan among them but I did see a familiar face grinning at me from one of the photographs. Tom Rustin. He'd been in his last month of residency at the halfway house when I'd arrived. I noticed him immediately because he and I were the only guys at the house who weren't white. I remembered his imperturbability and how, when he spoke at a meeting, he always began, "Hi, family." Now he was dead: "Complications from HIV. His only regret was not being able to pick up his nine-month AA chip at the Show of Shows."

I leafed through three more issues of the paper and fifty-seven obits before I found William Ryan's notice. The accompanying photograph showed an attractive, dark-haired man with light-colored eyes, a sharp nose and a forceful jaw, wearing a dress shirt and tie, a phone pressed to his ear.

> *Bill Ryan was born on August 18, 1955, in Eden Plains, Illinois. He came to San Francisco in 1971 and never left. He got an Associate Arts degree from City College and worked as real estate agent with Bay Realty before opening his own office in the Castro in 1977. Many of the neighborhood's Victorians were sold by Bill. In 1980, Bill turned his agency into the successful property management company he was running at the time of his sudden death. He is survived by his faithful office manager, Doris Chen, and his partner of five years, Nicholas Trejo. In keeping with Bill's wishes, there will be no memorial.*

It took me a couple of readings to decode the terse notice. Bill Ryan was clearly a guy in a hurry. He would only have been twenty-two when he started his own real estate agency and got caught up in the boom years when gay men were transforming a quiet Irish neighborhood called Eureka Valley into the epicenter of the city's gay life they renamed the Castro. Property management implied property to manage which made me think he had not just been a seller but a buyer. Like many other young men before him, going back to the Gold Rush, Ryan had come to California to make his fortune.

He was only eighteen when he uprooted himself from the Midwest and moved across the county. Surely, his reason for such a dramatic migration wasn't to attend a community college or work in real estate, things he could have done anywhere. No, I surmised that he, like thousands of other young men in the '70s in similar situations, had fled his small-minded Midwestern town for San Francisco to find a community of his own kind. And, because he was so young, I had to think there had been some serious trouble at home behind his move. The likeliest scenarios were either that he'd been discovered and his family had thrown him out, or, fearing imminent discovery, he'd run off before the shit hit the fan and become another gay refugee in a city filled with us.

Unlike other refugees, however, it did not appear he had immersed himself in that community. Their obituaries were filled with mention of gay clubs and groups to which the men had belonged, gay charitable organizations in which they had been active, and included long lists of surviving friends and personal messages of grief from them. Nothing like that for Bill Ryan. A casual reader of his circumspect death notice might not have even realized he was gay. Even the mention of his lover, Nick Trejo, was cast as his "partner" suggesting a professional rather than a personal relationship.

No family was mentioned among his survivors, confirming my suspicion that he was estranged from it. We were a generation of men who, when we had come out as gay, had been stricken from our family trees, and become non-persons whose names were spoken, if at all, in shamed whispers. Both my parents had died before I had to come out to them, and my only sibling, my sister, Elena, was also gay. But I did have uncles, aunts and cousins—none of whom I had seen since my mother's death a decade earlier because I hadn't wanted to come out to them. Maybe my Mexican, Catholic relatives would have been okay with a gay nephew and cousin but more likely they would have been disgusted or appalled. Even before my parents had died, and after I'd left home for school, I'd seen my relatives so rarely, it hardly seemed worth risking rejection, so I drifted away. The habit was so ingrained, I had even drifted away from my sister, though she had probably saved my life.

Brendan Scott's insurance agency was on the same block of Market Street as Ryan's property management company. Their two businesses were separated by a dry-cleaners, a camera shop and a coffee shop where, Scott was telling me, the two men sometimes met for coffee.

"Not that Bill had much time for socializing," Scott said. He was fiftyish, paunchy and going gray but he had a salesman's easy smile and twinkling eyes, as if he was about to tell you a particularly good joke. "Nope, it was always business with him. Terrible how he died, though I guess it was better than AIDS."

"What does that mean?"

The smile flickered off. "People would have thought he was one of those sleazy South of Market guys hanging out in bathhouses with their legs up in the air and a bottle of poppers stuffed up their nose."

"I don't think the virus limits itself to them," I said mildly.

He shrugged. "All I'm saying is Bill wasn't like that. He was about the straightest gay guy I knew. He worked long hours and then went home to Nick."

"You know Nick Trejo?"

"I only met him a couple of times," he corrected me. "Cute kid. Younger than Bill."

"You sold the policy to Bill."

He nodded. "Sure did. He came in one day out of the blue and said he wanted to make sure Nick was taken care of if something happened to him. Lots of gay guys do that, you know, to make sure there's something for the boyfriend the family can't get to." He frowned. "Of course, these days, with the virus, it's getting harder and harder to write a life insurance policy if the applicant's gay."

"How would your company know if someone's gay?"

"Red-lining," he replied. "If an application for life insurance comes out of certain zip codes where there's lots of gay men, the company rejects it."

"That's okay with you?"

"No," he replied firmly. "It's not. There are ways around it—" he paused. "I think I better keep them to myself."

"Sure, I understand. Getting back to Bill Ryan's policy. You filed the claim when he died. Did Nick ask you to?"

He shook his head. "I left him messages but he didn't call back so I went ahead and filed the claim to preserve his rights."

"Do you have any idea where he might be?"

"Sorry, no, but you let me know if you find him."

"Of course," I said, standing up. I noticed the gay paper on his cluttered desk was opened to the obituaries.

He noticed me noticing it. "My granddad called the obits the old man's sports page. Didn't think

Michael Nava

I'd be paying much attention to them before I was his age."

"Hard times," I said.

"You keep safe now," he replied.

Maybe too late for that, I thought, but did not say, not wanting him to write me off as one of those South of Market guys.

I went around to Ryan's office but the door was locked with a handwritten sign taped to it: CLOSED UNTIL FURTHER NOTICE.

A light drizzle fell from the darkening sky onto a narrow street in Hayes Valley where I stood before the tumbled-down, uninhabited, nineteenth-century cottage where Hugh Paris had lived. My lover. A recovering junkie, ex-rent boy, the black sheep of a wealthy family, whose murder remained officially unsolved. When I'd first returned here after leaving rehab, it was for evidence that Hugh had really existed and not been simply a figment of my alcohol-soaked imagination. In my mind, I walked myself up the creaky steps, through the door and the oddly barren living room into the bedroom. There, on a mattress on the floor, Billie Holiday crooning in the background, the damp sheet twisted around our feet, we had what was now called unsafe sex but which, at the time, I had thought of as making love. Standing there in the drizzle, I wondered if, in our heedless exchange of fluids, one of us

72

had passed the virus to the other. Not that it mattered to Hugh. He lay beneath the snow in a Boston graveyard. He was twenty-six when he was murdered and I remember thinking, how can that be? Who dies that young? Now the city was filled with gay men wondering if they would live to see thirty.

What if I got sober just so AIDS could kill me, I asked Larry one particularly anxious morning. Have you been sick, had any of the symptoms? he asked. No, I said, but—He cut me off. If you start down the road of what ifs, it's going to lead you back to the bottle. I'm afraid, Larry. Afraid of what? A possibility? Something that might never happen? It's more of a probability, I said. Is it happening today, he demanded with an asperity I realized later was a measure of his own anxiety. No, I said. Then stop these fantasies and learn to live in your body. What? You heard me, he said. Your mind lives in fear and regret but your body can only live right now, in this moment. So, take some deep breaths and live in your body. It's a safer place to be than in your head.

The drizzle turned into a cold, pelting rain. I opened my umbrella and headed home.

5.

I N THE DAYS FOLLOWING BILL'S arrival in San Francisco, Waldo waved off his offers to move out with, "Where would you go, hon? Stay as long as you want." In gratitude, Bill washed the dirty dishes, cleaned the apartment, used his dwindling stock of cash to fill the refrigerator and otherwise tried to make himself helpful to his friend. Waldo, returning home from work one evening, found Bill on his knees scrubbing decades of grime from the clawfoot bathtub and observed, "I guess you are gay."

Waldo worked as a file clerk in an obscure agency in the bowels of City Hall from eight thirty to five. Nights they spent at The Hide 'n Seek where Pete stationed Bill near the fire escape door in case the police came and he had to make a quick exit. Waldo introduced Bill to his many friends and protected him from what he called "the chicken hawks."

These, Waldo explained, were older men with a penchant for younger men "as close to illegal as they can get. And, hon, you're their wet dream.

They'll use you like a cum rag and throw you away." Bill appreciated that Waldo watched out for him, but he sometimes wished the older boy was a little less protective. He often felt like a child in a candy shop, permitted to look but not to touch the bright and delicious looking wares behind the glass counters. One night he was hanging around Pete, mooning over a guy playing pinball who looked like a grown-up version of Marco.

"What's wrong, pup?" Pete asked him.

"Um, nothing," Bill said, unconvincingly.

"Come on, Billy, you can tell daddy."

Bill shrugged. "I'm tired of just being gay in my head."

Pete looked at him, curiously. "You telling me you haven't had sex?"

Bill felt himself go red. "Well, there was one time, with my friend Marco."

"What did you do?"

Bill, still flushing, mumbled, "Um, I guess it was a blowjob?"

"You gave him one or he gave you one?"

"Me," Bill said.

"And that's it? Otherwise you're a virgin?"

"Yeah."

Pete lifted Bill's face in his hand and said, "Wow! A good-looking boy like you? That's a crime." With a slow, sexy smile, he said, "I could take care of that for you if want."

Mouth suddenly dry, Bill could only nod.

"I'll swing by your place tomorrow around noon."

When Bill let Pete into the apartment, he noticed Pete was older than he looked in the dimly lit bar. There were strands of gray in his thick black hair, wrinkles at the corners of his eyes, and the skin covering his big biceps was a little leathery. Somehow, though, these imperfections only made him sexier. Pete wore his customary black muscle shirt and tight Levi's, the ones with buttons instead of a zipper, sanded down at the crotch to emphasis his bulge.

Pete glanced around the apartment. "I never seen Waldo's pad this clean. That has to be your doing. He's a pig."

"Um, yeah, I wanted to do something for him for letting me stay here."

Pete nodded, closed the distance between them in a single step and put his arms around Bill's waist. "I've been thinking about you since I woke up. Had to keep from jerking off."

Bill, unsure what to say, let himself get pulled against the big man's chest. He tipped his head up and Pete mashed his mouth against Bill's, his tongue forcing Bill's mouth open. *This is French kissing,* Bill thought, before all thoughts went out of Bill's head as Pete's tongue made wet circles in his mouth, his thick chest rubbed against Bill's, and his hands kneaded Bill's butt. When the older man licked his neck and nibbled his ear, touching nerve endings Bill hadn't known existed, he got so hard it hurt.

"What do we have here?" Pete asked, grabbing Bill's cock through his pants.

Bill nearly apologized for his erection but Pete unzipped Bill's fly, stuck a finger into his crotch and rubbed the damp, sticky head of Bill's cock, making him gasp with pleasure.

"Fuck, baby, you're already leaking. That's so hot."

Pete released him, stepped back, pulled his shirt over his head and kicked off his shoes. Not only were Pete's chest and belly covered with hair, but there were tufts of hair on his shoulders. When he removed his Levi's, the dark pelt extended over his thighs and legs. He wore black briefs, his big, hard cock clearly outlined beneath the thin fabric. When he pulled them down, his dick, thick, purplish, and heavily veined, sprang free from a thatch of black hair.

"Your turn, Billy. Show me what you got."

Awkwardly, Bill pulled off his T-shirt, shoes, socks and pants and stood in his BVDs, in what felt like the furnace of Pete's maleness. He was overwhelmed by arousal and anxiety. To buy a little time, he stammered, "Um, I have to pee."

"Go ahead," Pete said. He lay down on the couch. "I'll be waiting for you right here."

Bill closed the door of the bathroom and stood at the toilet, his dick in his hand, pretending to pee. His heart pounded at the thought of the big, naked man waiting for him in the next room. He had no idea what he was supposed to do and he worried that his inexperience would annoy or disappoint Pete. Flushing the toilet, he decided he would do whatever Pete wanted him to do.

"Come here, pretty boy," Pete said, when Bill emerged from the bathroom. But Bill, mesmerized by the sprawl of Pete's naked body, could not move. After years of quick, furtive glances at other boys while they showered in the locker room, trying to memorizing the small details of their bodies to which he would silently masturbate later, Bill was free to look his fill and he could not stop staring.

"You're burning a hole in me with your eyes, Billy. It's okay to touch too." He patted the couch beside him. "Come on, baby. Come over here."

Bill lay down beside him awkwardly. Their bodies were a tight fit on the narrow couch. He felt the heat rising from Bill's skin and he inhaled his musk, a deep mixture of body odors, cigarettes and cologne. Pete reached down, hooked his fingers into the waistband of Bill's briefs, and said, with his white, irresistible smile, "You won't be needing these." He got them down to Bill's knees and then maneuvered his foot and pushed them down all the way to Bill's ankles where they slipped off. Bill had been naked thousands of times but he had never felt truly naked until that moment, his body utterly exposed and unprotected. He shook from head to toe.

"Hey, now," Pete said, gently. "Don't be scared. It's me, Pete. I'll take care of you."

Pete enfolded him in his arms. Their faces touched, their chests touched—the hair on Pete's chest was surprisingly soft—and then everything touched, bellies, thighs, cocks. Pete kissed his neck and whispered, "Relax, baby. I promise I'll make it good for you."

When Pete plunged his tongue into Bill's mouth again, Bill tentatively flicked his own tongue into Pete's mouth, tasting residue of tobacco and toothpaste. It should have been gross, but the slide of their tongues in and out of each other's mouths as, simultaneously, their bodies rubbed together sent ripples of pleasure through him that gave him goosebumps. He sank into the older man's naked embrace as if into a warm bath. Pete's fingers parted and then slipped between Bill's butt cheeks and he felt Pete's thumb press against his butthole, not hard, but purposefully.

"I can't wait to pop your cherry, Billy," Pete rasped.

A spasm of anxiety awoke Bill from the dreamy sensations of their mingled bodies. He knew what Pete meant, of course, but the thought of the older man's meaty purple-headed dick inside of him seemed both implausible and frightening. Before he could say anything, Pete flipped him on his back and shimmied down the couch until his head was level with Bill's crotch. He glanced at Bill with a devilish grin before closing his mouth around Bill's dick. He clenched Pete's shoulders and closed his eyes. A series of noises escaped his throat involuntarily, a combination of coos and moans as Pete moved his mouth faster and faster, his thick tongue teasing and stroking. And then, before he could warn Pete, he filled Pete's mouth in an orgasm that lifted his body off the sofa. Pete kept his mouth glued to Bill's dick, swallowing until there was not a drop left. Only then did he let go, sit up and, wiping his lips, exclaim, "Fuck, that was hot!"

"I didn't have time to tell you," Bill apologized.

"Tell me what? You were coming? I wanted you to come in my mouth." He smiled. "That feel good?"

"Yeah," Bill panted. "That was great."

"Good," Pete said. "Roll over on your belly. It's my turn."

His alarm when Pete licked and prodded his butthole with his tongue—he worried he was not clean down there—was nothing compared to his anxiety when the big bulb of Pete's cock head squeezed its way inside him. Pete had slicked his hole with Jergen's hand lotion and tried to loosen him up with his fingers but the jab of pain when Pete entered him still made Bill grind his teeth.

"You gotta breathe," Pete said hoarsely, his

weight driving Bill into the sofa's smelly cushions. "Ah, fuck, Billy, you're so tight."

He was entirely pinned beneath the older man's body now. Pete wrapped his arms around Bill's chest and pressed Bill's legs closed with his thighs. He sank his dick all the way into Bill's hole until Bill felt Pete's balls slap against his butt. He shut his eyes but the pain exploded little bursts of light beneath his eyelids.

"It hurts."

"Just keep breathing."

A tear gathered in the corner of Bill's eye. His shallow breaths were shudders of pain. "Take it out," he whispered.

"Shh, shh, shh, just breathe, baby. Oh, God, fuck, so good."

A tear ran down Bill's cheek, then another as Pete began to move in and out of him. After a few minutes, the pain lessened to a dull throb. Pete's body slapped against his until they were both slippery with sweat. Bill was conscious of each stroke, of the stink of hand lotion and shit, of the coarse grain of the sofa's fabric against his body, and Pete's hot, grunting breath on his neck. His cock had shriveled and his balls had become twisted up and ached. He waited for it to be over. Pete groaned, then drove himself even deeper and faster into Bill's body, growling Bill's name. Bill felt a hot spill of liquid fill him and then the pounding stopped. For a moment, Pete lay inertly on his body, his dick shriveling inside

Bill. He pulled himself out and panted into Bill's ear, "That was amazing."

Bill wriggled out from beneath Pete and retreated to a corner of the couch. He wiped his eyes and felt sticky liquid dribbling out his butt.

"It hurt," he said accusingly.

Pete grinned. "It always hurts the first time. You'll get used to it and then you'll be begging for it."

Bill, not knowing what else to say, said nothing.

"Ah, don't be mad, Billy. Come over here. Sit on daddy's lap."

Reluctantly, Bill got up and sat on Pete's thighs, ready to spring off if Pete tried to put his dick back into his butt.

"Lean back," Pete said.

Bill leaned against Pete's body. Pete licked his neck, ran his hands over Bill's chest and belly, teased his nipples between thumb and forefinger and made them hard.

"You're a beautiful boy," Pete said. "Your skin's so soft and smooth. You have those pretty blue eyes, those thick lips..."

As he continued complimenting Bill's body, his hand slipped down to Bill's crotch and he began, gently, to stroke his dick.

"Beautiful, tight little ass," he said. "Being inside you was so mind-blowing, Billy, so hot and wet in there. You just gobbled me up. Like you were born to be fucked."

That none of this sounded true to Bill did not prevent him from getting hard in Pete's hand.

"Yeah, that's right. Billy, fuck my hand. Fuck it hard. Come for me."

Bill twisted his head back, caught Pete's mouth and stuck his tongue into it, feeling at the same moment the bristle of Pete's chest hair against his back, the heft of Pete's thighs beneath his butt, the heat of Pete's dick against the small of his back, the smell of Pete's sweat and the sound of his own whimpers; all these sensations and smells and sounds built up in his belly and flushed his chest. A jolt of almost unbearable pleasure coursed through his body, curling his toes, and he gushed semen into Pete's hand. Grinning, Pete slowly spread the cum across Bill's torso, saying, "This will put hair on your chest."

He sat there for a moment with his arms around Pete's neck until Pete said, "Get up, Billy. I got to go home and get ready for work."

The encounter with Pete confused Bill. Pete had hurt him and when he had asked him to stop had ignored him and yet, at the end, he had given Bill that second toe-curling orgasm, the mere memory of which made his dick jump to attention. Maybe the roughness, the borderline brutality, was simply part of sex between men. Still, the experience troubled him and he thought long and hard about why before concluding that it had felt like he was part of Pete's fantasy, a fantasy that, except for the convenience of his body, excluded Bill. He remembered the exchange of warm, low laughter between Waldo and Eddie when they had sex, like two people sharing a private joke, a private happiness. Sex with Pete had been arduous, painful, bewildering and ultimately stupefying pleasurable—but it had not been fun or happy. And yet, though it bothered him, and he was relieved that Pete showed no signs of wanting a repeat, the memory of sex with Pete completely supplanted any thought of Marco when Bill jerked off.

"How do you know if you're a top or a bottom?" Bill asked Waldo one night as they walked home from the bar.

"That's easy, hon, if it feels good when you're getting fucked, you're a bottom. If it feels good when you're doing the fucking, you're a top. If you like it both ways, you're vers."

"Vers?"

"Versatile. Why are you asking?"

They passed Madame Rosa's psychic shop, her name and a palm outlined in red and blue neon in the window.

"Pete fucked me. It hurt a lot. Is that normal?"

Waldo shook his head. "Pete! I was wondering when he'd make a move on you. Did it hurt the whole time?"

"Yeah."

"Do you want to try it again?"

"No way."

"Then you're a top," he said. "Congratulations!"

"Why?"

Waldo laughed. "Because this city is the planet of the bottoms, hon. You're going to be very popular." Then, serious again, Waldo said, "The thing is, Billy, you're like the all-American twink and most guys who cruise you are gonna want to fuck you. You don't have to let them, okay?"

"How will I know if someone's a bottom?"

"Ask," Waldo said.

Although Bill was eager to find another boy to practice with, he was still too shy to approach anyone, so he remained a top in theory only as he continued to relieve himself in his hand.

The first time he saw the Golden Gate Bridge it appeared at the end of a long walk that had taken him through Chinatown, where cooked ducks hung in the windows of restaurants and sidewalk grocery stalls were filled with fruits and vegetables for which he had no name. He had gone past Washington Square, where a white-faced mime followed him across the park parodying his walk, and to Aquatic Park where the fishing boats creaked in their berths like old beds. Looking up, there it was—the bridge—like an edifice on the cover of one of the science fiction paperbacks his brother Tom had left behind when

Michael Nava

he went to college. The bridge was not gold but orange, its graceful span less a structure than a gesture. But it was truly a gate, one that marked the border of the remarkable city from the great swath of sea beyond it. The city that was now his home.

Waldo's apartment was in the Tenderloin, a neighborhood Bill's mother would have called the wrong side of the tracks. It sometimes seemed to Bill that its noisy, crowded streets were composed entirely of gay bars and pizza joints. In back alleys, garbage was piled against the chain-link fences topped with barbed wire that ran along the ground floors of apartment buildings. The buildings themselves, three or four stories high, jostled together cheek to jowl. Whether their façades were wood or brick or plaster, they were equally filthy, the bottom-floor windows barred and the entrances plastered with warnings and advisories about drugs and loitering. Incongruously, above these same entrances he would sometimes see a stone scroll inscribed with a name—*The Windsor Arms, The Adagio, The Norma*—harkening back to the 1920s or '30s when their builders envisioned a sedate, tree-lined district of sophisticated urban dwellers.

The shabby Tenderloin burst with life. People shouted down from third-floor windows, lovers or drunks quarreled loudly in the street and anti-war posters peeled from the sides of walls. In little corner stores that reeked of insecticide the

86

Chinese owners sold single cans of beer to derelicts in rags. The streets, crisscrossed by overhead electrical wires, were slowly pulverized by the incessant flow of cars and delivery trucks and buses. Bums and hippies, buskers, men in suits, whores in miniskirts and bigwigs, off-duty MUNI drivers, anxious-eyed tourists, transvestites, boy prostitutes stroking their bejeaned crotches, brown-skinned children clutching the hands of their pregnant young mothers, Franciscans in long brown habits with rope belts, saffron-robed, shaved headed Buddhist monks, the crazy woman in her wheelchair and Kabuki makeup screaming on the corner, the Bible-thumping black street preacher with a rhinestone studded pectoral cross, the girl in a fringed leather jacket hawking the *Berkeley Barb,* and ordinary people with weary faces trudging home to their tiny apartments on tired feet; these were the people Bill encountered whenever he left the apartment.

In his first few weeks, this urban chaos terrified him because he had no point of reference for it. Eden Plains was a town of ten thousand people from working-class white families, each with its two- or three-bedroom tract house and a summer cottage in Michigan. The fathers worked at the Ford factory and complained about the union. The mothers were housewives who attended PTA meetings. No one locked their door at night. Once or twice a year, the dads might take the boys to a Cubs game at Wrigley or Soldier Field to see the Bears. Bill's life in Eden Plains was as hermetic and predictable as life at a monastery but now he been turned out into the world, noisy, unpredictable, and evidently indifferent to whether he sank or swam.

As the days passed, his fear began to abate, replaced by a new feeling he slowly recognized as freedom. If this urban world was indifferent to his survival, it was equally indifferent to his quirks and to who he was and what he desired. A city that could accommodate a six-foot, five-inch transvestite in a purple wig and fishnet stockings offering dates to passing motorists surely had room for an eighteen-year-old gay boy.

Waldo showed him what this freedom could mean; he was like a brightly colored bird who had escaped its cage and soared above the city. Waldo, who applied glitter to his eyelids and slashed his lips with deep red lipstick and, when Bill asked nervously, "Are you going out like that?" looked at him and said, "You're right, doll, I need some blush too." Waldo, who flipped off the teenage boys who screamed "Faggot!" at him while screaming back "Asshole punks! Suck my queer dick!" Waldo, who flirted with MUNI drivers who, to Bill's amazement, flirted back, and who cruised the young Mexican bagger at the roach-infested supermarket where they shopped and succeeded in getting him into his bed. And when, one night, Bill woke up screaming from a nightmare of being beaten by his father, it was

Waldo who held him and said, "Oh, honey, it's okay. You're not in Kansas anymore," and when Bill said, "I'm from Illinois," howled in laughter as if Bill had made the best joke ever, until Bill laughed too.

Waldo's apartment was too small for privacy, and in any event, Waldo kept little to himself. He always emerged naked from the bathroom after his morning shower. Bill became accustomed to Waldo's pale, skinny, nearly hairless body, his long, pencil-thin penis, flat butt, big feet and the jagged scars around his wrists.

"What happened?" Bill asked him, not the first time he saw them, but later, after they were friends.

"I didn't think pills would work fast enough," Waldo replied, "so I used daddy's straight-edged razor to teach the motherfucker a lesson." He sighed, "You know what they say about hating, Billy? Hating is like drinking poison and expecting the other guy to die. I lived and I had to stop hating them."

"Who? Your family?"

"Uh-huh," Waldo. "Well, my relatives. My friends are my family. Yeah, I stopped hating them but I don't want anything to do with them, either. We were strangers on a train." He peered at Bill. "Your relatives too, hon. They were just strangers on a train. That part of your trip is done and you don't ever have to see them again. You're free now, Billy. They can't hurt you anymore."

But despite what Waldo said, some part of Bill still ached for his family and though the ache faded, it never went away entirely. Sometimes he thought if he could make them proud of him, they would re-admit him but he could not imagine the kind of success he would have to achieve before they would forgive him for being what he was.

One night, at the end of a ten-hour shift, Bill trudged home from the supermarket carrying a bag filled with dented cans of fruit cocktail, soup and tomato sauce his boss had given him. Mr. Liu's generosity surprised him because usually the damaged cans were sold as markdowns but, Bill thought, a recent visit from the city's public health department might have had something to do with it. No matter, it was food. Waldo would be happy and Bill liked making Waldo happy because he owed him so much. It was Waldo who got him the job bagging at the Calimart when his boyfriend had quit and moved away. Well, not boyfriend. Eddie was Waldo's boyfriend. Carlos had been what Waldo called "a number."

Waldo had a lot of numbers and over time Bill realized he was attracted to a particular type of guy, what Bill referred to as a Negro or Mexican, ("No, doll," he heard Waldo saying, "we call them Afro-American and Chicano."), working men, usually married, barrel-chested, stocky and shorter than Waldo. "Fireplugs," he called them admiringly and confided to Bill, "But not

their dicks, honey. Nothing little about those."
They came and went, but Eddie was Waldo's
constant. Easygoing Eddie with his big smile and
rumbly, low voice who brought Waldo flowers,
opened the door for him and pulled out his chair
at restaurants. Eddie with his wife and two
daughters. Bill had given up trying to understand
the nature of Waldo and Eddie's relationship or
whether Eddie was gay or if his wife knew about
his nights with Waldo. "Not your circus, hon,"
Waldo snapped when Bill asked those questions.
"Not your monkeys."

Bill had a type, too, he realized, though he kept
it to himself. He liked Mexican boys— "Chicanos,"
he mentally corrected himself. Maybe it was
because they reminded him of olive-skinned
Marco, but in any gathering of gay men, in the
bars or the demonstrations Waldo dragged him
to, he was always drawn to Chicano boys with
their inky hair, dark eyes and smooth flesh the
color of walnut meat. They were, unfortunately,
in short supply. But there was Michael, the
beautiful boy at the *taqueria* at the corner of
Hyde and Ellis who smiled brightly whenever Bill
came in for his *pollo asado* burrito and always
managed to brush his fingers against Bill's hand
when he gave him his change. Bill wanted to ask
him out but was uncertain whether Michael was
gay. Waldo would know, but Waldo might also
tease him if he knew Bill liked the other boy so
Bill had, so far, kept mum.

He fumbled in his pocket for the key and when he pushed open the door to the apartment, the lights were all out. He stepped inside, closed the door behind him and touched the light switch.

A fistful of confetti grazed his face followed by male voices, shouting, "SURPRISE!"

Half the number 19 on the cake had been cut and served. In the corner, Pete and his new boyfriend, a seventeen-year-old named Hank, were slowly grinding against each other to *Me and Mrs. Jones* and every surface in the apartment was covered with paper plates and plastic glasses. The smells of lasagna, garlic bread and pot hung in the air.

"You didn't really think I was gonna forget your birthday, did you?" Waldo asked.

Bill was wedged between him and Eddie on the sofa. The other guests were sitting or standing wherever they could find a space. "I kinda forgot myself," Bill said. "So much has happened in the last six months."

"Nineteen," Eddie said. "Your last year as a teen. That's a big deal. Not as big as twenty-one, of course. When you hit that one, we're going to take you out and get you shit-faced, Billy. Show you a wild time!"

Waldo giggled. "Billy's idea of a wild time is leaving the cap off the toothpaste." He sucked on the joint he held delicately between his thumb and forefinger. "Come on, doll, live a little. Take a puff."

"You know it just makes me cough."

"I'll take it," Eddie said.

"Like your presents?" Waldo asked.

Bill snorted. All the presents involved sex. Poppers, lube, a dildo, a skin magazine.

"I think you're trying to tell me something."

"Yeah," Eddie said. "You need to get laid, pretty boy like you. It's a waste."

Bill shrugged. "I've had sex."

"Pete doesn't count," Waldo said. "Pete's like the welcome wagon, he fucks every new arrival to the city. So, what do you want for your birthday? What do you really want?"

He looked at his two friends, drew a deep breath and said, "I want to go to school. To college. To make something of myself."

"Good for you, Billy," Eddie said, with a fatherly smile of approval, toasting the air with his bottle of beer.

Waldo merely squinted at him and took another hit off the joint.

After everyone had gone, even Eddie, someone buzzed from the entrance.

"I'll get that," Waldo shouted, stopping Bill at the door. He grinned at him. "It's your last present."

A moment later, he returned to the apartment with Michael, the boy from the *taqueria*.

That night, Waldo took the couch and gave Bill and Michael the bed where Bill fucked a boy for the first time. After he and Michael had tussled for awhile on Waldo's bed, Michael rolled onto his belly and spread his legs, looked over his shoulder with a lascivious grin and whispered, "What are you waiting for?" Bill could scarcely believe Michael was going to let him do this to him. His hands shook so hard, he could not position his dick correctly. Michael lifted his pretty little rump, reached back and guided Bill in. "Now fuck me *guapito*," he said. As Bill sank his dick into the other boy every cell of his body groaned Yes.

Before he left the next morning, Michael explained that he had a boyfriend but Dennis wouldn't care if Bill fucked him too, though sometimes he might want to watch.

"It's cute how shy you were at the restaurant," he said. "I can come over on Sunday, okay?"

Bill drifted through work in an erotic daze, reliving every second of what it felt like being inside of Michael's yielding flesh and grateful that the long apron he wore hid his hard-on. When he got home that evening, Waldo was in the kitchen and the apartment smelled of curry.

"Look on the coffee table," he shouted over the sizzle of hot oil in a fry pan.

Bill looked at the shiny cover of a catalogue for San Francisco Community College.

"Classes start in March," Waldo said, coming into the room.

"Oh, Waldo," Bill said, seizing the catalogue. "Thank you!"

"Sure, Billy, but you know, doll, you don't have to make something of yourself. You already are somebody. You're Bill."

6.

I TRUDGED UP EUREKA STREET BENEATH leafless trees in a heavy mist to Bill Ryan's house and found myself standing before a beautifully restored Edwardian duplex. The body of the building was a warm, buttery yellow, the fretwork and Juliet balcony a creamy white. Elsewhere were touches of deep green while the capitals of the columns flanking the porch, the oak and acorn frieze, and the sunburst above the second-floor bay windows were gold-leafed. The house glistened in the damp and darkness of the morning as snug as a little ark ploughing briskly through rough waters. The Castro was filled with old houses like this, brought out of disrepair by the gay men who had settled the neighborhood in the previous decade. But I had never seen one so self-contained or that spoke so yearningly of refuge.

The doors were four-paneled and painted forest green, inset with a square, leaded glass window. A curtain was drawn over the door to my left. Above the door on the right was an address that matched the one on Ryan's insurance application. I peered through the uncurtained window at a carpeted stairway that disappeared into darkness. I could feel the emptiness but I rang the bell anyway and, when that failed to get a response, pounded on the door. Out of the corner of my eye, I saw the curtain on the left door flicker. I knocked again. The other door opened a crack and a shadow in the doorway said in an old woman's irritated croak, "Nobody's home."

She didn't slam the door shut, so I said, "I'm looking for Nick Trejo."

"You won't find him here," she replied, but her tone was less annoyed than curious, so I went on.

"I work for an insurance company. Nick's friend, Bill Ryan, took out a life insurance policy and made Nick the beneficiary. The company won't pay out on the policy until I find him."

The door opened wide to reveal a small woman in a flowery housecoat, silver hair carefully arranged around a pink face whose features had dissolved into a puddle of sags and wrinkles. She looked me up and down with sharp blue eyes.

"You say Nick has money coming to him?"

"If I can find him, Missus..." I said politely.

"Donohue," she allowed.

"My name is Henry. Henry Rios."

Curiosity warred with suspicion in those bright, shrewd eyes. Curiosity won. "You better come in out of the damp, Mister Henry Rios."

Mrs. Donohue's apartment was a typical San

Francisco railroad flat, all the rooms opening off a long, dark, narrow hallway that led from the front door to a small, sunlit space at the back. The high-ceilinged hallway was half paneled in narrow slats of oak. Above the paneling was a gallery of framed family photographs. She led me into a front room that faced the street by way of three tall, lace-curtained bay windows through which, no doubt, she had been seen me come up the stairs. Above a gas fireplace was a faded, hand-tinted photograph of a stern-faced young man in a navy uniform. Mr. Donohue, I assumed. The parlor—I couldn't imagine she called it anything else—featured Oriental carpets, large, dark pieces of furniture and Staffordshire bric-a-brac. Doilies covered the end tables and antimacassars were strategically deployed on the backs of the armchairs and the sofa. A built-in bookshelf held rows of Reader's Digest Condensed Books dating to the '50s. On the wall opposite the fireplace was a large, framed colored print of a severe looking Jesus parting his robe to reveal a heart crowned with a circlet of thorns and a flame. Through the open pocket doors, I saw a dining room filled with the same heavy furniture. The table was covered with a lace tablecloth and, in its center, was a blue and white ceramic bowl filled with plastic fruit. The place smelled like old wool and attar of rose. There was not a speck of dust anywhere.

I had stepped back in time to when the Castro, then called Eureka Valley, was home to working-class Irish families. I had occasionally seen an old Irish widow—for it seemed the only remnants of that era were women—trudging up Castro Street, retaining custody of their eyes just as the nuns had taught them, by looking straight ahead and ignoring the hordes of young men that engulfed them. The spire of their parish church, Blessed Savior, was, along with the bright neon Castro Theater sign, one of the neighborhood's two signature landmarks.

"Sit down," Mrs. Donohue commanded and when I did, said, "How do I know you're who you say you are?"

I handed her a business card.

"This says you're a lawyer, not an insurance man."

"I am a lawyer, but I also work part-time for Western States Insurance Company as a claims investigator."

"You're sure you're not working for *them*," she said, laying hostile emphasis on the last word.

"For who, Missus Donohue?"

"Them that's swooped in from Chicago and turned Nick out of his house. Bill Ryan's kin."

"No, ma'am. I'm just trying to find Nick to confirm the details of Bill Ryan's death so we can pay out the policy. I had no idea Bill Ryan's family was here."

"Came in like locusts before the body was cold," she said, bitterly. "Put a new lock on the door while Nick was still in the hospital and wouldn't let him back in even to get his clothes, poor boy."

"They have no legal right to keep him from getting his things out of the apartment," I said. "When I find him, I'll tell him so."

Her face softened. "I'm forgetting my manners. Let me make you a cup of tea."

Over Irish Breakfast tea and Vanilla Wafers, I learned quite a bit about Mrs. Peggy Donohue and her upstairs neighbors.

"I grew up around the corner, on Diamond Street," she began. "Married a boy from down the block."

"Childhood sweetheart?" I ventured.

"No, his best friend. The one who came back from the war alive. Married thirty-five years, two kids. Maggie met a boy from L.A. when she was at State and they live down south now. Timmy was drafted to Viet Nam in sixty-seven. He died there." She tipped her head toward a folded flag mounted in a shadow box on the wall. "That's all I have left of him."

"I'm sorry, Mrs. Donohue."

"Oh, call me Peg." She sipped her tea. She made it as strong as my grandmother had brewed her Lipton, to rouse her ancient taste buds. "The kids were right about that war. We had no business there. Too late now. Have another cookie."

"Thank you." I bit into the brown wafer and felt I had entered, not her house, but the old woman's memory. Even the light smearing the windows seemed to be falling from a long-ago sun.

"My husband Jim died in nineteen-seventy-one. The neighborhood was already changing by then. The old folks were dying. Their kids were moving out, down to the peninsula to those new houses where their kids had yards to play in, instead of the streets. I stayed put, with the other old women, the widows." She fixed her blue eyes on me. "Jim and I bought this place after the war and rented out the top to help with the mortgage. In seventy-three, my tenants moved out. By then, young men had started to move into the neighborhood. The church says it's a sin, what these boys were, so a lot of us old people wanted nothing to do with them."

I sipped my tea as she collected her thoughts,

"Why they came to Eureka Valley, I don't know. But pretty soon, they were buying up the old houses and opening businesses in the boarded-up shops on Castro Street. The neighborhood came back to life, but it was all these men, not women with strollers or kids headed to the parish school. Around that time, we got a new priest down at Blessed Savior, Father Toby. Some of the old folks went to him and asked him if there wasn't something they could do to save the valley from these boys. Fairies, they called them, and worse than that. He told them he would give them his answer on Sunday at the ten o'clock Mass."

"Well," she continued, "the church was packed. Father Toby stood up to give the homily on some verses in Deuteronomy."

She got up from her armchair, went to the bookshelf and returned with a thick oversized book, bound in dark leather, *The Holy Bible* emblazoned in gold lettering on its cover. When she opened it, a piece of official looking paper slipped out and fell to the floor. I retrieved it, glancing at it as I returned it to her: her son's death certificate.

"Here," she said, and began to read reverently. "'The great God, mighty and awesome, has no favorites, accepts no bribes, executes justice for the orphan and the widow, and loves the stranger, giving them food and clothing. So, you too should love the stranger, for that is what you were in the land of Egypt.' Then he told us these boys—these strangers—were beloved of God, and that we had to love them. Take them into our neighborhood." She closed the book and set it aside. "Well! Down at the coffee hour after Mass some of the old men were saying things to Father Toby that you don't say to priests, but he stuck to his guns."

"A few days later, these two boys came to my door to see about the upstairs apartment. Waldo and Billy. Now Waldo," she said, and smiled. "You could have picked him for a fairy if he was standing still. Billy, he could have been one of my son Timmy's school friends."

"Billy was Bill Ryan?"

She nodded. "He and Waldo couldn't have been more different, but they were best friends. Waldo was—" she smiled softly, reminiscently, "a sprite. A skinny little thing with a bushel of red hair and bright blue eyes. Polish boy. He had time for everyone and not a care in the world. A teasing sort of boy, but never mean. No, he was softhearted, kind. Billy was quiet and solid and handsome. He had a big flop of black hair falling over his forehead and worried eyes. Anyway, they wanted to see the apartment. Well, I'm ashamed to say that I hemmed and hawed because I wasn't sure I wanted to rent to them."

"What changed your mind?"

"It was something Waldo said about the old movie I was watching when they came to the door. I don't remember what, exactly, but he made me laugh, so I let them see the place. I watched them as they looked around, whispering and giggling, and I thought, Peg, they're just boys. No horns or tails. And I remembered what Father Toby said. Welcome the strangers. So, I rented to them."

"How did Bill Ryan come to own the building?"

"After he got his real estate business going strong, I told him I couldn't keep up with the property taxes that kept rising and rising and asked him to sell the place for me. He offered to buy it and let me stay in the apartment rent-free for the rest of my life. Wrote it into our contract."

"That was generous of him."

Her eyes misted and it was a moment before

she spoke. "Bill Ryan had his troubles, but he was a good man."

"What kind of troubles, Peg?" I ventured.

"Waldo told me Bill's family threw him out for being gay when he was only eighteen. Gave him a bit of money and told him to get lost." She glanced at the flag on the opposite wall. "What kind of people throw away their child?"

"Unfortunately, that's not an unusual story."

She gave me a sharp, shrewd look. "That doesn't make it right. I don't think Bill ever got over it."

"I don't imagine he did," I said, thinking about all the other refugees from disapproving families wandering around the neighborhood. "What else can you tell me about him?"

She smiled. "Well, Waldo would come downstairs to watch old movies with me and make me laugh with his comments but Bill, he made sure the rent was paid and the plumbing worked."

"He was responsible."

"Very," she said. "Bill was a regular man, not like the other gays flitting from boy to boy like butterflies going from flower to flower. He was what we used to call the marrying kind. I know he was happy when he found Nick."

"When was that?"

"It was after Waldo moved out," she said. "After Bill took this old dump and made it beautiful."

"The restoration was Bill's idea?"

She nodded. "Back in the fifties, my husband covered the house with vinyl siding and painted it gray to save on the upkeep. When Bill bought the place from me, he took down the siding and went to work putting it back the way it was when it was first built. Spent a fortune. Why? I asked him. It's just somewhere to live."

"What did he say?"

"He said houses have souls, just like people, and he was going to uncover this one's. For such a practical man, that was a funny thing to say, but I could tell he believed it. He loved the city, loved the buildings, the streets. Anyway, he made this place into his home and after that, all he needed was someone to share it with him."

"Nick," I said. "Do you know how they met?"

She shook her head. "No. I started seeing Nick leaving Bill's apartment in the morning. I was a little shocked because he was so young. Bill was young too, of course, but he was a man and Nick was still a boy. The first time I saw them together, Bill seemed a little embarrassed. Later he told me, Peg, I swear he's legal. I laughed and said, well I didn't think he wasn't and Lord knows you're not the first man who likes them young, Bill, as long as he makes you happy. I guess he did, because he moved in not too long after they met. Nick was a good boy," she continued. "He reminded me of Waldo. Not that he was as light in his loafers as my Waldo, but he was just as sweet. That boy," she continued, "had been well loved by someone.

His family, I imagine. Raised a good Catholic, too. We got into the habit of going to the ten o'clock Mass down at Blessed Savior."

"Just you and Nick? Bill didn't go?"

She shook her head. "The church was part of the hatefulness he left behind when he came to California. He wanted nothing to do with it, but he would meet us after Mass and we would go to breakfast. It was a happy time until, you know, the AIDS started."

"Yes," I said. "AIDS has ended a lot of happy times."

She sighed deeply. "This morning on my way to the bank I saw a boy, why he couldn't have been more than twenty-one, shuffling across the street on two canes. So skinny you could almost see through him. The old convent at Blessed Savior, the one where the nuns lived who used to teach at the school? We want to make it into a hospice. For our boys."

A familiar fear squeezed my heart like a cold hand, silencing me.

"My Waldo died," she said. "Died hard." She fumbled in the pocket of her housecoat for a handkerchief and wiped her eyes. "It was like all the plagues of Egypt were visited on him before the Lord in His mercy took him. It was horrible, just horrible. Billy was there for the whole thing and I could see how hard it was for him."

"Yes," I said. "To lose a friend..."

"And wonder if you're next," she said, completing my thought.

"Yes," I said, to my lap. When I met her eyes, they were filled with sympathy.

"That not knowing can change you. It changed Bill for the worse and he took out his worry on Nick."

"How?"

"Nick stopped taking communion. When I asked him about it, he said Bill was worried about Nick sharing the communion cup with men who had the virus or taking the host from someone who was sick. Then he stopped going to Mass completely. Dropped out of school. It was like Bill couldn't let him out of his sight."

"To protect him?"

"But you can't," she said. "That's what I told Bill. You can't lock him up against something you can't see. Bill told me to mind my own business. He had never spoken to me like that before and afterward we didn't have much to say to each other. Except for the time Nick came down with a black eye."

I replied with a startled, "Bill hit him?"

"Nick said it was an accident but I know all about women who had those kinds of accidents from their husbands. This was no different. I told Bill if he ever laid hands on the boy again, he would have to answer to me. If he hit him again," she said, "he was careful that it wasn't anywhere I could see."

"What happened the night Bill died?"

Her face sagged and it was a moment before she answered. "I can't tell you much. It was very late and I was sound asleep when the firemen pounded on my door. They took me outside and told me they needed to check my apartment for a gas leak. I was scared and confused. I saw Nick in the back of an ambulance with one of his brothers, Sal, I think his name is, and then they took him away. I watched them bring down a big black bag all zipped up from Bill's place. What's that, I asked a fireman. The other man, he said. Another fireman asked me if I had somewhere I could go because it wasn't safe in my apartment with all the gas upstairs. A police car came and took me to my friend Edith's house where I stayed until the gas company said I could come home."

She wiped her eyes again. "A few days later, Bill's brother showed up, put a new lock on Bill's door and asked me a lot of questions. I played dumb. I was coming home from the store and saw Nick on the porch. They wouldn't let him in the apartment to get his things."

"Do you know where Nick is now?"

"He gave me an address to forward his mail," she said. She got up and went to a secretary in the corner of the room. She returned with a slip of paper. "Here. It's his parents' house, I think."

"Thank you, Peg."

"Waldo and Billy, both gone," she said. "Gone so young, their whole lives ahead of them. And me still here at eighty. Does that seem right to you?"

The mist had turned to rain as I walked back to my office. On the side of a building on 18th Street near Castro someone had written in red spray paint, *Where's the outrage!* The first time I saw someone dying from the disease was shortly after I got out of rehab. I'd met some men at a Thursday night AA meeting in the Castro who invited me out to coffee afterward. Still feeling fragile, I would have passed except that I was under orders from Larry to accept such invitations.

You're an isolator, Henry. I don't even think that's a real word, Larry. Don't be a smartass. If someone reaches out to you, you say yes. I'm no good at small talk. This isn't small talk, my friend, this is recovery. Alcoholism is a disease of isolation. You need to put as many sober people as you can between you and the bottle. So, go have a damn cup of coffee with these guys.

Larry was right. There wasn't much small talk with these guys; coffee was a continuation of the meeting as they talked about their fears and their hopes and the road they were trying to construct that would take them from one to the other. One evening, one of them said, "Chris's in the hospital and wanted us to bring a meeting to him." That's how I found myself with six other men encircling a hospital bed at SF General. We all wore gowns and masks and plastic gloves. Jack was probably in his late twenties, though the disease had leeched the youthfulness from him. I remember, especially, that his hair was lifeless and brittle and he stank of piss and medicine. His face and hands were covered with purple lesions, the mark of Kaposi sarcoma, one of the more common opportunistic diseases. His tongue was covered with a fungus. He was going blind from CMV. The informal leader of our group, the man who had brought us here to have an AA meeting, asked Jack to pick a topic for discussion. "Gratitude," he whispered.

When I got home to my apartment from the hospital, I stripped naked and inspected every inch of my body for lesions. I did not sleep that night, thinking about the man dying in the hospital bed. Would I be next? *Where's the outrage?* Most of us had yet to arrive at outrage. We were still traveling through horror.

I'd had to maintain a professional detachment while I interviewed Peg Donohue, concealing, as best I could, how deeply affected I was by her talk of Bill Ryan's life and death. The fact was that his life and mine were not so dissimilar. We had both been forced to choose between our families and their cultures—his Irish Catholic, mine Mexican Catholic—and the freedom we needed to express our deepest sense of ourselves. Well, not chosen, exactly. Apparently, his family had made the choice for him. I had not been so explicitly rejected by my family, but only because my parents died before I had a chance to come out to them. Had they not, I'm sure I would have been violently disowned by my father with my passive mother going along.

Both of us—Bill Ryan and I—seem to have responded in the same way to having been cast out of our tribes, by becoming over-conscientious overachievers, as if our successes and accomplishments could compensate for our deficiencies as sons. We weren't unique. There was even a name for this reaction—the best little boy in the world syndrome. I had spent hours talking about this with Larry, who himself suffered from this syndrome.

It's like, I said, I have to justify the air I breathe by being better than everyone else at my job. That's a tough way to live, he replied. Waiting for the other shoe to drop. Yeah, that's exactly how it feels. That dread of being exposed as—As what? he asked. A faggot? A queer? That ship has already sailed for both of us, Henry. I know, I know. I started coming out of the closet when I was seventeen, so why do I still feel like I have to prove myself? Because, Larry said, it's hard to be hated and to never know when that hatred's going to slap you in the face.

After my morning, it was a relief to step into the Gold Mountain, where Adam greeted me with a dazzling smile, and to turn my head off. Today he was cooking but, after I got my food, he came out of the kitchen to take his break with me.

"How's your day going?" he asked.

For a moment, I thought about telling him Bill Ryan's story, if only to relieve myself of the sadness it had caused me, but Adam was untouched by a world where parents rejected their children and men died ghastly deaths. I wanted to keep it that way.

"Just putting one foot in front of the other." I replied. I looked at the plate in front of me, piled high with broccoli and beef and rice. "This is a lot of food. Did you make up my plate?"

He grinned. "You need to eat, Henry. You're all skin and bones."

"We can't all be gym rats."

"Do you get any exercise?"

"I run five miles a day."

"That's great for cardio and legs but it doesn't do anything for your upper body."

"I could lift weights until I was a quivering mass of jelly but I'd never look like you."

He smiled. "You don't have to be a muscle head to be fit."

"How did you get started bodybuilding?"

He laughed. "I'm not a bodybuilder, that's a full-time job and I've already got one, in case you hadn't noticed. I lift for fun. I started in high school and took to it right away. I liked the workouts, liked the pump, liked the way I looked. Plus, people don't expect a Chinese guy to be built like the Hulk. It makes them nervous."

"I bet."

"Yeah, I flex my biceps and put on my mean face and they don't ask stupid questions like, where were you born or say stuff like, you speak really good English. And I don't have to tell them I was born at St. Mary's on Stanyan Street and I speak good English because I'm a fucking American." He smiled. "White devils. You get that too?"

"One of my first clients took one look at me and said he wanted a real lawyer, not some wetback," I said. "Ironically, he was a black guy."

"What happened?"

"We worked it out, but there have been other clients who plain refused to let me represent them." I speared some meat and vegetable with my fork. "Where do you lift?"

"A buddy owns a gym south of Market. Nothing fancy. Basically, a warehouse with weights and a bunch of muscle heads grunting and calling each other 'fag.'"

I froze and something shattered inside of me. I forced myself to swallow the food in my mouth. Heart pounding, I lifted my head, met his eyes, and said, as calmly as I could, "I'm gay, Adam, and I prefer you not use that word around me."

I braced myself for his response.

He flushed dark red and sputtered, "Oh, fuck! Oh, fuck! I'm so sorry."

I relaxed a fraction.

"You must think I'm an asshole," he continued. "I swear I didn't mean anything by it. I was just talking shit."

"You want to be careful who you talk shit to," I said. "In this city, at this moment."

We stared at each other, a gulf between us where none had been before.

"Man, I feel so bad." His distress seemed genuine. "What can I say?"

I was torn being wanted to console him and wanting to get away from him as quickly as I could. The latter impulse won out.

"I've had a tough morning. You mind bringing the check? I have to get going."

"You haven't touched your food."

"I'll take it with me."

In a shaky voice, he said, "Listen, please, you don't have to go. I am so sorry."

He sounded sincere, but my nerves were raw.

"I can't talk to you now," I said, more sharply than I'd intended.

He fled into the kitchen. A moment later, Mr. Chu boxed my lunch for me and when I asked for the check, grunted, "On the house."

As soon as I was out of eyesight of the restaurant, in a burst of delayed fury, I tossed the takeout bag into a trashcan.

7.

THE SECOND TIME BILL SLEPT with Michael, he learned Michael's last name was Vega and that he came from a Mexican-American family ("Chicano," Waldo automatically corrected him) in Riverside from which he too had been banished for being gay. On their third date, Michael told him that Dennis—the older man he had called his boyfriend—actually had another lover and was seeing Michael on the sly. After their fourth date, Michael said there was something he wanted to show Bill, a surprise. The two of them took the number 21 MUNI to Alamo Square Park and hiked to the top, above Steiner Street. Just before they reached the summit, Michael told Bill to shut his eyes and led him by the hand the rest of the way. They came to a stop and Michael said, "Look."

Below them was a row of seven restored Victorian houses. The body of each house was painted a different color—sky blue, emerald, cinereal, apricot, wheat—but the fretwork, lattices, columns, pediments, bas relief, were white- or gold-leafed. Behind them the city calmly unfurled itself in the cantaloupe-colored light of late afternoon.

Bill managed a stunned, "Wow!"

Michael said, "They're called the painted ladies."

Bill squeezed Michael's hand. "They're beautiful."

"Can you imagine living in a house like that?" Michael asked, returning the pressure. "You and me?"

"Yeah," Bill said, eagerly, throwing his arm around the other boy's shoulder and squeezing him close. "I can."

On their fifth date, Bill blurted out, "I love you."

Behind those words were a thousand nights of lonely fantasies and a notion of love formed by his observations of the dating rituals in Eden Plains. There, when a boy and a girl were going steady, he displayed his ownership by giving her his letter jacket and escorting her to classes. With these and countless other small intimacies—passed notes, shared lunches, hasty kisses at classroom doorways—they created a closed world in which, having found each other, they had no need of anyone else. At the junior prom, they slow danced in the corner, even though a fast song was playing, moving to a music only they could hear. Bill's declaration of love to Michael was an invitation to separate themselves from the gyrating crowd and slow dance forever.

Michael's offhanded, "I love you too, hon," accompanied by a pert kiss, left Bill thrilled but uncertain. His confusion turned to anger when Michael refused to stop seeing Dennis.

"You're my boyfriend now," Bill told him as they lay naked on the fold-out couch.

"Yeah, sure, but," Michael scrunched his nose, "Dennis pays my rent."

"He what?" Bill said, angrily.

"Oh, papi, don't be pissed. I make shit working at that burrito place and I'm trying to save up to go to beauty school. Dennis helps me out, that's all."

"He gives you money to have sex with him."

"Well," Michael replied, annoyed, "when you say it like that, you make me sound like a whore."

"Isn't that what you are if someone pays you for sex?"

"Fuck you." Michael jumped out of bed and pulled on his clothes. "You think I want to spend my life in shitholes like this with losers like you? Hell, no." He finished dressing and, hands on his hips, declared, "You're cute and a good lay, but I'm looking for someone to take care of me."

"I can take care of you," Bill insisted angrily.

"Grow up, Billy. You can barely take care of yourself." And with that, he flounced out of the apartment.

In tears, he related the argument to Waldo,

who told him, "Don't cry, hon. She'll cool down and be back in your bed in no time."

"What about that Dennis guy giving him money for sex? That's wrong."

Waldo lifted a pale eyebrow. "I wouldn't be so quick to judge. We do what we have to survive."

"Like what, being a whore?" Bill replied bitterly.

Waldo shook his head. "Jeez, you can take the boy out of the sticks but you can't take the sticks out of the boy."

"What's that supposed to mean?" Bill snapped.

"I mean," Waldo replied pointedly, "we ain't living in your little white fence fantasy world where if you fuck somebody you own them. That's for boys and girls. Boys and boys play by different rules. You really need to get out more, doll."

Waldo's response left him feeling more alone than he had since stepping off the Greyhound. The gratitude and relief he had felt at stumbling into this world of men like himself had, through familiarity, begun to wear off. He had begun to notice how rootless his friends were, how improvised their lives. They drifted from little job to little job, from one ratty apartment to the next, from one dark bar to another and from bed to bed with partners whose names, if they knew them at all, they quickly forgot.

Bill was still the same boy his parents had raised him to be, for the life they had raised him to expect—a good job, a nice house, and someone he loved, and who loved him, waiting for him at the end of the day. He didn't sleep around, or drink or take drugs. He worked and went to school and came home. Straight lines on narrow paths while he waited, as Waldo once said, impatiently, for his prince to come. As time passed, he began to wonder if all he was saving himself for was, paradoxically, the same lonely life he had feared when he lay alone at night in his bedroom in Eden Plains. There, he really had been alone but here, in San Francisco, he was surrounded by other gay men. What was it his grandmother liked to say when some little plan was foiled by circumstances beyond her control? *Water, water everywhere, but not a drop to drink!* That was how he felt, parched in an oasis because the water on offer seemed tainted to him.

Maybe the problem was not with the water, but his attitude. Maybe he was holding on to his virtue not because he was virtuous but because it made him feel superior to the men around him. Made him feel, *I'm not like those other—* Other what? he asked himself. Other *faggots? Queers?* Maybe it all came down to his need to believe that, after all, in some fundamental way he was not gay. But he knew he was. Was gay. Was like other gay men. That, when catching the lust in a stranger's eyes as they passed on Polk Street, he felt an answering heat. That his most thrilling sexual fantasies were coarse and hot and anonymous. There were places all over the city where he knew he could act them out. Water, water, everywhere—maybe it was time to take the plunge and overcome that last resistance he felt within himself to being who he was.

And so, late one night he entered a bathhouse off Polk Street where he was greeted by pulsing disco music, the stink of poppers, and a gimlet-eyed attendant at a counter who took his money and gave him a towel and a key to a locker to store his clothes. The reception area was harshly lit but once he pushed through the interior doors, he entered a red haze of near darkness. Off to one side was a bank of gym lockers. On the other a dimly lit corridor, studded with doors, led into the gloom. Men in towels shuttled in and out of the doors. Someone laughed, someone else moaned. The music thudded overhead. Bill's heart raced and not for the first time in the gay world he was unable to distinguish whether he felt fear or excitement, attraction or repulsion. He had just stowed his clothes into his locker and tied the towel around his waist when a man came up, leaned against the lockers, looked him over, and said, in a friendly voice, "Hi, I'm Jack. What's your name?"

Jack towered above him, his massive body sculpted at one of the gyms that advertised in the gay newspapers, and he had the requisite buzzed hair and moustache. Billy would have been completely intimidated had Jack's face, plain almost to the point of homeliness, not reminded him of a friendly dog.

"I'm Billy."

"How are you doing tonight, Billy?"

"Um, I'm a little nervous. I never been here before."

Jack smiled. "Nothing to be scared about. We're all friends here." He brushed his big fingers across Bill's chest. "Why don't you come to my room."

The touch of Jack's fingertips startled him into hyper-alertness. He was suddenly and keenly aware of being nearly naked in a pit of heat and darkness thick with the musk and noises of sex. He had expected to be repulsed but instead the blood surged to the surface of his skin and his cock stiffened. Jack, who noticed the sudden movement beneath the thin towel, grinned and said, "That a yes?"

Bill managed a hoarse, "Uh-huh."

Jack dropped a friendly arm around Bill's shoulders and shepherded him down the murky corridor to a door he unlocked to reveal a tiny cubicle. Inside was a single bed covered with a rumpled sheet and a metal bedside table. On the table was a piece of cardboard, a razor, and a nub of something white.

"What's that?" Bill asked, alarmed at the sight of the razor.

"Blow," Jack said. "You've never done it before?"

"No," Bill said.

"Watch me." He took the razor and cut the white nub into powder and then knelt beside the table, lowered his head, pinched one nostril shut and inhaled a line of the powder with the other. He threw his head back, sniffed loudly, and then cut another line. He grinned at Bill. "Your turn."

Bill hesitated. He associated drugs with the long-haired stoners in high school who hung out in the student parking lot, furtively sharing joints between classes. "Degenerates," his father called the potheads. It was the same word he used for homosexuals and it was enough to scare Bill off drugs.

"I don't know," Bill said.

"Hey," Jack said, standing up and wrapping his big arms around Bill's chest. "It's okay, baby. Relax. I'll take care of you."

Bill imitated Jack's movements, from inhaling the powder to tipping his head back and sniffing it into his nose. Jack watched him from the edge of the bed. He had tossed his towel aside and was completely naked, his big cock recumbent between veiny, muscled thighs.

"Feel it?" he asked.

Bill mumbled, "No."

"You will."

He yanked Bill toward him, pulled off his towel and reached around with a big calloused hand and pressed his thumb against Bill's hole.

When Bill tried to back away, Jack gripped him tighter. He no longer looked like a friendly dog.

Bill wasn't sure how he got back to the apartment but the next morning he kept his eyes shut, pretending to sleep until after Waldo was gone. Images of the previous night seeped into his head—Jack pinning him to the narrow bed; more lines of coke; other men coming into the room and fucking him, one after another. When he went to the toilet, the pain was excruciating and there was blood in the water. He stood at the chipped bathroom mirror mechanically brushing his teeth and avoiding his own eyes. Back in bed he sorted through the emotions that churned in his chest. Shame, guilt, disbelief. He had expected those.

What surprised and alarmed him was how aroused he felt when he thought about what he allowed those men to do to him in that little room. It wasn't just sex. He had allowed himself to be humiliated and abused and he had liked it. More than liked it. He had felt as if a void inside him had been filled by his degradation. His hand was on his cock and his cock was hard. Guiltily, he jerked off to the remembered images: Jack choking him almost to the point of passing out as he fucked him, another man yanking Bill to his knees, slapping him and pissing on him. He came in an obliterating orgasm and then lay in bed, semen running down his hand, mortified but still aroused. Something had been revealed to him about himself he had not wanted to know. Now that he knew it, he could not unknow it. He wiped his hand on a tissue and promised himself he would never act on the knowledge again.

Bill enrolled at City College and got a job waiting tables at a gay restaurant on Fillmore Street frequented by older, professional men. His preppy looks earned him more money in tips in a single night than he had made in a month bagging groceries. He and Michael continued to date and to fight, break up and get back together. He played shortstop in the gay softball league on a team sponsored by The Hide 'n Seek, bought Lacoste alligator shirts and 510 jeans at All American Boy on Castro Street and *The Joy of Gay Sex* and *The Frontrunner* from Paperback Traffic on Polk Street. He worked out at Muscle Systems on Hayes Street and learned to dance at the I-Beam's Sunday afternoon tea dances on Haight Street. And, despite his resolutions, he still sometimes secretly veered off alone to the city's seedier bathhouses and backroom bars where he engaged in activities he kept to himself.

Waldo told him he looked like the poster boy for gay San Francisco. Yet, the longer Bill lived in San Francisco, the lonelier he felt. Back in Eden Plains, wanting sex with other boys was only part of what he had been concealing, and it wasn't even the most shameful part. Everyone talked about sex. His high school baseball teammates constantly joked about butt fucking and blowjobs and the size of their cocks. Probably, Bill realized in retrospect, at least a couple of them would have gladly allowed him to blow them had he had the courage and the finesse to hit on them. But, with the possible exception of Marco, he doubted his teammates' fantasies included holding hands at the movies and making out in the front seat of his dad's car at the end of a date. Had any of them dreamed of the moment when he would look into another boy's eyes and say, "I love you?" Or imagined the house where they would spend the rest of their lives together?

This is still what Bill believed he wanted, even if he couldn't square it with the coke and rough sex he secretly indulged in. Those nights of raw exhilaration were followed by days of regret during which he could scarcely face the memory of what he had allowed to be done to him. The names he had let men call him—faggot, bitch, queer—as they plundered his body. He could barely acknowledge that the humiliation as much as the coke or the ecstasy or the meth was what made the sex so gut-wrenchingly intense and, almost more than the drugs, was why he went back for more. Unable to face whatever truth about himself his secret life might reveal, he hid that life from Waldo, from everyone, thus exchanging one closet for another and dividing himself into two: Good Bill and Bad Bill.

Waldo dragged him to political meetings where people talked about changing laws and rewriting the medical books that classed gays as mentally ill. Not just talk, as it turned out. Within three years of his arrival in San Francisco, the psychiatrists had declassified homosexuality as a mental illness and the legislature had abolished California's sodomy law. Waldo was gleeful. "See, hon, the shrinks say we're not sick and the government says we're not criminals!" When Bill brought up the Church's strictures against homosexuality, Waldo rolled his eyes and said, "Honey, if you're going to take sex advice from a bunch of men in dresses, I'd choose drag queens over priests. At least drag queens have had sex."

Bill went to the meetings and the marches and the gay pride parades, a gay face in the gay crowd, but he never felt entirely included in the celebrations. While these advances in law and society allowed gay men to live as they wanted, none of them, Bill observed, seemed to want what he wanted; what Waldo teasingly called, "A cunning little cottage and your lover in an apron making you dinner when you get home from work."

"What's wrong with wanting something like that?"

"Guys aren't made that way, Billy."

"I am," Bill said.

Waldo shook his head. "That's what they

want you to think you want. Your family, society, the schools, the fucking billboards and TV ads. That's their world, Bill, not ours. We're making our own world here."

"What world is that?" Bill asked bitterly. "Bathhouses and fist fucking and guys pissing on each other."

Waldo compressed his lips into a tight, angry line. "You sound just like them. First off, yeah that's part of our world, but it's part of their world too. You don't think women let their husbands fuck them in the ass or guys don't ask their girlfriends to piss on them? Sure they do. The difference is we're not goddammned hypocrites about sex. Second, who cares if some guy gets off by having other guys pee on him or getting a fist up his butt. It's none of your business. No one said you had to do it. Third, is that what you see when you walk down Castro Street? Sex? That's not what I see, hon. I see freedom. I see courage. You're the one with sex on his brain."

Bill walked away from the argument because Waldo's words about hypocrites hit too close to home. He came close to telling Waldo about Bad Bill, but the shame and guilt were too deep, so he pushed them down where they festered and drove him back to the dark places where Bad Bill emerged.

Bill had never forgotten the afternoon Michael showed him the Painted Ladies of Alamo Square.

Until then he had thought of houses, if he thought of them at all, as mere shelter. Nothing in Eden Plains' cookie-cutter tract houses had given him any reason to think differently. But the Painted Ladies were like no houses he had ever seen and he returned to them again and again. They were alive with distinct histories and personalities. They spoke to him of a gracious and placid past when there was time to dwell on small, ornamental details that served no purpose other than to be beautiful. They spoke to his longings for home and family and a place in the world that was solid and tangible and unchanging.

One afternoon, he walked past a real estate agency at the corner of Market and Church Streets on the fringe of the Castro district. In its windows were photographs of Victorian houses, most in need of rehabilitation, that were for sale in the neighborhood. At that moment, Bill was floundering at school, taking a course or two a semester without any clear notion of where this education would lead. He sorted through the possibilities—lawyer, doctor, teacher—but these were mere clichés, the sort of thing he offered up when someone asked him about the future, not professions in which he had any actual interest.

He stood at the window of the realty company studying the photographs of the Victorian and Edwardian bungalows, cottages and demi-mansions. None of them looked remotely like the Painted Ladies. They were in various states of ruin, neglected, weather-worn, denuded of their ornamentation, slapped with vinyl siding and cheaply painted in white or gray. He grazed the windows with his fingertips as if to comfort the old girls from whom he seemed to hear a plaintive cry of *Save Me*. Out of the corner of his eye, he noticed a small, handwritten sign taped to the inside of the window: Help Wanted. He went in and inquired. The position was for an office assistant, someone to answer phones, file and do light typing. Ten minutes later, Bill walked out with the job.

He soon proved to be so industrious, curious and eager that the four owners of the agency began to take him with them when they went out to look at properties. They had him take notes at their meetings with prospective sellers and buyers and sent him to City Hall where he negotiated the labyrinthine bureaucracy to obtain title records and permit histories. They trusted him with keys to the properties and he would often go alone to some nineteenth-century wreck and walk lovingly through its rooms, imagining what it had once been and what it could be again. Invigorated, Bill returned to City College with new purpose and graduated with a degree in real estate. Two days after he turned twenty-one he passed his licensing examination and became a real estate agent.

Waldo stood in the middle of the apartment,

hands on hips, and announced, "This place is a dump. We have to move."

Bill, rubbing the sleep from his eyes, yawned, and said, "What?"

"We've outgrown this place. I mean, between Eddie coming over and you and Michael bumping uglies on the couch at three in the morning while I'm trying to get some shuteye, I'm on my last nerve." He headed into the kitchen to make coffee. "Besides, I got a raise and now that you're working at the agency, we can afford it."

Bill sat up, awake and excited. "Yeah, we should move! We could find a big two-bedroom."

"Uh-huh, and a real kitchen for me to cook in."

"You know where we should look? The Castro."

"The place where all the other queens are moving?"

"Yeah, there are lots of beautiful old houses. I bet we could get a place cheap."

"Well, what are we waiting for?"

"I'll start looking today."

"Let me do the talking," Bill told Waldo as they turned off 18th Street to Diamond Street. They passed Blessed Savior and headed up the hill to the address Bill had written on a scrap of paper.

"Who died and made you queen?" Waldo asked, a little breathless from the walk. "Why do you have to do the talking?"

"Because when you open your mouth a purse falls out."

Waldo stopped, breathing hard, and said, "You don't think the landlord's going to figure out we're gay as soon as he opens the door and gets a gander?"

"The landlord's a woman," Bill corrected him. "Some of the old timers don't like all the gays moving into the neighborhood. I don't know if this lady is one of them so I should talk first because—"

"If you say 'the normal one,' I will bitch slap you so hard."

"Come on, Waldo," Bill pleaded. "Behave yourself."

The woman who answered the door was small and plump and pink. Steam rose from the mug in her hand. Her silvery hair was carefully set and she wore a flowery apron over her house dress. Her face bore only a trace of rouge and lipstick. A TV played in the background, the volume turned up high, and they spoke to her over snatches of movie dialogue.

"Yes," she said, giving them a long once over. "Can I help you boys?"

"Mrs. Donohue? I'm Bill Ryan. I called about the upstairs apartment?"

"Oh, yes."

"Is it still available?"

"Uh-huh," she said, dubiously.

"My friend and I are interested in renting it."

132

She looked at them skeptically, as if a pair of leprechauns had rung her doorbell and asked about the rental. In the awkward silence, a woman's voice from the TV exclaimed, "Jerry, don't let's ask for the moon, we have the stars!'

"Are you watching *Now Voyager?*" Waldo asked, eagerly.

"Yes," Mrs. Donohue said, surprised.

"Don't you just adore Bette Davis?" Waldo continued, enthusiastically.

That earned him a smile from Mrs. Donohue who said, "What do you know about Bette Davis? She was way before your time."

"I know everything about Bette Davis," Waldo said. "My ma parked me in front of the TV when she cleaned the house and I saw all the old movies. *Jezebel*, *Dark Victory* and my absolute favorite, *All About Eve.*" He put his hands on his hips and declaimed, 'I may have seen better days, but I'm still not to be had for the price of a cocktail, like a salted peanut.'"

Mrs. Donohue laughed. "What's your name?"

"Waldo, missus. Waldo Kornowsky and you met my friend Billy Ryan. Don't ask him about old movies, though. He don't know Joan Crawford from Jean Harlow."

She shook her head, her eyes mirthful. "Come inside, boys. I'll make you some tea and we can talk about the rental."

As they headed down the hill, key to their new

apartment in hand, Waldo said, "Sure glad I let you do all the talking."

Within the month, he and Waldo had moved into the spacious apartment above Mrs. Donohue, he sold his first house and earned his first commission, and he had two new listings in the neighborhood. He should have been happy but as he lay in bed watching Michael tie his shoes, sadness impaled him.

"I don't understand why you won't move in," he said. "Your place is a dump and we've been going out for almost two years. It's time."

Michael looked up. "Time for what, Billy?"

"I earn good money and I got a nice apartment. You told me you wanted someone to take care of you. I can do that now, baby. Let me."

Michael sighed. "Comes with too many strings. I like my freedom."

"You like tricking with other guys, you mean," Bill said bitterly.

"Yeah, hon, that too."

"Don't you love me?"

"Oh, Bill, stop with the guilt tripping. Yeah, I love you but if I lived here, you'd drive me crazy. Honestly, you're so jealous. You should be the Mexican."

"I want to settle down."

Michael sat at the edge of the bed and took his hand. "It don't mean anything if I trick with someone else. Don't I always come back to you?"

"I don't understand why you need to do it in the first place."

"Oh, honey, this city—it's like living in a candy shop and all the candy is free and you can eat as much as you want. Grab it with both hands and stuff your face. Don't you ever want a taste?"

"I only want you, Mikey."

Michael kissed his forehead. "You got me baby, but you got to share. I have a break between appointments at three. You come into the shop and I'll cut your hair, okay?"

"Yeah, okay," Bill said, sullenly.

Michael stood up and said, a little sadly, "Billy, you are the straightest gay boy I ever met. I wish you would loosen up."

"You sound like Waldo, now," Bill said.

"That's because we both love you and we want you to be happy."

"Then come and live with me."

Michael shook his head. "I'll see you at three."

After Michael left, Bill threw himself into the bed and shed some tears. In the back of his mind, however, he wondered if the reason he wanted Michael to move in was not only that he loved him but also because, with Michael there, Bad Bill would disappear once and for all.

Two years after he got his realtor's license, Bill started his own agency with money saved from his commissions and a surprisingly large investment from Waldo. He scanned the obituaries, visited the residences of the newly departed old people and, if the houses were Victorians, contacted the heirs who were usually only too glad to rid themselves of these white elephants. Then he found buyers, usually gay men, who were prepared to put the time and money needed to restore the old ladies to their former glory. He bought a small apartment building in Hayes Valley and restored it himself. When property taxes and upkeep became too much for Mrs. Donohue, he quietly bought her duplex, stipulating she could live there for the rest of her life, rent free. Well before he turned thirty his assets amounted to half a million dollars, a fact he never disclosed to anyone.

He still thought of his family from time to time. He wondered how his grandmother was, if his eldest brother had finally married his college girlfriend and whether he was an uncle. Memories and imaginings were all he had of Eden Plains. No photographs, no high school friends, no family, not even a yearbook. It was as if that life had never existed except as a dream. Nonetheless, he sent Christmas cards, Mother's Day cards and birthday cards to his mother and his grandmother, sometimes with the circular for a house he had sold. He heard back only once when he received, from his mother, an obituary clipped from the Eden Plains newspaper for his grandmother. No note or message. He wept like a child.

Eddie finally left his wife and Waldo announced

that they wanted their own place. Bill helped them find one, not far from the old apartment, and sobbed himself to sleep the night Waldo moved out. He presented Waldo with a Cuisinart as a housewarming gift, observing, "I never thought you'd settle down before me." He and Michael broke up for the last time and Michael slowly transitioned from lover to friend. When that transition was complete, Bill found himself truly alone for the first time since he had arrived in the city. His solitude terrified him because now, he worried, there was nothing to stop Bad Bill and, for a while, he went wild, reaching depths of degradation he had not imagined existed until he found himself dragged along their bottom. Self-disgust finally stopped him and he searched desperately for a distraction.

That was when he threw himself into the task of restoring Mrs. Donohue's duplex—now, his—to its 1878 glory. The Donohues had purchased the house just after Mr. Donohue returned from the war and married his best friend's high school sweetheart. To them the duplex was simply an old, cheap house near their families with a rental to help pay the mortgage. Mr. Donohue covered it in vinyl siding. The stately Queen Anne, submerged and denuded, faded from view, replaced by the family house of a plumber and his wife and their two kids with an upstairs tenant. Fortunately, Mrs. Donohue had kept some old photographs, black-and-white, curling at the edges, of what the house had looked like when she and her husband had bought it. She gave them to Bill with the comment, "I don't know why you want to change it back, dear, it's so much trouble to paint."

He studied the pictures carefully and spent his spare time walking through the Castro, the Haight and Hayes Valley photographing similar houses. The Donohue's house, like most of the survivors of the 1906 earthquake and fire, was a row house intended for the middle class; the mansions of the rich had perished in that disaster. The row houses were two stories, some with attics, under steeply pitched roofs, each floor with its characteristic bay windows. The entrances were set back on porches framed by columns. The sides and backs of the houses were plain; all the distinction was in the street-facing facades where, it seemed to Bill, the builders had vied with each other to see who could ornament them with the most detail. Like master bakers in a wedding cake competition, the builders buried the redwood planks in friezes, shingles, brackets, scrolls, wreaths and garlands and pilasters; put up Juliet balconies above the porches and crowned it all with elaborate finials.

After months of consulting with contractors, woodworkers, tile-makers and architects, he began the restoration. The vinyl siding was removed, revealing, beneath nine layers of peeling paint, the redwood planks of which the house was constructed. Mr. Donohue had chiseled off some of the decorative woodwork, but most of it he had simply covered over. Now Bill saw what had been there before: traces of a carved frieze of oak leaves and acorns, decorative shingles on the upper floor, scrolls upholding the second-floor bay window and a sunburst above it. The columns framing the porch had Corinthian capitals and the entrance archway was decorated with carved serpentine designs that still bore traces of gold leaf. When he beheld all this, once lost and now revealed, he wept.

Misunderstanding his tears, Mrs. Donohue said, "I told you she was a wreck. It would have been better to leave her be."

"No," he said, wiping his eyes on his sleeve. "She's beautiful."

"Then why are you crying?"

"Because under all that crap, the paint and the vinyl and everyone neglecting her for so long, her heart is still beating."

"Houses don't have hearts."

"They do," he insisted. "Hearts and souls."

By then, Mrs. Donohue had come to love her "boys," the Bills and the Waldos, who had brought her dying neighborhood back to life. They, responding to her kindness, confided their stories to her, stories of being discarded, rejected and despised for something over which they sincerely believed they had no control and which was part of them. She understood that Bill wasn't talking about the house, he was talking about himself.

"Why, yes," she said, patting his arm. "I see that now. She was just waiting for someone like you to appreciate her."

Six months later, the renovations were done. He had had the body of the house painted a creamy yellow, the balcony and the fretwork white, other details in forest green and had gold leafed the Corinthian capitals, the oak and acorn frieze and the sunburst above the second-floor bay window. To him, it was like the prow of a glorious vessel cutting through the sea of time, a voyage that would continue long after he was gone. Mrs. Donohue had exacted his promise that he would leave the interior of her apartment alone but in the upper unit, where he now lived alone, walls had come down, windows had been enlarged and a skylight installed to flood the space with light. The old wood floors were sanded and refinished, the chimney retiled, the walls painted in the spectrum of browns that ran from cinnamon to sand, and furnished by an interior decorator in beige and ivory, glass, chrome and leather in compliance with Bill's single directive: "Modern and nothing queeny."

From the kitchen window, as he poured himself a glass of wine, he could see Castro Street begin to throb with life on another Saturday night. He wondered, not for the first time, is this it? If only, he thought, he could restore himself as he had his house and peel back the accretions built up by the years of struggle and shame. Would he find that his heart was still beating? Would he then at last look upon Bill Ryan's soul?

8.

FOUND PERFECTLY PLAUSIBLE REASONS TO eat my meals in restaurants other than Gold Mountain after my last run-in with Adam when he had dropped the f-word, but the mere fact I had to justify to myself avoiding the place proved how deeply the incident had affected me. It was the last thing I thought about before I went to sleep and the first thing I thought about when I woke up. Well, not so much thought about as obsessively reenacted in my head, triggering over and over the shock, anger and hurt Adam's casual use of "fag" had caused me, and then wondering whether I had overreacted.

One evening, on my way home from an AA meeting in the Castro, my head once more spinning over the incident, I peered into the Twin Peaks bar and thought, *I could really use a drink.* Instead, I found a payphone, called Larry and blubbered the whole story to him, ending my incoherent narrative with, "I don't understand why I can't let go of this."

"Isn't it obvious?" Larry replied. "You're attracted to him."

A chilly, overcast night had fallen on the city and the smell of incipient rain was in the air. I watched a line of headlights move slowly down Market Street beneath leafless trees and a grid of wires and my heart sank because this was the thing I had refused to admit to myself and it was hard to hear.

"Adam's straight," I mumbled.

"But you're not," Larry countered. "You're gay and you like him. You've been flirting with him and you thought he was flirting back until he said this ugly thing. What are you feeling?"

"Anger."

"Yeah, sure, but if it was only anger, you'd have told him off and let it go."

"Yeah," I admitted. "I was hurt too. And, I guess," I hesitated because it was painful to say. "I guess I was disappointed that, you know—"

"That he doesn't feel the same way about you," Larry said, finishing my thought. "I understand, but hurt and disappointment isn't what's keeping you awake at night."

A male couple walked passed me holding hands, one leaning into the other affectionately.

"What is it then?" I said quietly, watching the men.

"It's shame."

"Shame? I don't understand."

"If you were a straight guy and Adam was a

girl who had rejected you, you might feel hurt and disappointed, but you wouldn't feel bad for having had feelings for her in the first place because the world has told you all your life that those feelings are normal. That's not what the world tells you about your feelings for other guys. The world tells you those feelings are unnatural. So, when a guy rejects you, in addition to everything else, you feel shame."

"I thought I got over that when I came out to myself."

"How old were you?"

"Seventeen, eighteen."

"The damage was already been done by then. You'd already been taught to be ashamed of yourself. Getting over that shame is a process, not a one-time event. Coming out's only the beginning. So, with this kid, you got to meet the shame again. Now you get to practice an even deeper level of self-acceptance."

"So, I should thank Adam for calling me a faggot?"

"He didn't call you a faggot. That's just what you heard."

A sudden gust of wind lifted leaves and debris from the gutter and chilled me, but I felt, not cold, but relief.

"Yeah, you're right. This doesn't have anything to do with Adam. It's all me."

"Go home. Have a cup of tea, do some writing

about shame and we'll talk some more in the morning."

"Thank you." I glanced at my watch; it was a quarter to ten. "Why are you still at work?"

"There's no rest for the wicked in Hollywood. Goodnight, Henry. I love you."

Adam was making change at the cash register when I came in the next day for lunch. He waved at me as I headed to my usual booth. I pasted a smile on my face and waved back. I spread out my files on the table, ordered chicken lo mien and tea from Mrs. Chu and began to read the paramedic and autopsy reports in the Ryan case that arrived that morning from Ruth Fleming.

EMT Incident Report

Medic: I responded to above location on a report of gas leak victims. Upon arrival, found Pt. 1 nearly unconscious on steps to apts. Pt. 1 was dizzy, having difficulty breathing, disoriented. Pt. 2 discovered in bed in upstairs apt. Attempts to resuscitate Pt. 2 unsuccessful. Pt. 3 removed from downstairs apt. Examined and appears unaffected by leak.

Pt. 1: "I woke up and smelled gas. My friend is still upstairs."

Pt. 1, male, 23, with no reported health problems. Pt. 2, male, early 30s. Medical history unknown at this point. Pt. 3, female, 79, no significant health problem reported.

Assessment: Pt. 1, symptoms of carbon monoxide poisoning from gas leak of as yet unknown origins. Pt. 2, death apparently result of carbon monoxide poisoning from same gas leak. Pt. 3, no injuries.

Transport: Pt. 1 transferred to gurney and then ambulance. Pt. 1 transported to hospital without incident. Pt. 2 body removed to county morgue for autopsy. Pt. 3 released into custody of SFPD for transport to friend's home.

The medical examiner's report confirmed Bill Ryan's cause of death as carbon monoxide poisoning. A report from the gas company attributed the leak to a faulty hose connecting the gas line to the oven and suggested the line had been slowly leaking for some time. I slipped the reports into the envelope in which Ruth Fleming had sent them with a scrawled note: *These just arrived. No surprises. Find the roommate and wrap it up.*

"Hey, Henry, what are you working on?"

Adam stood tentatively at the edge of the table. His smile was subdued and ended at his eyes, which were watchful and worried.

"I'm investigating an insurance claim," I said, "and I'm a little out of my depth."

"What do you mean?"

He had been holding himself stiffly, evidently uncertain of his welcome, but now he relaxed a bit though I could still see anxiety in his eyes.

"Can you sit for a minute?"

He slid into the booth. "You haven't been here since—" He hesitated. "Since I said that dumb thing to you. I thought maybe you weren't coming back." He looked at me with unconcealed distress. "I felt awful."

"I'm sorry you felt bad. I felt bad too." I took a breath. "I'd like to be friends again, but I have to know if you have a problem with gay guys."

He dropped his voice. "I don't, I swear, but I can't talk about this here."

"What?" I said, startled. This was not the response I had anticipated.

"I don't have a problem with gay guys," he repeated in the same low voice. "But it's complicated."

"Complicated how?"

"That's what I can't talk about. Not at work and not with them around."

"Your grandparents?"

He nodded. He reached into his shirt pocket and extracted my card. I remember I'd given it to him half-jokingly, telling him I hoped he'd never have to use it.

"If you hadn't come in today, I was planning on showing up at your office. I need to talk to you."

147

Michael Nava

"I have to drive out to the East Bay but I should be back in my office by four,"

"I work 'til eight," he replied. "Would you be okay coming to my place tonight? To talk?"

I nodded. "Yeah, I have a meeting at seven but I could come after that."

He borrowed a pen, wrote his phone number and address on the back of my card and slipped it across the table. "I have to get back to work. See you tonight, okay?"

"Yeah. See you tonight."

As I watched him disappear into the kitchen, I felt puzzled but also hopeful and excited for reasons I preferred not to examine too closely.

Mrs. Chu set my lunch before me with a curious expression, but said only, "Enjoy." I picked at my meal, occasionally glancing toward the cash register where Adam and his grandfather seemed to be going through stacks of old receipts. Once he looked up, met my eyes, and nodded. I nodded back and reluctantly turned my attention back to the Ryan case.

If, as I'd told Adam, I felt out of my depth on the case, it wasn't because it was complex but because it seemed so simple and I was used to the complexity of criminal law. Those complexities arose not from the whodunit—more often than not, the evidence was such that the cops had my clients dead to rights—but why. Although motive was not formally an element of crime, it could be a powerful factor in aggravation or mitigation when the time came to argue moral, if not legal, responsibility for the act. Why someone broke the law could be the difference between conviction of a greater crime or a lesser one or could add to or take off years of a prison sentence. I was trained to seek out the why of my cases, but here, the why seemed both irrelevant and self-evident. While there was a death, there was no crime, and therefore no one's motive to examine. As to why Bill Ryan died, the answer was a faulty gas line. Hence, Fleming's curt *wrap it up.*

Probably, I was overthinking it, and yet, something bothered me about Bill Ryan's death. As I put the reports into the case file and the case file into my briefcase, it occurred me that what was bothering me wasn't so much the circumstances of the case as the victim. Bill Ryan: a thirty-something gay man, tossed out by his family, steeped in a culture hostile to his very existence who had, nonetheless, remained a basically decent human being—*Bill Ryan had his troubles, but he was a good man*, Mrs. Donohue had told me—and led a successful, productive life—only to die an untimely and pointless death. Who did that remind me of? Oh, right, me, and just about every gay man I knew, all of us standing at the brink of an epidemic. How many more untimely and pointless deaths lay in store for us? Would one of them be mine?

I glanced again at Fleming's note—*find the roommate.* The roommate? Fuck you, Mrs.

Fleming. Nick Trejo was Bill's lover. He had awakened in the middle of that night to discover Bill lying dead beside him, nearly choked to death himself, and had then been locked out of the house they shared by the family that had thrown Bill away in the first place. I would find Nick Trejo, all right, if only to make sure he squeezed out every cent coming to him from Western States Insurance Company.

Before heading out to the address Mrs. Donohue had given me for Nick Trejo, I tried Bill Ryan's office again. The closure sign was gone and the door was unlocked. Inside a woman was speaking Cantonese into a phone at a desk strewn with files. Almost buried in the papers was a plastic nameplate: Doris Chen. Behind her, an open door revealed a private office I assumed had been Ryan's. She saw me and pointed at the two chairs on either side of a coffee table. Her voice climbed with exasperation and then she slammed down the phone.

"Contractors," she grumbled, sweeping a manicured hand through thick black hair shot through with silver. With a tight smile, she said, "Hello, can I help you?"

Before I could respond, the phone rang again. She held up a hand and answered it, speaking this time in English. "No, that bill was paid... I have the receipt right here in front of me." She dug through some papers. "Yes, three hundred and eighty-three dollars and fifty-five cents. Okay, well, check your records I'm sure you'll... What? No, I haven't seen that bill. How much? Can you send someone here to pick up a check? We need the power back on today. Okay, thank you."

She hung up. "Sorry, this is my first day back in the office and I'm swamped. Who are you?"

"My name is Henry Rios. I'm a claims investigator for Western States Insurance. I'm looking into Bill Ryan's life insurance policy."

"I didn't know Bill had life insurance," she said. "You probably want to talk to his lawyer, Randy Gifford. I've got his number here somewhere." The phone rang again. She looked at it distastefully. "Here's Randy's card. Is there anything else?"

"Do you know Nick Trejo?"

She frowned. "Why are you asking?"

"He's the beneficiary."

"You really need to talk to Randy," she said, picking up the phone. "Excuse me."

"Thanks," I said, pocketing the attorney's card.

Nick Trejo lived in Linwood, one of the string of towns in the urban corridor that stretched along Interstate 80 across the bay from San Francisco. From the freeway, they were an indistinguishable series of shopping malls and housing developments but once off the freeway they retained vestiges of the old railroad or farm towns they had once been. Linwood had been a farm town—there was still a grain and feed store housed in an old brick building on its two-block Main Street. Nick Trejo's neighborhood seemed to be original to the old town because it was unlike the surrounding 1950s and '60s ranch-style house tracts. The houses on Jefferson Avenue, where he lived, were constructed from wood, not stucco, and were of different shapes and sizes on irregularly sized lots. Dobermans and Rottweilers patrolled unkempt yards behind chain link fences where even now in mid-November, ancient, leggy rosebushes produced a few blowsy blooms. I had grown up on a street like this, in a town not a hundred miles away, in another neighborhood on the wrong side of the tracks and I felt at home here.

I parked in front of the Trejo residence, a single-story, white wooden house set back from the street and shaded by a venerable oak tree. An oversize tire hung from its branches and its leaves littered the lawn. Flower beds on either side of the porch had been planted with herbs—mint, oregano, thyme, rosemary. A wooden placard, the kind boys made in high school shop class, hung above the porch proclaiming *Familia Trejo*. I rang the doorbell. A moment later a girl of eight or nine was staring at me from behind the screen door.

"Hi," I said. "I'm looking for Nick Trejo."

Without turning her head, she screamed, "*Manito*, there's a man at the door for you!"

Manito. Little brother.

"How come you're all dressed up?" the girl asked.

"I'm working."

She seemed skeptical but before she could say anything else, a soft male voice behind her said, "Go help my mom in the kitchen, Adela."

She ran off and a tall, skinny boy in sagging jeans and an SF State sweatshirt came to the screen. Thick black hair, parted in the middle into wings, framed a narrow face. A wispy goatee only made him look younger than twenty-three, his age on the EMT report. Blunt eyebrows like soot smudges above his dark, mild eyes gave his face a male forcefulness but he was undeniably pretty. Long nose, thick lips, big ears, seamless cinnamon-colored skin. He looked every bit the little brother.

"Nick? I'm Henry Rios. I work for Western States Insurance Company. They sent me out here to talk to you about Bill Ryan's life insurance policy. He made you the beneficiary."

"How did you know I was here?" he asked worriedly.

"Peg Donohue gave me this address."

He smiled briefly. "Oh, I see. How is Peg?"

"She's fine. She says to tell you hello. Can I come in?"

"Um, wait here a minute, okay?"

He stepped back into the house and I heard him talking to a woman in Spanish. My Spanish was marginal but I understood he was telling her about me. I could not hear her end of the conversation but then she appeared at the door, Nick behind her. She was short, gray-haired, stocky and as primally female as the Venus of Willendorf. Mrs. Trejo, I assumed.

Wiping her hands on her apron, she asked, bluntly, "Who are you, mister?"

I again explained who I was and why I was there.

"Does Nick have some money coming to him from this life insurance?"

"Yes," I said. "Maybe as much as a hundred thousand dollars."

"I didn't know about any insurance," Nick said.

"Well, regardless, the policy was in force when Bill died and the insurance agent who wrote it made the claim on your behalf. If I could just have a few minutes of your time."

She looked me up and down, then said, "*Eres mexicano, no?*"

"My dad was from Mexico, my mom was Mexican-American. You'll have to excuse me though, I don't speak Spanish very well."

"Shame on you," she said, mildly, as she opened the door. "Come in, Mister Rios. We can talk in the kitchen."

We passed through a living room carpeted

in gold shag. Well-worn armchairs and a couch covered in a blue chenille bedspread were arranged around a big screen TV. A ceramic panther with green glass eyes guarded a *TV Guide* opened to the half-completed crossword on the coffee table. Atop the TV was a planter filled with plastic roses. The wall above the couch was lined with framed high school graduation photos of three boys and one girl, each in a robe and mortar board, one of them Nick. The air was warm, musty and lived in, the product of years of bodies in close quarters; the smell of family.

The kitchen, painted sunshine yellow, was almost as big as the living room. Dominating the room was a large square table covered by a flower-patterned oilcloth and surrounded by six cane-backed chairs. Built-in shelves held plates, glasses and cups. There was a five-gallon tin of lard in one corner and beside it a big sack of flour. On the table was a bowl of oranges, a plastic red tortilla warmer, a bowl of salsa covered with plastic wrap, and the morning paper. A pot of beans simmered on a four-burner gas stove. Adela, the little girl, was sitting at the table with a coloring book. I felt like I'd stepped back into my maternal grandmother's house where I'd once been the child at the table, only with a book for reading, not coloring.

Mrs. Trejo said, "Adelita, go watch TV. The grownups have to talk." Uncomplainingly, the girl took her book and crayons and left the room.

"Your daughter?"

"The neighbor's girl," she said. "I watch her after school until her mom gets home from work. Sit down, Mister Rios. You want coffee?"

"Call me Henry," I said. "Coffee would be nice." The earthy scent of beans made my stomach growl, more out of memory than appetite. "Sorry."

"You're hungry," Mrs. Trejo said.

"No, I'm—"

"I'll make you a taco. Sit, sit."

I pulled out a chair. Nick sat down across from me, where the newspaper was spread. He watched me warily as I removed a legal pad from my briefcase, laid it on the table, and took a pen from my pocket.

"I just have a couple of questions to ask," I said. "About the accident."

He took a deep breath but it was his mother who spoke.

"Nick is still very upset about what happened to Bill."

"I can understand that. You were close."

"They were together for four years," she continued, setting a mug of coffee before me. "There's sugar in the bowl. You want milk?"

"No, black is fine," I said, grappling with the implication that Nick's mother seemed to know about his relationship, but I had probably misunderstood her meaning; she must have meant only that they had been *roommates* for four years.

Then Nick said, "He was my first boyfriend."

I glanced at Mrs. Trejo who went on warming a tortilla on a griddle. I had not been mistaken. She was a Mexican mother who knew her son was gay, had had a boyfriend and seemed unbothered by either fact. It was completely alien to my own experience and it took me a moment to refocus my attention to the task at hand.

"You must have been very young when you met him."

"Eighteen," Nick said. "Ma, can I have some coffee too?"

"How did you meet?"

He glanced at his mother while she filled the mug in front of him. He spooned sugar into it and said, "I was a freshman at SF State. Some friends of mine and I would go down to the Castro and hang out near the bars. We couldn't go in, but we liked being close to the action. One night I was wandering around alone and ran into Bill. We got to talking and he gave me a ride back to my dorm. I asked him for his number and called him up the next day. That's how it started."

Mrs. Trejo snorted skeptically as she set a plate before me with a taco of beans. "There's salsa if you want."

The skepticism seemed directed at Nick's version of the meeting, but there was no note of disapproval. I tried, but utterly failed, to imagine how my mother would have reacted had I told her a similar story when I was Nick's age. And as for my father—I again had to bring myself back into the present and bit into the taco. The beans were a perfect consistency and had been stewed with onion, garlic, Mexican oregano and cumin.

"This is delicious."

She shrugged. "It's just *frijoles*."

She sat down between us, pulled a pack of cigarettes out of her apron, and lit one. When Nick reached for her pack, she slapped his hand away.

"I want one," he whined.

"They're bad for you."

"You smoke."

"Because I didn't know no better and got hooked. You're educated."

The phone rang in the other room and Mrs. Trejo got up to answer it. When she was out of the room, I asked Nick, "Your family knows you're gay?"

"Uh-huh," he said.

"And they're okay with it?"

"With my brothers, it was one more thing to tease the kid brother about," he said. "But they'd beat the crap out of anyone else who picked on me. My sister never had a problem."

"Your parents?"

"My dad died before I could tell him, but he wouldn't have minded. My mom doesn't care."

"Your dad's dead," I said. "I'm sorry."

"Yeah," he said. "I miss him every day."

I wanted to ask him more about his family's

acceptance, but I reminded myself I was here on business. I took a sip of strong coffee and smiled at him. "The story of how you met Bill, is that all there is to it?"

He eyed me uncertainly. "What do you mean?"

"Nick, I'm gay too, okay?"

His eyes widened. "You are?"

"A card-carrying homosexual, and I have a feeling you left something out about how you met Bill because your mom was in the room."

"It was more or less true," he said, "except I was really drunk. Bill was walking home and saw me stumbling around like a fool. He grabbed me by the shirt collar and said, 'Hey, kid, what are doing out here like this.' He says I told him I was looking for Prince Charming. He asked me how old I was and I said 'I'm legal, let's go to your place.' Instead, he took me to a diner on Castro and fed me a burger and some coffee to sober up. He was so handsome." He laughed. "I did everything but stick my hand down his pants to get him to take me home with him, but all he wanted to do was talk. He did drive me back to my dorm. As soon as he parked, I grabbed him and kissed him. He just laughed and told me to go to bed and sleep it off. I said I wouldn't get out of the car without his number, so he gave me his card. I found it the next morning in my pants pocket between runs to the toilet to puke. I called him to thank him for taking care of me and he invited me to lunch. We hung out after that, but he never tried anything with me until I pretty much attacked him. He said I was too young. I told him I was old enough to know what I wanted. I wanted him." He looked at the paper. "Bill was my first."

"Your first boyfriend?"

"First anything," he replied. "I talked a good game but I was a total virgin. For me it was love at first sight. Took him a little longer."

"When did you move in together?"

"Six months later, maybe? Yeah, it was that summer because I was going to come back here to live with my mom and I didn't have a car, so it would have been hard to get into the city to see him. Bill said I should move in for the summer and we'd see how we got along. I never left."

"Even after he hit you?" I asked.

He frowned. "What are you talking about? Bill never touched me that way."

"Peg Donohue said he gave you a black eye."

"That was an accident. I told her."

"She didn't believe you."

Before he could respond, his mother returned to the kitchen and joined us at the table. She looked at him and said, "Is everything okay here?"

"I was just asking Nick about Bill," I said.

"Bill was family," she said firmly.

Nick nodded. "Yeah, we all loved him."

I felt a wall descend that ended any further questioning of Nick's relationship with Bill Ryan.

"Okay," I said. "Nick, can you tell me what happened the night of the accident?"

He took a deep breath. "We went to bed around eleven. I woke up from a nightmare that I was drowning. My head hurt and I felt like I was going to throw up. I could barely breathe. That's when I smelled the gas. I tried to wake Bill, but he just lay there." He mother took his hand as he paused to compose himself. "I got out of bed and called my brother Sal."

"Why didn't you call 911?"

"Uh, I was confused, you know, and half unconscious. I smelled the gas and Sal knows about gas, so that's why, I guess."

"His brother works for PG and E," Mrs. Trejo said.

Pacific Gas and Electric, the local utility monopoly. "I see. What happened next?"

"Sal said to get out of the apartment and he would call 911. I told him Bill wasn't moving. He said, 'Get out of the apartment now.'"

"And did you?"

He shook his head. "I went back into the bedroom and tried to wake Bill up. I grabbed him and shook him. I shook him and shook him, but he wouldn't wake up. I started to pass out and I knew I had to get out. So, I... I left him there and went downstairs. I made it to the porch and blacked out. The next thing I knew I was in the ambulance with Sal."

"Your brother?"

He nodded. "Then the ambulance took me to the hospital." He gripped his mother's hand. "I never saw Bill again. His family came, from Illinois."

"And locked you out of the apartment," I said.

"Yes."

"They're bad people," Mrs. Trejo said.

Nick looked at me, his eyes bright with tears. "Bill said they threw him out like a stray dog."

I nodded. "Thank you. I know this must be hard for you."

I scanned my checklist of questions to see if I'd forgotten anything. "Oh," I said. "Do you know what caused the gas leak?"

Nick glanced anxiously at his mother. She responded with a nearly imperceptible nod.

"Uh-huh," he said.

"That's a no?" I pressed, curious about the exchange between mother and son. He looked at her again, this time even more anxiously.

"We don't know," she said. "Those old houses. Something's always going wrong with them." She smiled, insincerely. "Can I get you more coffee? Another taquito for the road?"

She was nice about it, but I was being given the bum's rush. From years of cross-examining evasive witnesses, I had developed an acute sense of when I was being lied to. I was being lied to now on a point where a lie made no sense. I hadn't expected Nick to know what caused the gas leak: it was a rote question required by the

Western States handbook in all accidental death investigations.

"No, thank you, I'm fine." I closed my notebook. "That's it, for now. I'll be on my way."

Nick remained in the kitchen while Mrs. Trejo walked me out. I indicated the four graduation photographs on the living room wall.

"Your kids?"

"Yes. My daughter Isabel and my boys, Tomás, Salvador and Nick."

"Nick said your husband passed," I said. "I'm very sorry."

"He worked in the shipyards in Oakland," she said, "and he got the asbestosis."

"Nick's your baby."

"Nick is everyone's baby," she said, at the door. "Drive back safe to the city."

I was halfway across the Bay Bridge when it occurred to me that neither of the Trejos had asked when my investigation would be completed and they could expect a check. A hundred thousand dollars would be a fortune to the Trejos. I didn't doubt Mrs. Trejo's sincerity when she called Bill Ryan family or that Nick's grief was real. Still, it seemed an odd omission which, with the lie about the source of the gas leak, raised a flicker of suspicion in my mind which as yet had no label.

That night I went to an AA meeting in Blessed Savior's community hall. I'd been a lot of meetings there, but I'd never given much thought to what went on upstairs, in the chapel. From what I knew of the church's position on homosexuality— "an objective disorder," was the official line—Peg Donohue's description of a parish that welcomed gays and lesbians seemed pretty implausible. The chapel was set between the rectory and the community hall. I stood on the sidewalk waiting for the meeting to start and watched parishioners climb the steep set of stairs from the sidewalk to the entrance of the chapel. Some, like Peg Donohue, were older people, women mostly, clinging to the handrails as they made their way up the stairs. Others were younger, male, and unmistakably gay. A couple of the men, with tell-tale marks of AIDS wasting upon them, were assisted up the steps by friends. I searched my limited recollection of the Catholic liturgy but failed to recall any regular services conducted on weekday evenings. I stopped a man who, down to the dark blue bandana hanging from the left back pocket of his very tight Levi's, was a Castro clone incarnate.

"What's going on up there?" I asked.

"Forty hours," he said, and hurried up the stairs as the church bell tolled seven o'clock. I headed into the community hall for the meeting.

The doors to the church were still open when the meeting ended an hour later. Somewhat hesitantly, I made my way up the stairs. I paused at the entrance, sniffing incense. As I stepped inside, I could not remember the last time I had darkened the threshold of any kind of church.

My first impression was of darkness. Dark pews, dark carpeting, the overhead lights dimmed to obscurity, the flicker of votive candles at various altars serving only to emphasize the absence of light. It was a big, high-ceilinged room, the walls bearing large, stained-glass windows that depicted episodes from the ministry of Jesus in scarlet, azure, emerald and gold. Beneath the windows, oil paintings illustrated the fourteen stations of the cross. There were maybe fifty people in the pews, clumped together or solitary, some sitting, some kneeling. Exposed on the altar was an ornate gold vessel designed like a sunburst. I slipped into a pew at the back of the church and picked up a prayer card:

Blessed are you, Lord of All, giving new life and health to those who call upon you.

Usher in your kingdom and manifest your power to heal those with AIDS.

Blessed are You, Lord of Wisdom, who pushes back the borders of darkness and disease.

Enlighten those who search for a cure for AIDS
And strengthen those who care for our suffering brothers and sisters.

Blessed are you, Lord of Love and Peace.

Be with the families and loved ones of those who live with this disease.

Touch us all with your love and make us instruments of your healing...

"Henry, is that you?"

"Hello, Peg."

I scooted over to make room for Peg Donohue. She carefully removed her coat, scarf, and gloves, beamed at me, and said, "You're a Catholic boy."

"Lapsed. What is this service?"

"The forty hours. It's a very old devotion. Father Toby says it goes back to the Middle Ages when people prayed for forty hours in front of the Blessed Sacrament to stop the black plague. And, well, we have another plague today, so we started it up again here."

"You mean these people," I said, indicating the other parishioners, "are going to pray nonstop for forty hours?"

"Not the same people," she laughed. "We're all too old or tired, but the church stays open for forty hours and someone will come, even if it's in the middle of the night, to pray for a cure for AIDS and for the people who are suffering from it. Did you find Nick?"

"Yes. His family's taking care of him."

She nodded. "They're good people, those Trejos."

"I wanted to talk to Bill's ex-boyfriend, Michael. Do you know where I can find him?"

She nodded, "I have his address."

At that moment the man I had seen earlier, the one who advertised his sexual specialty with the blue hankie in his left pocket, made his way to the pulpit, unfolded a sheet of paper, set it down and began intoning names.

"What's he doing?" I asked Peg.

She took a fresh linen handkerchief out of her purse and dabbed the corners of her eyes, bright with tears, before she answered, "He's reading the names of the all the neighborhood boys who have died."

The address Adam had given me led me to an old apartment building at the outskirts of the Tenderloin, not far from the restaurant. I rang the doorbell and he buzzed me into the building. The tiny lobby was clean but bleak and smelled of insecticide and musty wool carpet. I skipped the ancient, gated elevator and climbed the dimly lit stairs to the fourth floor where he was standing outside his apartment in a pair of black sweatpants and a gray SF State T-shirt.

"Hi, Adam. Sorry I'm a little late."

He looked at me with uncertain eyes, and then, taking a deep breath, he pulled me against his chest, immobilizing me in a tight embrace and kissed me full on, tongue and all.

"What the hell? Is this what you wanted to tell me? That you're gay?"

"I'm not gay," he replied. "Uh, maybe you should come inside."

9.

BILL WAS DRINKING AT THE bar on Castro everyone called the Petrified Forest because all anyone ever did there was stand and stare, waiting for the blond who had been cruising him to work up his nerve and approach him. Once, Bill would have gone over and chatted up the guy but that was before he had learned The Rules. The Rules, unwritten and largely unspoken, were more about power than sex, and while he disliked them, it was impossible not to play by them when everyone else was. Rule One: wait for the other guy to make the first move.

He didn't remember whether The Rules applied when he had first stumbled into The Hide 'n Seek almost a decade earlier. If they had, he hadn't noticed, being too thrilled and too terrified to be aware of much more than that he was in a room full of other gay guys. After that first night he always went out with Waldo, who had no patience for rules and had been known to approach stuck-up, posing queens and ask, in his most honeyed voice, "Girl, you need some help taking the broomstick out of your ass?" He smiled to himself, thinking about his friend. Waldo was most likely curled up at home with Eddie watching *Dynasty*, his latest craze. Tomorrow morning, Bill could expect a call in which Waldo would describe in detail not only the plot but Joan Collins's outfits. Not for the first time he thought how ironic it was that Waldo, a self-described slut, had settled into a monogamous relationship, while Bill, who had wanted just that, was still on the hunt for Mr. Right ("Or," he could hear Waldo add snidely, "Mr. Right Now"). He was more likely to find the latter than the former at the Petrified Forest.

The lights were carefully dimmed to cast everyone's face in seductive shadows with the added benefit of erasing sags and wrinkles, not that many were to be found among the predominantly thirty-something clientele. Discreet speakers mounted on the ceiling seemed to play a ceaseless loop of *Bette Davis Eyes, Just the Two of Us, Endless Love,* and *Angel of the Morning,* above the coiffed heads and cologned, gym-toned, and casually but expensively dressed bodies of the patrons. They posed like statues at and around the bar, but their eyes darted wildly back and forth across the room like goldfish swimming circles in a fishbowl. God, he was tired of the scene. Had he not spent the previous weekend at a bathhouse in San Jose on a coke and sex binge, he would have left and gone to the Club Baths. That, however, would have broken his own rule—only one Bad Bill binge a month—to which he grimly adhered.

His best bet was still the blond in the black Lacoste alligator shirt and pressed Levi's who looked at him again with a half-smile before examining his tasseled loafers, worn, of course, without socks. Ugh, Bill thought, I don't even like blonds. Still, a bed warmer was a bed warmer. But it was nearly midnight. He wasn't going to wait until the guy had consumed enough liquid courage to make his move so Bill plastered a smile on his face and walked across the bar with his hand out. As soon as he approached, the blond turned his back. His smile curdling on his lips, Bill dropped his hand and headed for the exit, more rueful than angry, thinking, that's what you get when you break The Rules.

It was a cold, clear night in March. A full moon shone above Castro Street. The shops were shuttered but the bars and a few food places remained open. The Castro Theater was letting out after a late showing of a Marilyn Monroe double feature—*Niagara* and *The Misfits*—and the sidewalks were crowded with men in flannel shirts, 501 Levi's and leather bomber jackets, hair and moustaches clipped to perfection. The thump of disco music poured into the crisp air each time someone pushed open a bar door. On the corner of Castro and 18th' the small plaza, christened Hibernia Beach after the bank it fronted, was filled to capacity with gay men laughing, chatting, smoking and cruising.

Another night in the Castro, where the party never ended. Yet it seemed to Bill that much of the levity had gone out of the street, replaced by darker notes of anxiety and paranoia. Only a year earlier, Harvey Milk had been assassinated and the previous May, after the verdict was announced virtually acquitting his murderer, a gay riot at city hall was answered by a police riot on Castro Street. Gay bashings were on the rise and even as he headed down brightly lit 18th Street toward home, he remained on alert, scanning the sidewalk ahead of him and listening for footsteps behind him.

He was passing Badlands when the door swung open and the bouncer forcibly escorted a tall, skinny boy onto the sidewalk saying, "Come back when you're legal, kid." The boy staggered into Bill's path, stumbled, and reeking of beer and pot, fell into Bill's arms.

"Hi!" he said brightly, throwing his arms around Bill as if the collision was an intentional embrace. His cheek, smooth and almost feverishly hot, brushed Bill's. He was all arms and legs in baggy, no label jeans and an SF State sweatshirt. He had, Bill noticed, the most adorable, oversized ears. Bill freed himself from the boy's sloppy embrace and stood him against the wall. The boy's stuporous grin and glazed eyes indicated either that he was extremely drunk or an inexperienced drinker. Since he looked like he was in high school, Bill guessed the latter.

"Hey," he said. "Look at me. What's your name?"

"Nick," the boy said. "Wow, you look just like a Ken doll! I had a Ken doll," the boy confided. "I used to sleep with him. Can I sleep with you?"

"Uh, no. How old are you?"

"Twenty-one!"

"Bullshit."

The boy grinned and shrugged. "Eighteen."

"Where do you live?"

"Um, in the dorms at State," he smiled crookedly. "But we can't go there. I have a roommate."

"Are you alone, or do you have some friends around here who can take you home?"

He gave an elaborate shrug. "They're still at the party."

"Where's the party?"

He grinned again. "I don't remember, Ken."

"My name is Bill," he said. "Did you drive here from State?"

He shook his head violently. "Um, I don't have a car. Jimmy drove."

He started to slide down the wall. Bill grabbed him by his armpits and pulled him up.

"Shit," Bill muttered. "You are royally drunk. You can't be wandering around the Castro like this. People are getting jumped."

"Okay," Nick said. He broke into another big grin. "I have an idea, Bill. Let's go to your place."

"That's not going to happen. Can you walk?"

"Since I was two years old," Nick replied with a giggle.

In spite of himself, Bill laughed. "Smart ass. Put your arm around my shoulders."

Nick put one lanky arm around Bill's shoulder and squeezed Bill's ass with his other hand. "Wow," he said. "You have a nice butt, Bill." He tried to touch Bill's crotch but Bill batted his hand away.

"Behave."

Nick pouted and said, "You're no fun," but let Bill walk him up Castro into Coming Home.

When he hauled Nick into the diner, his favorite waiter, Freddy, raised a shaggy eyebrow and said, "Well, well. Look what the cat dragged in."

"I found him outside Badlands," Bill said. "I'm going to get some food into him and drive him home."

Freddy smirked. "Sure, and I am Marie of Romania."

"Give me a break. I'm not a child molester."

Nick squeaked, indignantly, "I'm not a child!"

Freddy laughed and said, "Sit him down and I'll bring him coffee."

"Bring him a cheeseburger too," Bill said. "And one for me, with a Coke."

Watching Nick demolish his burger, Bill thought: *Eighteen*. The kid barely looked sixteen. Whatever his age, the boy, swiping a paper napkin across his grease-coated lips and sucking down Bill's Coke, seemed fearless even though he was drunk, stranded, and sitting with a man who had just picked him up off the street. No, Bill corrected himself, not fearless. Innocent. Like someone who didn't worry about bad things happening to him because nothing bad ever had. Nothing seriously bad, anyway. The kid probably wasn't even gay. More likely he was a curious straight boy who had wandered into the queer neighborhood filled with liquid courage and decided to check out the local fauna.

But then Nick reached his hand across the table and grabbed Bill's hand and said, "Are we going to your place now, Bill?"

"No, I'm driving you back to school. What were you doing trying to sneak into Badlands?"

"Looking for Prince Charming. I guess I found him."

The food had sobered him up a bit, dissolving the alcoholic glaze in his eyes. Bill allowed himself the thought that had the kid been just a few years older and not so drunk, he would have happily taken him to bed. He was exactly Bill's type: cinnamon-skinned, his eyes coffee bean brown and bright in a narrow, pretty face framed by long, black hair parted in the middle. A small patch of hair was making a gallant stand on his chin; his eyebrows were sexy black smudges and those ears—a little floppy but perfectly shaped. Bill imagined nibbling them and then licking the boy's long, flawless neck.

"Like my friend Waldo says, the city's full of queens, but not too many princes."

Nick giggled. "I like your friend Waldo." He rested his face between his hands and said, with a note in his voice, almost of awe, "You are so handsome."

Bill felt absurdly touched by the compliment. "You're pretty cute yourself, kid."

"No, my nose is too big and, um, I have ears like Dumbo, and I'm really skinny."

"You're adorable," Bill said.

"Does that mean we're going to your place?"

"I'm not taking advantage of a drunk teenager."

"I'm not that drunk," Nick argued.

"You're shit-faced."

"No," Nick said, quietly. "Really, I'm not and... I like you. You're nice."

"Not everyone is. Remember that."

Nick dipped a cold French fry into a pool of ketchup, popped it into his mouth and said, "My dad always told me people are as nice to you as you are to them."

"Does your dad know where you are tonight?"

Nick's face fell. "He died when I was fifteen. I miss him every day."

"I'm sorry to hear that," Bill said. "What about the rest of your family? Do they know?"

Nick peered at him quizzically. "Know what?

That I'm gay?" He giggled. "I told you I used to sleep with my Ken doll. Yeah, they know."

"And what? They just accept it?"

He picked up the last of his burger from a blob of congealing grease and scarfed it down. "Yeah. Sure. They're my family."

"You have brothers?"

"Two," he said. "And my sister. They're all older." He sucked the last of the Coke loudly through the plastic straw. "Where's your family, Bill?"

"Illinois," Bill said. "I'm going to drive you to your dorm."

Nick rubbed his fingers on the back of Bill's hand. "Are you sure?"

"Yeah," Bill said, reluctantly. "I'm sure."

Nick lived in a high-rise dorm at the edge of campus. On the drive there, he had chattered on about school, his family and his friends; a stream of untroubled talk frequently punctuated by a bark of goofy laughter and a hand laid on Bill's knee for emphasis. A couple of times, Nick's hand strayed up Bill's thigh and Bill pushed it away, not wanting Nick to touch his dick, which had been hard almost the entire drive. Unlike the contrived blond guy posing in the swirls of cigarette smoke and the dim light of the Petrified Forest, Nick was almost unbearably sexy. He was undeniably cute, but it was more than his looks that made Bill want to pull the car over and bruise the boy's lips with hard, deep kisses and slip his hand beneath Nick's hoodie and T-shirt. Nick's sexiness was more a matter of his guilelessness, his unaffected physicality and his apparently uncomplicated happiness. But then again, he was only eighteen, a freshman in college, ten years younger than Bill. Ten years might not have mattered had Nick been in his twenties and Bill in his thirties because both would have been men. Nick, however, was a boy who looked and acted like a boy.

Bill pulled into a space in front of the dorm. Nick stopped mid-sentence, looked at the entrance to the dorm, then at Bill. Abruptly, he grabbed Bill by the shoulders, kissed him hard and quick, then fell back with a guilty look as if he expected to be reprimanded. Instead, Bill pulled him in and kissed him back, slowly, open-mouthed. When he released the boy, Nick said, "No one has ever kissed me like that before."

"Just how many men have you kissed?"

"Counting you? Um, four. You're the best."

"Not much of a sample."

"Will you kiss me again?" Nick asked, moving in.

"I can't. You're too goddamn young, Nick."

"You like me, I like you, what's the problem?" Nick asked, genuinely puzzled.

Bill, not knowing where to begin, nor even fully understanding his reservations, shook his head.

Nick crossed his arms defiantly and said, "I'm not leaving this car until you give me your phone number."

Bill dug into his pants pocket for his wallet and took out his business card. He reached past Nick for the glove compartment, got out a pen and wrote his home number on the back of the card.

"If you still want to see me when you're sober, call me."

Nick looked at the card. "You sell houses?"

"Yeah. Okay, time for you to go inside."

Nick slipped the card into his pocket. "Can I call you in the morning?"

Bill laughed. "It is the morning."

"Bye-bye, Bill," Nick said, suddenly shy, and slipped out of the car. He was still standing on the sidewalk, staring after Bill's car, when Bill turned the corner. Bill caught his tall, skinny figure in his rearview mirror and smiled.

The little speech Bill had prepared for Nick when he called about why he couldn't date him went out of his head as soon as he heard Nick's cheerful voice on the other end of the line, and Bill agreed to lunch. When he arrived at the restaurant, a Mexican place near the college, Nick was already at a table waiting. As he had on the phone, Bill intended to let Nick down, gently but firmly, but the words caught in his throat when he saw the artless joy in Nick's eyes as he sat down across from him. He could not remember anyone ever having been so happy to see him.

"Um, hi, Bill," Nick said, nervously. He pointed at an empty plastic bowl. "Sorry, I was hungry and I ate all the chips but I asked her to bring more. I hope you like Mexican food, I should have asked you. This place is good, not good as my mom, she makes the best chili *rellenos*. Thank you for taking care of me the other night. How are you?"

"Hi, Nick. I'm good."

"I talk too much when I'm nervous," Nick said, unnecessarily.

The waitress came with another bowl of chips and menus.

After she departed, Bill said, "You don't have to be nervous. It's just a lunch."

But Bill was nervous too, though he concealed it, and the conversation moved awkwardly until Nick asked him about his work. When Bill began to talk about the houses he sold and what they meant to him his nervousness faded away. Nick, leaning toward him, listened with rapt attention and asked him questions that displayed intelligence and sensitivity. A different Nick emerged—not the callow eighteen-year-old boy—but a curious, thoughtful young man with definite opinions he was not shy about expressing. As he had at the diner, Bill's impression of Nick was of someone who had been protected from the worst of life and that this had produced an innocent self-confidence Bill found moving and hugely attractive. Bill could not help but contrast his own terrified and injured eighteen-year-old self with the cheerful, assertive boy talking through a mouthful of food, oblivious to what anyone else might think when he put his hand on Bill's and squeezed it. Bill, who in this situation might have self-protectively withdrawn his hand, was emboldened by Nick's openness and instead squeezed back. He experienced with Nick a moment of true freedom—liberated from his own self-consciousness and anxieties, and in that moment, he could almost forget that he and Nick were gay. They were simply two people, mutually attracted, enjoying each other's company, as if it were the most natural thing in the world.

After their meal, Bill offered Nick a ride back to school.

"I'm done with my classes for today. I thought, um, maybe we could go for a walk."

Bill thought about the piles of paperwork on his desk and the sheaf of phone messages waiting for return calls. "A short walk."

"Ocean Beach?" Nick suggested.

It was one of those afternoons, rare in San Francisco, of such clarity that the blues of ocean and sky blurred together at the horizon. Nick, gazing at it with his hand shading his eyes, murmured, "And yet this great wink of eternity."

Sitting beside him on a log someone had

dragged to the edge of the sea, watching a flock of gulls scribble their way across the sky, dipping and rising, Bill said, "What?"

"Oh, that's from a poem about the sea I read in my American lit class."

"Wink of eternity," Bill repeated. He could see it—the sea one eyelid and the sky the other, slowly closing and opening. "Who wrote it?"

"His name was Hart Crane. He was gay. He threw himself off a boat."

"Because he was gay?"

"I don't know why," Nick replied. "A lot of poets kill themselves. Like Sylvia Plath. She stuck her head in an oven. Um, it's what you call an occupational hazard, I guess. I want to be a writer."

"And jump off a boat?" Bill laughed. "Or stick your head in the oven? No way. I'm not letting anything like that happen to you."

With a shy smile, Nick said, "You're not?"

And just as it had once before, when he'd stood at twilight on Polk Street in front of City Hall and come out to himself, for a split second, time froze, allowing him to study every detail of Nick's face. He glowed as if his skin were illuminated from within, and a strand of his dense, dark hair fell forward, grazing his cheek. His full, firm lips formed a small, questioning "O" making a shallow dimple in his chin. But there was no question in Nick's eyes, only a happiness that made Bill's chest swell protectively. *It would be so easy to love you,* Bill thought.

"What did you say?" Nick's question startled Bill out of his trance and the world moved around him again.

"What?" Bill repeated.

"You said something about loving me."

"I did?" Bill said, realizing too late that he had spoken the words aloud.

Nick offered a puzzled, "Yeah. Um, I mean, I thought that's what you said."

Bill shook his head. "We just met, Nick, and like I said the other night, you're really young."

"You're not that old," Nick countered.

"Twenty-eight."

"So, when you're a hundred, I'll be ninety! What difference will it make then?"

"But you're not ninety. You're eighteen," he said, adding, with more bitterness than he'd intended, "What do you know about life?"

"Not so much, but you could teach me."

"Life's not college. Life's hard. It roughs you up."

Nick said quietly, "Is that what happened to you, Bill?"

"You think I'm rough?"

Nick scooped a handful of sand and let it run through his fingers. "I did hear you. You said you could love me. I know I could love you."

"I don't even know your last name," Bill said.

"Trejo," Nick said. "T-R-E-J-O. Nicolás Alejandro Trejo, but everyone calls me Nick."

"That's a beautiful name," Bill said. "I have to get back to work now. Let me drive you back to school."

Nick got up, dusted the sand from the seat of his pants, and said, "I'll walk back to the dorm, it's not so far."

Bill reached up and grabbed his hand. "Are you okay?"

Nick nodded. "I just have to think."

"About what?"

"About you." He bent down and kissed Bill's mouth. "How I can make you not be afraid to like me."

Bill stood up. "You're just so young."

"Stop saying that!" Nick snapped. "I can't help being eighteen, but that doesn't mean I don't know what I want. I want to date you. There, see, it's not hard to say. Why can't you say what you want?"

Bill pulled the boy into his arms, touching his forehead to Nick's. "I want to date you too. Okay?"

Nick nodded. "Okay. I'm still walking back to school. Can I call you tonight?"

"I'll call you."

"Promise?"

"At seven o'clock," Bill said. "I promise."

The naturalness Bill had felt with Nick at the

Mexican restaurant deepened each time they were alone together, surprising Bill with the realization he had never experienced this feeling with other guys. When he went on a date or had sex with another man, he was always conscious of the censuring world peering through a keyhole. Bill could ignore or reject the censure but he could not escape its presence, reminding him that what he and the other men were doing violated the rules of nature the world had set down. Nick in his spontaneity and happiness seemed entirely oblivious to the disapproving world; while he was undeniably male he was, above all, simply himself. No shadows seemed to cling to him, no history of hurts deformed him and, in his presence, Bill felt as if he could shed his own shadows and hurts. He could, for a little while, forget even that he was gay and be, simply, a man in love.

The freedom he felt with Nick when they were alone, however, was tested every time they left Bill's apartment, where the disapproving world waited for them. Outside the Castro, Bill could not shed his cautious habits. If Nick grabbed for his hand when they were walking down Market Street, he would gently bat it away. When they sat together on MUNI, he kept an inch distance from his lover. When Nick once tried to kiss him while they were shopping in Union Square, Bill turned his face away. He knew these deflections were upsetting to Nick, and he tried to explain them, but, while Nick nodded in apparent understanding, he saw the skepticism in Nick's eyes.

"Um, if we're afraid to hold hands," Nick said once, "how will guys ever be able to hold hands? I mean, what's the worst that can happen? Getting called names?"

"No, we could be get beaten up."

He watched Nick digest this, a tiny glimmer of fear entering his eyes, and felt immediately regretful. He wanted to take it back, but because he believed it, he could not. He told himself he was only teaching Nick survival techniques but by doing so, he knew he was also teaching Nick to be afraid and it weighed on him.

In the Castro, they faced a different challenge. The disparity in their ages was accentuated by their appearance. Nick, with his long, usually disheveled hair, baby face and sloppy schoolboy clothes, looked younger than eighteen while Bill, in his businessman's coat and tie, clipped hair and with a habitually serious demeanor projected a maturity much older than twenty-eight. This disparity drew remarks that ranged from the jokey—the ticket taker at the Castro theater who greeted them with "tonight's feature, the return of the cradle snatcher"—to the judgmental—the aging queen at the Neon Chicken who hissed to his companion, "He should be ashamed, the boy's not even legal, gives all of us a bad name."

Nick's school friends were divided between

those who thought Bill was "hot" and those who thought dating an older man was "gross." Then there was the question of where to go. Bars and over 21 clubs were out. Bill let Nick drag him to a dance sponsored by the university's gay club but he felt so awkwardly out of place he bailed after twenty minutes, leaving Nick hurt and fuming. Eventually, it seemed more comfortable to both of them to spend the evenings alone at Bill's flat where they ate takeout, watched movies on Bill's new VCR and kept each other awake half the night having sex.

In clothes, Nick looked skinny but naked, Bill discovered, he was slender, elegant rather than awkward, long-limbed, wasp-waisted and with a surprisingly plump butt. He claimed his only exercise was walking to classes but he was as muscled as Bill, though Nick's muscles were lean and long, a gift of genetics and youth, rather than weights and workouts. He had three wiry chest hairs—he called them Larry, Moe and Curly Joe—and light aureoles of hair around his nipples which Bill soon discovered were extremely sensitive. His lower legs were shaggy but the hair ended at his thighs and, except for his pubic patch, he was otherwise smooth. His cock was long and thin, uncircumcised and purplish against the lighter skin of his thighs. It dripped threads of precum when Bill grazed it with his fingertips. His puckered hole was dark too, and the first time Bill entered him, slowly and only after he had readied it with copious amounts of lube, it sent a shudder through both their bodies that was, for Bill, greater than pleasure; it seemed to Bill, when he thought about it later, that he had fucked Nick's heart. They moved in a single wave, Nick on his belly, his face in the pillow, Bill pressing down on him, chest to back, nibbling those delicious ears. Nick yelped and came without touching himself, smearing the sheet beneath him with semen. When, a moment later, Bill emptied himself into Nick, tears oozed from the corners of his eyes, streaked his face and splashed Nick's back. Bill wiped them away before Nick could see them, unable to explain even to himself where the tears had come from or what they meant.

Late one night, Nick nestled against Bill in bed and said, "My mom wants us to come to dinner on Sunday so you can meet my family."

"You told your mom about me?" Bill asked, startled.

"Uh-huh," Nick replied sleepily. "She asked me if I was dating anyone."

"Who's coming?" Bill asked uneasily.

"My brother Tom and his wife, Sara, and Sal and his girlfriend—this is a new one, I don't remember her name, Betty or Bonnie or something like that—and my sister Izzy and her daughter, Lila, my niece. Izzy's divorced, I liked her ex-husband Joey but he doesn't come anymore. And me and you. Oh, and my mom. That's all."

"Do they know about me?" he asked, unable to keep the harshness and worry out of his voice.

Nick, now fully awake, replied slowly, "If my mom knows, everyone knows." He raised himself up on an elbow and forced Bill to meet his eyes. "What's wrong?"

"That's a lot of family to meet all at once."

Nick, grasping Bill's reservations, replied, "They're not like your family. They'll love you."

"You don't know that."

"They love me, so they'll love you too," Nick said, with syllogistic certainty.

Bill's worry that he would be the unwelcome center of attention at the Trejo family dinner was quickly dispelled. Three-year-old Lila in a pink confection and a princess crown was the star of the gathering, running from uncle to uncle and from aunt to grandmother and back to her mother. Sister Isabel was tall and thin and dark like Nick, but not half as pretty; she had a square-jawed intensity that set her apart from her laid-back, good-looking brothers and marked her as their leader. Freshly divorced, she worked at the phone company during the day and went to law school at night. When Bill asked her why she wanted to be a lawyer, she replied, curtly, "Didn't Nick tell you about my dad?"

"Yes, I'm sorry. It was cancer, wasn't it?"

"Mesothelioma," she said, the intricate word slipping easily off her tongue. "The company knew the risks of asbestos for years, but they still exposed my dad and the guys he worked with. They call it business. I call it murder."

At that moment Lila called, "Mommy, mommy, look at me! I'm flying!"

Nick was spinning Lila in his arms.

"Nick, you be careful with her." She turned her eyes away from them, fixed Bill with a fierce look and said, "Nick likes you. Don't hurt him."

"Never," Bill said.

Isabel rolled her eyes. "Listen, there's bound to be fighting, just don't do what me and Joe did. Don't take your arguments to bed with you. Don't make resentment part of your relationship. There's not enough room for three."

Nick's mother bounded into the room and said, "Come and eat."

The meal was loud and long and he thought he had never eaten so well. The rice and beans were familiar to him, but the roast chicken was served with a sweet and savory meat dressing Nick called *picadillo* accompanied by a platter of his mother's famous chili *rellenos* that were better than anything Bill had ever eaten at a restaurant. The stacks of tortillas quickly disappeared; the salsa burned his tongue to the amusement of Nick's brothers, Tom and Sal, who were sitting across the table from him. When they weren't teasing Nick directly, the brothers told Bill embarrassing stories about him when he was a child. Sara, Tom's wife, three months pregnant, engaged in a long conversation with Mrs. Trejo about herbal remedies for her morning sickness. Sal's girlfriend, Beth, was telling Isabel about her custody fight with her ex-husband who was trying to get full custody of their four-year-old son claiming that Beth, who had gone back to school to get her nursing degree, could no longer properly care for him. Beneath the table, Nick squeezed Bill's knee reassuringly. Bill slipped his hand over Nick's and speculated with his brothers about the upcoming baseball season now that the Giants had named Frank Robinson as their new manager.

Hours later, loaded with leftovers, they drove home across the bridge.

Bill said, quietly, "I like your family. Now you'll have to meet mine."

"Are we going to Illinois?"

"No, not those people," Bill said. "My real family."

Bill had worried what his friends might think of him dating an eighteen-year-old but after the dinner with the Trejos, he wanted them to meet Nick. So, one Sunday morning he invited them to brunch. Nick had gone to Mass with Mrs. Donohue who had taken to Nick immediately after he had moved in with Bill. When Bill had first told her about Nick, abashed and worried about her response, she had laughed and said,

"Do you think you're the first man who likes them young?" Once she had met him, Nick delighted her.

Waldo arrived first with a baked concoction of eggs, bread, cheese, milk and bacon he called strata. He set it down on the table Bill had covered with bagels and cream cheese, lox and pastries, all store bought since Bill did not cook. Waldo made himself a mimosa and walked around the apartment, shaking his head.

"Honey, I can't get over what you did to this dump. It looks like a room out of a magazine."

Bill laughed. "It is, Waldo. Where's Eddie?"

"He has his girls this weekend and they take forever to get ready. I got tired of waiting, but they'll be along."

"How old are they now?"

Waldo said, fondly, "Yvette is eight and Marie is six. He's trying to get joint custody but, you know, the ex-wife's being a bitch about it and the lawyer says it's gonna be hard to find a judge who's gonna give kids to a pair of faggots."

"He said that?" Bill replied, indignantly.

"Oh, no, hon, he was all mushy mouthed, the way lawyers are, but that's what he meant. Anyway, I'd love to have them living with us. They're feisty little bitches."

"You'll make a good mom."

Waldo smiled and sat. "I know I will. Where's the boyfriend?"

"At church with Mrs. D."

"Oh, that's nice. I like him already."

"I hope you will. He's young."

"I know, hon, that's all any of us know about him. You say it like it's some kind of disease but it ain't." He sipped his cocktail. "He'll grow out of it. Just like you did."

Bill sipped his own drink, plain orange juice. "I was never young, Waldo."

"No," Waldo said. "I guess none of us were."

"Nick is, though. He really is. His family, they don't care he's gay. They love him. He doesn't have our hang ups."

"That's a good thing, Billy."

"I don't want to fuck that up for him."

"How would you do that?"

"Sometimes I think I'm still the kid that got off that bus ten years ago. Scared, confused. Still looking over my shoulder, still waiting for the other shoe to fall. Afraid of everything." He looked at his friend. "That's not who I want to be for Nick. I want to be brave."

"Oh, honey, your family threw you out with the trash and you picked yourself up and came here and made all this for yourself." He spread his arms, embracing the room and the city visible in the windows. "You are brave, Billy."

"You don't know everything. I've done things I'm not proud of. Sex things."

"I know all about that."

Bill stared at him. "You do?"

Waldo finished his drink. "It's a small town full of gossipy queens. Whatever you do with your body is your business." He handed his glass to Bill. "Here, mix me another since I'm drinking for two." Bill poured champagne and orange juice into the glass and brought it to Waldo. "Thanks, hon. So, you like sex rough sometimes, you don't have to be ashamed of it."

Bill tried to find words to express that it wasn't the sex itself, but what he was thinking when he did it; that the sex was not for pleasure but a punishment. The best he could do was, "I wanted someone to hurt me."

"Billy, we've been hurt enough, don't you think?" Waldo said. "We don't have to go looking for it. Listen, if this boy makes you happy, hang on to him. You deserve to be happy. We all fucking do."

The door opened and there were steps up the stairs and then Nick appeared with Mrs. Donohue. She and Waldo saw each other and he got up and scooped her in his arms. Nick stood behind them, his eyes bright and happy at their reunion.

"Oh my God, Mrs. D.," Waldo was saying. "I swear you look younger every time I see you."

She laughed. "You are such a liar, Waldo, but I love it."

Waldo looked at Nick. "You must be Nick. I'm

Waldo, Billy's mom. Come here and give me a hug."

As he watched them hug, Mrs. Donohue beaming at all of them, Bill thought with simple and complete joy, *this is my family.*

10.

I STEPPED INTO A DARK, NARROW hallway and followed Adam into a small living room furnished monastically with a couch, coffee table and a single chair but also a large screen TV and expensive sound system. The street noise squawked through an open window that framed the neon sign of a shabby hotel called the Excelsior. I noticed a series of photographs on the wall above the nondescript sofa, striking black-and-white shots of wooden buildings that looked like barracks, a long room filled with narrow beds, and an unpainted wooden wall carved with Chinese characters.

"What are these?" I asked Adam.

"Angel Island," he said, coming up behind me. "My ex took them."

I turned. "And your ex would be a boy or a girl?"

"Candace," he replied, "and don't call her Candy. Hey, you want something to drink? I could use a beer."

"A glass of water."

He left the room and padded down the hall toward what I assumed was a kitchen. On either side of the window were tall bookcases filled with books in English and Chinese and a photo of Adam and a beautiful girl with sleek black hair and intelligent eyes. Candace, I guessed.

"That's her," Adam said. He offered me a glass of ice water.

"What happened between you?"

"We dated our junior and senior years at State, and then she went to Boston for med school. We tried the long-distance thing but neither one of us has the time or money to be flying back and forth across the country. She doesn't know if she'll be coming back to California and I plan to stay here for biz school, so it didn't look like it was going to work out."

"I'm sorry."

"Yeah," he said. "Me too."

"And guys?"

He sat on the beat-up sofa and patted the cushion beside him. "Have a seat. Stay awhile, okay?"

I sat down. "That depends on what you tell me."

He took a swig of his Tsingtao. "I'm a straight guy who likes having sex with other guys once in a while," he said. "It's the same thing as, you know, once a year I crave Indian food so I go out for curry, and it's great, but the rest of the time I don't think about it."

In law school, I'd slept with a closeted classmate who ended up marrying a woman because he wanted the kind of career in the law he didn't think would be possible if he was openly gay. I remembered there was a tension in his face that nothing could dissipate. Even in sleep, there were faint frown lines at the corners of his mouth and a seam etched between his eyebrows, the visible marks of his internal conflict between who he was and who he pretended to be. I searched Adam's face carefully, looking for the same lines, the same conflict, but found no trace of it and it occurred to me, as improbable as it sounded, he was telling the truth about who he was.

My silence must have begun to worry him because he said, "Hey? You there?"

"Yeah, sorry. I don't know what to say. No one's ever compared me to curry before."

He grinned. "I didn't know you were gay until you told me. Well, I thought you might be, but I wasn't sure. You aren't married and never talk about women, and a couple of times I thought I caught you checking out my butt, so I was hopeful."

"Did you say fag to see how I'd react?" I asked.

"No, I swear. That was just stupid locker room talk. I'm really sorry about that. But," he added, throwing his arm around my shoulder, "at least I know for sure you're gay."

"I'm still not sure what you are."

"I'm into you," he said, "and I thought maybe you're into me too. Isn't that enough?"

I stood up and went back to the photographs on the wall, to buy time while I processed the moment. A straight guy who liked having sex with guys sometimes? What did that even mean? I had no frame of reference here.

"Angel Island," I said. "That was the immigration center. The Ellis Island of the west."

From the couch, he replied, "Not really. At Ellis Island, they let people in. Angel Island was there to keep people out. Chinese people, mostly."

"The writing on the walls of the barracks? What does it say?"

He was standing behind me, peering at the photographs. "They're poems written by the men who got stuck on the island. This one says, 'For what reason must I sit in jail? It is only because my country is weak and family poor. Even if my petition is approved and I can enter the country, when can I return to the mountains of Tang?'" He put his hand on my shoulder. "My people suffered trying to get here."

"And when they made it to the mainland, they died in the thousands building the railroads for the Stanfords and the Crockers at half the pay the white workers got."

"See, that's the other thing I like about you," he said, squeezing my shoulder. "You fight for the little guy."

I moved away. "Do you want to have sex with me because you like me or am I just convenient?"

"Huh?"

"You're not gay? Fine. I am. I like you too. When I have sex with a guy I like, it's more than a physical thing. I won't have sex with you just because you're tired of jerking off."

He frowned. "If getting off was all I wanted, I could've picked anyone. I picked you because... we're friends, right. I thought we could help each other out and have some fun while we were doing it. It doesn't have to be complicated."

He really meant that last bit. There was no guile in Adam Chu. He was exactly what he seemed to be: a bluff, friendly, hard-working, straightforward boy. Maybe I was so used to shadows, ambiguity, struggle I couldn't see what was in front of me anymore. Adam was offering me warmth, companionship, sex—all things that, once he offered them to me, I was keenly aware were absent in my life. That kiss at the door—I wanted more of that but—

"What about AIDS?"

He froze. "Do you have it?'

"No. Well, I haven't been sick or had any symptoms but any guy who's had sex with another guy has been exposed to the virus. I could be carrying it."

"I know. I read the papers. The last guy I had sex with, that was a couple of years ago before people knew and we didn't use condoms, so maybe I've been exposed too. There's nothing we can do now except protect ourselves."

"Did you tell Candace?"

"Yeah, of course. We used protection." He shrugged. "I'm sure I don't have it."

"How can you be sure?"

"I just am," he said, with the invulnerable certainty of youth.

"I'm not."

"Like I said, we can protect ourselves."

It occurred to me that, unlike my friends and me, Adam had no firsthand experience of the virus and what it did to people. That explained his nonchalance. On the one hand, I wanted to bear down and lecture him on the seriousness of the disease. On the other, it was a relief to be with someone who wasn't haunted by what was happening in the city. Was I being irresponsible? Should I walk away from him? If I did, should I then avoid all sex until I knew, one way or the other, about my status? Or, by doing that, would I be imprisoning myself in fear? As Adam had said, there were ways we could protect ourselves.

"Hey," he said. "You okay?"

"I was thinking—"

"Are you one of those guys who thinks too much?"

"Probably."

He stepped toward me, crowding me, forcing my back to the wall. His Adam's apple shifted in his thick, strong throat. His lips were full and dark. His gray tee was stretched tight across his heroically broad chest. I could feel the heat coming off his body.

"Stop thinking," he said, pulled me against him and kissed me.

After a couple of minutes, he broke away long enough to ask, "You wanna go to bed?"

"Yeah," I said.

Adam lifted himself off me, dug around the twisted sheets until he found the condom, picked it up and went into the bathroom. I heard the toilet flush and then running water. He returned to the room with a damp hand towel he used to wipe our mingled semen off my belly and chest. Smiling, he dabbed my chin.

"Sorry about that," he said. "It's been a while."

"I'm not complaining. That was incredible."

"Really?" he asked, sinking back into bed and pulling my arm around his shoulder.

"Really," I replied. "For someone who says he's not gay, you do a damn good impression of a gay guy."

Even after we were naked, I hadn't known what to expect. Maybe some more rolling around and then mutual masturbation but, gay or not, Adam had no inhibitions about sex with another guy. Even so, I was momentarily at a loss for words when he whispered, "Wanna fuck me, Henry?"

When I recovered, the first words out of my

mouth were, "I don't know if that's safe for us to do."

He rolled over, opened the drawer of the bed stand, reached in and then tossed me a condom and a bottle of lube.

"You sure about this?"

"You don't want to fuck me?" he asked with a grin.

"I've never wanted anything more."

"Then put that thing on."

"Here's a better idea," I said, handing him the foil. "You put it on me."

We lay face to face, knees touching, hands idly stroking each other's chests and bellies. The dark flush of arousal had faded from beneath his skin.

"So, this is the part where you tell me your story," I said. "How many other guys have you been with?"

"Three. A friend in high school, but all we did was look at porn and jerk each other off. I liked how it felt, you know, being with another guy, having his hand on my cock, but it was no big deal. I liked girls better. Then when I was a freshman, I messed around with another guy for a while. Learned to do some other things."

"What happened then?"

"I met Candace."

"Oh," I said. "You said you told her about the guys."

"Yeah."

"And she was—okay with it?"

"She's a scientist," he replied, as if this explained everything.

"And the third guy?"

"That was after Candace and me broke up. A guy who cruised me on the street. I was lonely and horny, so I went home with him. That lasted a couple of months but he kept telling me I was a closet case and I had to come out. I got tired of arguing with him, so that was the end of that."

"Why aren't you dating women?"

"I do. Shit, between my mom and my grandma trying to set me up, it's like I have my own personal dating service." He sighed. "But, it's complicated. I'm still not over Candace, plus depending on where I get accepted to biz school, I might not even be in the city next fall and then there's the restaurant. I'm working ten, twelve hours a day there, six days a week. A girlfriend is the last thing I need right now. I want something simple."

"Why not a woman for that?"

"Women want more," he said, "at the least the ones I meet, and right now I can't give them more. I like sex with guys and guys aren't thinking that maybe I'll propose to them somewhere down the line." He yawned. "You ask a lot of questions."

"I'm trying to understand you."

"I'm not complicated."

"I have to think about this," I said, getting out

of bed, and searching for my clothes on the floor.
"I'll get back to you."

"I hope you don't think yourself out of it,
because this was fun."

Later, lying awake in my own bed, I remembered
a conversation I'd had with Larry when we got to
step three of AA's twelve steps.

Step three, Larry intoned, we made a decision
to turn our will and our lives over to the care of
God, as we understood Him. What does that mean
to you, Henry? I don't believe in God, I replied, so
I don't believe that God has a plan for me, if that's
what you're asking. No, he snapped. I'm asking
whether you can accept the distinction between
what you want and what's good for you and that
left to your own devices you're more likely to
choose the first instead of the second. I'm asking
whether you accept that fact that you have a deep
streak of self-destructiveness in you that you need
help controlling. Yeah, I replied, humbled, I can
accept all that. Because? he persisted. Because
I nearly drank myself to death, I said, and if I
hadn't gone to rehab and met you, I might have
succeeded. Good boy, he said. Now, he continued,
the bad news is that your propensity to make
stupid choices isn't limited to drinking. Any time
you get yourself into a situation where you have
a choice of action, and one road leads to chaos,
you need to run it by me. Because you're God, I
snarked. No, he said, because I'm not you. Your

ideas of what's good for you, Henry, are mostly wrong, but you can't see that and you're so smart you can always rationalize your bad decisions. You need someone to call bullshit on you. That's my job. Got it? Yes, boss, I said. Got it.

The taste of beer in Adam's mouth when I kissed him was thrilling and dangerous, not because it made me want to drink, but because it savored of the forbidden. Was it a good idea for me to take up with a straight guy who wanted sex without strings when most days, emotionally flayed as I was, I was nothing but strings? I knew I should run it by Larry. Then I thought about how Adam's body had felt against mine, like steel sheathed in silk, and the way his stomach muscles bunched when he came beneath me as I fucked him. I remembered his mouth on mine, his hand gripping my hand, our legs tangled together. In my chilly bed, I remembered his warmth. Maybe Larry didn't need to know yet, I told myself. After all, it was only sex. There was no step in AA against that.

I called Michael Lauro and explained who I was and what I was doing.

"Well," he said, hesitantly, "I wasn't there when Billy died. I can't tell you anything about that."

"I'm more interested in his background. Mrs.

Donohue said you and he were boyfriends, before he met Nick."

"You say Nick's gonna get the insurance money?"

"If everything checks out."

"Well, I guess she put in the time," Lauro replied. "On her back."

"I beg your pardon?"

"You want to know about Bill? Come over Saturday morning."

The address he gave me led me to an Art Deco apartment building on a street midway between Union Square and the Tenderloin. Two blocks east were posh restaurants, the American Conservatory Theater, the St. Francis hotel and Macy's; two blocks west and junkies were shooting up in the doorways of shuttered storefronts. It was the San Francisco out of a 'thirties noir novel. When the intricately ornamented bronze elevator door slid open to take me up to Michael Lauro's apartment, I half expected Joel Cairo to step out into the marble lobby. Instead, a girl in jogging sweats emerged, twisting her long hair into a ponytail for her morning run.

I took the elevator to the fourteenth floor and as I stepped out of the elevator, a male voice said, "Henry? Over here."

Michael Lauro was medium height with a gym-built body accentuated by tight Levi's and a clinging gray T-shirt. He would have been a twink when he was younger—that gay term for boyish

and cute—but now there was gray in his stubble
and short black hair and his features were settling
into middle age. He gave me a friendly smile as he
waved me into his apartment, a one-room studio
artfully arranged to appear bigger than it was.

"Sit down," he said, indicating the black
leather sofa. "You want some coffee?"

"Thanks."

The small kitchen was partitioned off from
the main room by a low counter. He made the
coffee on the granite countertop using a French
press. He pushed down on the plunger, poured
the coffee into two gold-rimmed coffee cups and
brought them, with cream, sugar, napkins and
spoons, on a lacquered tray that he set down on
the coffee table.

"So," he said, "little Nick's gonna get his
payoff."

"You have a problem with that?" I asked
neutrally.

He spooned sugar into his coffee. "The kid
was a gold-digger. We all knew, but Bill couldn't
see it, and when I tried to tell him we had a big
fight and he stopped talking to me."

I tried to square my impressions of Nick with
Lauro's accusation. "Why do you say Nick was a
gold-digger?"

"Well, it's obvious, isn't it? He got Bill to move
him into his flat and pay for everything and now
he gets the insurance money. Listen, the kid was
eighteen when Billy met him. Bill was handsome

and successful. All Nick brought to the party was his twink ass."

I sipped my coffee, stifling the distaste I was beginning to feel for Michael Lauro.

"Maybe Bill did all that because he loved Nick."

"You know Bill's story?"

"Somewhat," I replied. "Why don't you tell me."

Lauro got up and crossed the room to a curtained alcove. He pulled open the curtains to reveal a bed, got on his knees, lifted the bed ruffle and rummaged around, emerging with a photo album bound in red leather. He came back to the sofa and opened the album on his lap. He flipped though pages of fading photographs, then stopped and pointed to a snapshot of a very tall, skinny young man with a comic face, a big grin, and a shock of orange hair. He had his arm around a shorter, unsmiling, dark-haired boy I recognized as a young Bill Ryan.

"Waldo," he said. "And Billy."

"How old was Bill when this was taken?"

"They're standing in front of the old Hide 'n Seek, so he must have just got to San Francisco. Eighteen or nineteen, maybe."

"Bill looks scared."

"When Billy was eighteen, his dad found him with another boy's cock in his mouth and beat him so bad they had to take out his spleen. After he got out of the hospital, they gave him a one-way ticket to San Francisco and told him, don't come back. He got here with nothing but the clothes on his back. If he hadn't met Waldo, he would have had to peddle his ass on Polk Street to survive. So, yeah, he was scared."

"Waldo Kornowsky. You knew him?"

"Everyone knew Waldo. He was Polk Street's official welcome wagon. He knew all about boys like Billy."

"What do you mean?"

He turned the pages of the album, pointing out other photographs of Waldo, at parties, in the park, at a bar, always with friends and always smiling or laughing. "Notice anything unusual about Waldo's shirts?"

"No, not really."

"He always wore long sleeves, whatever the weather was like."

I looked again. In every photo his arms were covered. "Yeah, I see that now."

"They covered the scars on his wrists where he cut himself when he tried to commit suicide," Lauro said. "They were deep and ugly like he'd been handcuffed with barbed wire. Waldo knew what it was like to be thrown away and live on the streets. That's why he went around saving people like Bill. And me." He thumbed to a photo of Waldo in full drag. "She was loud, opinionated and sloppy but once that queen took you in, you were family and no one messed with her family."

"What does this have to do with Nick?"

He closed the album and sipped some coffee, pinkie extended out. "Billy came from the streets, like me and Waldo, but Nick? He was a spoiled kid who didn't even break a fingernail coming out of the closet. He couldn't know what we had been through."

"Isn't that a good thing?" I asked, mildly. "Shouldn't it be easier for kids Nick's age than it was for us?"

He eyed me. "That's right, I forget. You said you were one of us." He delicately set his cup down. "Why should it be easier for them? Why shouldn't they suffer like we did?"

"Well, they do have AIDS to worry about."

"Honey, we all have AIDS to worry about."

"Of course, you're right." I said. "I'm still not sure what this has to do with Nick being a gold-digger."

"He took advantage of Billy. You see, he was the same age when Bill met him that Bill was when he got thrown out by his family. Billy took up with him because he wanted a do-over. He wanted to be eighteen again himself and for it to be different this time. Nick was his second chance. But," he continued, bitterly, "there ain't no second chances. Nick should have left Bill alone."

"You think Nick knew Bill was vulnerable and exploited him."

"Exactly."

"Bill was older than Nick. Some people might say Bill was the exploiter."

Lauro shook his head. "Bill never got over what happened to him when he was eighteen. In a way, he was eighteen his whole life. Hurt and scared and ashamed of himself. Waldo used to say we queens are born behind enemy lines and once you figured that out, you had to blend in 'til you could make a run for the border. The thing is, the more you blended in, the more you could pass for one of them, the harder it was to shake it off when you finally escaped. Now, take me. I was always a little bit of a sissy and Waldo, well, he came out of the womb singing show tunes, you know. We didn't blend in so good. That made it really hard while we had to live with the breeders, but at least we never figured ourselves for one of them. We always knew who we were and once we got out we could be ourselves and, you know, fuck them." The anger in those last words was still fresh. "But Billy, he blended in until his dad caught him with that boy's dick in his mouth. Until then, everyone thought he was a straight jock kid, and it wasn't just pretending either. He drank the Kool-Aid. He thought if he couldn't be like them, then something was wrong with him. Even after they threw him away, he thought it was all his fault because he was..."

"Defective," I said.

Lauro nodded. "Yeah. Like that. Waldo said Billy was held together with spit and baling wire.

Waldo was always telling Billy there was nothing wrong with him. He was gay, is all. And Waldo kept telling him that, day after day, month after month, year after year, until Billy almost believed it."

"Almost?"

"Yeah, almost," Lauro said. He crossed his legs and leaned back against the couch, like an actor in a play. "Now I'm gonna to tell you something about Bill you have to swear you won't tell anyone else."

"I can't promise that if it's relevant to my investigation."

Lauro waved an unconcerned hand at me and plunged on, almost gleefully. "Bill had a secret life."

"What kind of secret life?"

"Drugs," he said. "Rough sex. He liked—" he arranged his mouth into a moue, "to be humiliated."

It bothered me that he was enjoying this. "Yeah, it's not relevant."

"Waldo told me," he continued, oblivious of my disinterest, "but I didn't believe him until—well, I went to the baths one night and saw Bill laying naked in a bathtub in the orgy room getting pissed on by—"

"As I said, that's not relevant to my investigation."

"But this happened when he was already living with Nick. What does that say about their relationship? Bill wouldn't have needed that if he was happy with the kid."

"When was the last time you talked to Bill?" I asked to change the subject.

"A couple of months ago, he called me out of the blue and asked me to lunch. We met and talked about nothing until I got tired of it and said, why did you call me, Bill? What do you want? He hemmed and hawed some more, and then he said, do you have it? Are you sick? I almost threw my wine in the bitch's face. I told him, I'm fine. What about you? He said, I'm fine too. A couple of weeks before he died, I got another call from him. Same thing, lots of small talk but I could tell something was bothering him. He really wanted to tell me, but he couldn't."

"What do you think it was?"

"What do most men feel guilty about?" Lauro asked archly. "Cheating on the wife. I think he wanted to tell me I was right about Nick and that he was going to dump him."

"That was the last time you heard from him?

"Yes," Lauro said. "I don't mean to rush you, but I have to get to the salon. Can't keep the blue rinse ladies waiting."

"Of course," I said, rising. "Thanks for your time."

I had an arraignment the next morning at the Hall of Justice—a dismal misnomer if ever there was one. While I waited for my client to be brought up from the holding cells, the Public Defender declared a conflict of interest in two cases, much to the irritation of the arraignment judge. She brusquely appointed me to represent the defendants so I didn't get to my office until after lunch. Our receptionist handed me a half-dozen pink message slips from my cubbyhole that I perused as I headed to my office. The one that caught my attention was from Isabel Trejo: "Called re her brother."

I replayed my conversation with Michael Lauro in my head. His description of Nick Trejo as a gold-digger didn't jive with my own impressions of Trejo or what Mrs. Donohue had told me about him and his relationship with Bill Ryan. Moreover, Michael Lauro struck me as a mean-mouthed gossip who dined on the misfortunes of others. That being said, bitter old queens could be surprisingly perceptive and if what he said about Nick Trejo rang false, his insights into Bill Ryan seemed accurate enough: A deeply injured man trying through his relationship with Nick to heal the wounds inflicted on him by the family that rejected him when he was a boy. The Castro was filled with such men—wasn't I one of them? — embedded with the shrapnel of hatred who tried to ease the pain with whatever analgesic was at hand, sometimes drugs and booze, sometimes compulsive sex and misguided relationships. That line of thinking brought me dangerously close to my situation with Adam, so I set it aside and called Isabel Trejo.

To my surprise, the call was answered with, "Law offices."

"Yes, hello, I'm returning Isabel Trejo's call from this morning. My name is Henry Rios."

"Hold, please." I listened to canned music and wondered why Nick and his mother had failed to mention that Nick's sister was a lawyer. My thoughts were interrupted with a brisk, "This is Isabel Trejo."

"Miss Trejo, I'm Henry Rios. I'm returning your call."

"You're the claims investigator for Bill Ryan's life insurance policy?"

"Yes. I'm also a lawyer but I do some work for Western States."

"Oh," she replied. "A lawyer. Why does Western States need a lawyer to look at a death claim? Is there something else going on?"

"No, it's a standard investigation. You're Nick's sister?"

"Nick called me after you came and talked to him and my mother about Bill's policy."

"Why would they think they need a lawyer?"

This conversation was beginning to sound like a negotiation between adversaries, a cat-and-mouse game where each side was trying to ferret out information without giving any up.

"I'm not calling you as their lawyer. I'm calling as a concerned family member."

"Concerned about what?" I prodded. "It's all pretty straightforward. Bill Ryan took out a life insurance policy with your brother as the beneficiary. Once I confirm the basic facts surrounding his death, the company will pay the claim."

"Nick's still very upset about Bill's death. All he wants is to put it behind him, go back to school and get on with his life."

"I can understand that. Sounds like they had a complicated relationship."

She bristled. "I don't know who told you that. They were fine. Bill was family."

"So your mother said."

"Look," she snapped, "let me shortcut this for you. Nick doesn't want the money."

"He what?" I said, astonished.

"Nick doesn't want the money from the policy."

"You realize we're talking about a hundred thousand dollars?"

Now it was her turn to be astonished. "That much?"

"It's a fifty-thousand-dollar policy that pays double in the event of accidental death."

"Of course, it was an accident," she said, brusquely.

"No one is saying it was anything else."

"Then why are you investigating?"

"Standard procedure," I replied. "What kind of law do you practice, Miss Trejo?"

That got a bitten off, "Plaintiff's personal injury, not that it's relevant."

"But it is. You must deal with insurance companies all the time. You know how reluctant they are to part with money until every 't' is crossed and every 'i' is dotted."

"Sure," she said. "I understand that, but that's business and this is my family. Nick's very sensitive. He's already been through our dad's death and now Bill's. You can't imagine how tough this has been on him."

"You're right. I can't, but even so, I don't understand why he would reject the money."

"He doesn't want to profit off Bill's death."

Profit off Ryan's death? That was an odd way of putting it.

"The policy was Bill Ryan's way of taking care of him."

"Nick doesn't see it that way. To him, it's blood money."

"I could see that if Nick felt he was in some way responsible for Bill's death, but as you said, Miss Trejo, it was an accident."

There was a fraught silence that went on so long, I thought she'd hung up on me, but then she said, "It's Nick's decision and that's what he's decided. If he needs to sign something, you can messenger it to my office and I'll take care of it."

She rattled off an address before I could respond.

"Okay," I said, scribbling it down. "I'm not

sure what the procedure is when a beneficiary declines the benefit. I'll have to check with the company and get back to you."

"Fine. But talk to me, okay, not Nick. Like I said, Nick's—"

"Upset," I said.

"That's right. Thanks."

She hung up.

I put the phone down and thought about Nick Trejo. Sensitive? Yes, I could believe that. But so sensitive he couldn't bear the thought of taking the insurance money because it derived from Bill Ryan's completely unforeseen and accidental death? That didn't pass the smell test. There were only two reasons I could think of for why he would reject the money. One, to end my investigation. Two, Ryan's death was something other than the result of an accident. This line of thinking led to reason three: *Mens rea. Mens rea* was law school Latin for guilty mind; one of the two elements that had to be present before a crime was committed. The other was *actus rea*, a guilty act. I was beginning to think some kind of crime had been committed. Rejecting the money might be circumstantial evidence of Nick's *mens rea* but what could the *actus rea* have been?

Whatever my suspicions, however, I had no jurisdiction to pursue them. My job was limited to the investigation of the death claim. If Nick renounced the money, Western States was off the hook, and the circumstances of Ryan's death were moot. My work for Western State was privileged so I couldn't go to the police, even had I wanted to which, given my deep-seated aversion to cops, I did not. In any event, all I had were gut feelings and suspicions. The sensible course was to call Ruth Fleming, fill her in on the details, and find out the procedure for renunciation of a claim.

I might have done that, too, had I not glanced at the remaining message slips on my desk. Atop the pile was one from Randy Gifford, Bill Ryan's attorney, returning my call. I picked it up. As I studied the name and number, it occurred to me how I could keep the investigation open and answer the nagging questions I had about Bill Ryan's death.

Randy Gifford's office was on Castro Street above a fancy furniture and *tchotchke* shop across the road from what had been Harvey Milk's camera store. He may well have furnished his handsome office from his downstairs neighbor with distressed leather armchairs, heavy crystal knickknacks and the elegant antique library table he used as his desk. He was pretty well put together himself in a French blue broadcloth shirt, blue and yellow rep tie and pale, yellow suspenders. His pleasant, friendly, forty-something face was the kind of face that, if encountered on the next barstool or beside you on an airplane, invited confidences. Now this, I thought, is what a lawyer is supposed to look like, prosperous and discreet. Not a look I'd ever been able to master.

We made our introductions and then he asked, in a deep as soothing as his appearance, "What can I do for you, Henry?"

"I'm investigating a claim made on a life insurance policy your client Bill Ryan took out with Western States."

Surprise momentarily rippled his smooth countenance. "Really? Bill never mentioned an insurance policy."

"He named Nick Trejo as the beneficiary."

He nodded. "Yes, that makes sense. They were partners."

"Boyfriends," I said with a smile to let him know I was in the club.

"The things we're forced to call ourselves." He frowned. "Boyfriends, as if we're teenagers, or lovers, as if it were only about sex, or partners, which makes it sound like we're running an antique store together. It's demeaning."

"What should we call ourselves?"

"Spouse. Husband. Not that that day will ever come." He smiled. "Sorry, let me climb off my soapbox. How can I help your investigation?"

"Actually, I'm here because I have information that would be of interest to the executor of Bill Ryan's estate."

"That would be me."

"Nick Trejo declined the death benefit."

Another surprised look. "He did? Why would he do that?"

"According to his family, he doesn't want to profit from Ryan's death."

Gifford raised an eyebrow. "Too late for that. Bill left him almost his entire estate."

"Really? Does Nick know?"

"He was sitting in your chair when Bill signed his will," Gifford said. "I've been trying to reach him since Bill died but he seems to have disappeared."

"He's staying with his mother in Linwood. I have the address and a number."

"That's great. Will you give it to me? I really need to talk to him. I've been fending off Bill's family and it's getting ugly."

"I understand they've laid claim to his apartment."

He didn't try to keep the anger out of his voice. "Those people. They swoop down like vultures to pick at Bill's carcass after they threw him into the streets. I told their lawyer they better be ready for a fight because I will take them down."

"My understanding is that Bill was estranged from them. How did they even find out about his death?"

"They were estranged from him," Ryan replied. "Evidently, Bill never gave up hoping they would come around someday. He wrote to his mother about his career and he instructed his office manager—Doris something—to contact his parents in the event anything ever happened to him. She's the one who notified the family."

"And his parents were on the next plane," I suggested.

"No, actually, a brother—Tom. He sat there and told me Bill owes the family for what he put them through."

"What he put *them* through?"

"The shame of having a faggot brother," Gifford answered. "The father lost his job, had a heart attack. The house got foreclosed on. Somehow, all of this was Bill's fault. Lost in the recitation was how his father beat him up so badly he had to have his spleen removed."

"You knew Bill's story, then. You were friends."

"I don't know if having a drink now and then qualifies as friendship, but then Bill was kind of a loner."

"You knew Nick?"

"I met him."

"How were things between them?"

He gazed at me steadily. "Why would you ask me that?"

"I'm trying to understand why Nick would turn down a hundred thousand dollars. My sense, from talking to his sister, is that he feels guilty about something."

"His sister?"

"Isabel Trejo. She's a P.I. lawyer. She's the one who called me and told me Nick didn't want the money."

He shrugged. "I don't know how things were with Bill and Nick. We mostly talked business and baseball. I can tell you he became obsessed with AIDS, but then who isn't around here? I gather a couple of his friends died early on. I told him to do what I do, assume you're infected and get on with life."

"Did he take your advice?"

"I don't know. Bill Ryan was like a lot of us in this neighborhood. He came here from East Jesus after his family threw him out and found a community and a life he could never have imagined, only to watch it slip away when AIDS hit. I wouldn't blame him if he ignored me. How do you get on with your life when you can see a tsunami coming at you?"

"That's a good question."

He turned his chair to face the window that looked out on Castro Street. "I used to sit in the barber chair in Harvey's store across the street with all the other young refugees and plot how we would turn San Francisco into the gay homeland. A gay Israel with the Castro as our Jerusalem." He turned back to me. "Now it looks like that's all going to end with us."

It sounded like an epitaph. Something in me resisted. "Some of us will survive."

"Traumatized and disillusioned, and more stigmatized than ever. We had one generation of liberation and now it's back to the dark ages." He smiled dolefully. "Excuse me, Henry. One

223

friend died this morning and I have to speak at a memorial for another one tonight. It's not a good day."

That explained his funereal mood. I wanted to console this elegant, decent man, but couldn't come up with anything better, "I'm very sorry."

"Back to business," he said briskly. "You were telling me about the insurance policy."

I nodded. "Since Nick declined the benefit, I assumed the estate would want to claim it."

"How much did you say it was?"

"Fifty thousand doubled to a hundred thousand for accidental death."

"Wow. I'd be violating my fiduciary duties to the estate if I didn't make a claim. Have you finished your investigation?"

"Not quite yet. But soon."

"Could you give me a copy of the policy?"

"I have one here for you," I said, removing the file from my briefcase and handing it to him.

"Thanks," he said. "Yes, if Nick actually declines the benefit, the estate will claim it." He smiled. "You know what's ironic?"

"No, what?"

"As Bill's sole heir, Nick will get this money whether he wants or not."

Without, I thought, having to answer any more of my questions.

Aloud, I said, "At least that's one asset Bill's family can't claim."

"I'm sure they'll try. They've laid a stake to everything but Bill's body."

"What?"

"They left Bill lying in the morgue. The morgue called me. I couldn't reach Nick about what he wanted to do, so I had him cremated." He gestured to a small, rectangular antique-looking rosewood box on a bookshelf and said, "Meet Bill Ryan."

11.

"**Y**OU DON'T HAVE TO DRIVE me to school every day," Nick said, easing himself into Bill's Mercedes. "I can take the bus."

"I like driving you," Bill replied, locking Nick's door from the driver's side.

Nick smiled. "At least let me lock my own door."

"Someone has to protect you."

Nick started to reply but apparently thought better of it. Bill knew Nick disliked it when Bill mentioned protecting or taking care of him because, he told Bill, as the youngest child in his family, he'd had enough of being taken care of. His brothers could still get a rise out of him simply by calling him "baby bro" and he complained that his sister mothered him more than his mother did. Nick wanted to be treated like a grownup but, from Bill's perspective, Nick did not understand—because he'd had no experience of it—that what mostly comprised the grownup world was uncertainty, fear, regret and loss. That's really what Bill wanted to protect Nick from: all that.

If he was being honest, he also wanted to protect himself, or, rather, to protect the happiness Nick had brought into his life. That happiness, like the touch of Nick's breath on his face when they lay in bed at night, was pervasive but fragile. The joy Nick gave him could often completely still the small throb of anxiety that had been like a second heartbeat since he had boarded the Greyhound bus to San Francisco on that long-ago summer day in Eden Plains. For a little while, the world faded from view and it was as if he and Nick were sitting at a campfire, wrapped in and warmed by the simple fact of each other's existence. But then Bill would become aware that the fire was a small one, the reach of its light was limited, and that behind them, above them and around them was a creaking, teeming, devouring, primeval darkness. When that happened, he was terror-stricken and he grabbed at a startled Nick, unable to explain fears so overwhelming he did not have words for them, only sensations, above all, the sensation of impending loss.

Bill had never been in love before. What he'd felt for Marco had been a schoolboy crush coupled with the ache of sexual loneliness. The dust of his quarrelsome affair with Michael—all fighting and fucking—had never settled long enough for real feelings to emerge. He loved Nick and it was not at all what he had expected it to be, the mushy sentimentality of pop songs, a warm and homey sentiment, the emotional equivalent of oatmeal and raisins on a cold morning. Love was exhilaration alternating with terror, a steep and jagged path through a dark tangle of fear that led him to a mountaintop. It was all-consuming and exhausting. He had never been happier; he had never been more anxious.

Nick opened the *San Francisco Chronicle* he had picked up at the doorstep and began to read the front page.

"Reagan thinks ketchup should count as a vegetable for school kids," he said disgustedly. "That asshole. I still can't believe he's president."

After a moment, Bill said, quietly, "I voted for him."

Nick crumpled the corners of the newspaper. "You what?"

"I'm a businessman. He was the better candidate for business."

"You're also gay, and this guy is surrounded by religious anti-gay bigots like Falwell and that woman, Schlafly."

"Like I said, baby, I'm in business. I have to think about more than being gay."

"Not me," Nick said. "If I'd know you were a Republican, I would never have dated you."

"I didn't say I was a Republican," Bill replied, soothingly. "All I said was that I voted for Reagan. Are we really going to fight about ketchup?" He rounded the curve at the top of Portola where the city spread out beneath them in the glittering, autumn sunlight. "Look at the city, like Norma Desmond ready for her closeup."

Nick guffawed. "Did you just make a campy reference to *Sunset Boulevard*?"

"I guess all those years of rooming with Waldo rubbed off on me." He reached over and clasped Nick's hand. "No more talking about politics, okay?"

Nick returned the pressure of his hand but said, "Oh, we will talk about it again, but not now."

He fiddled with the radio dial, restlessly switching one station after another.

"Wait, stop," Bill said. "I like this song."

A group called Ambrosia sang:

"Need your lovin' here beside me
(Shine the light) Need it close enough to
guide me
(All my life) I've been hopin' you would
find me
You're the biggest part of me..."

"It's corny," Nick said.

"I don't care. Whenever I hear it, I think of you."

They listened to the song in silence until it ended.

Nick said, "Uh, when I think of the biggest part of you, I think of this." He ran his finger lightly back and forth above Bill's crotch.

Bill's cock jumped to attention. "Hey, stop that. I'm driving."

He began to unzip Bill's trousers. "I could give you a blowjob."

Bill flicked his hand away. "And get us both killed."

"You'd die with a smile on your face."

"You're being a bad boy. I'm going to have to spank you tonight."

"Promise?"

"Yeah, now keep your hands to yourself. What are you doing at school today?"

Nick babbled happily about his classes until they arrived at the school and Bill dropped him off with a quick kiss. He idled the car, watching his lover melt into a mob of other students.

Bill had not expected his affair with Nick to be much more than casual fun given Nick's age. Bill had imagined that once the first blush of lust had passed, they would settle into an unequal friendship in which he would guide eighteen-year-old Nick as he had been guided by Waldo through the byways and backwaters of the gay world. He had imagined that eventually Nick would find someone his own age and their friendship would devolve into occasional meals and phone calls whenever Nick needed his advice.

But Nick was not a confused gay boy in need of a steady hand. Beneath the awkward innocence that had drunkenly propelled him into

Bill's arms the night they met was a core of self-assurance. Nick, it seemed, had been undamaged by the revelation he was gay. Unlike most gay men, including, Bill knew, himself, Nick wasn't constantly glancing over his shoulder—sometimes figuratively, sometimes literally—anxious about who or what might be gaining on him.

Once, on the bus home from the hospital where they had visited a friend who had tried to kill himself, Waldo had answered Bill's "Why?" with a philosophical, "It's hard to be hated, hon. Being a fag ain't for sissies." Bill had understood perfectly: the boy in the hospital, Waldo, and he himself were hated not for something they had done, for which amends might be possible, but for their unchangeable nature, for which no forgiveness was possible, a point first made for all of them by their families.

Not Nick. Nick was the little brother, teased but loved by his siblings and cherished by his parents, above all, by his father—also named Nicolas—whose death was so painful that after three years it was still hard for Nick to speak about him. It was his sister, Isabel, who had told Bill about him. Nick, Sr. was a Mexican immigrant who drove a forklift in a cannery, spoke English with a heavy accent, had married a Mexican-American woman and had a single driving passion: his children.

"Dad was more like a mother than Mom was," Isabel told him at a Trejo family gathering, of which there were many. "After dinner he'd sit us down one by one and ask us about our day even when we were little kids and our days were like going to kindergarten and finger-painting and taking naps. He tucked us in at night and got us up for school, not because Mom wouldn't have done it, but because he wanted to. When the other neighborhood dads were spending the weekend watching sports on TV and drinking beer, Dad was taking us to the park or the zoo, to the swimming pool, to Funland, to the drive-in. He tried not to play favorites but we all knew Nick was his *hombrecito*, his little man. Dad knew Nick was gay before Nick did."

"He what?" Bill asked, astounded. "How?"

"When Nick was about four, he found a doll my folks had given me that I never played with because I didn't have any use for dolls. Nick loved her. He named her Maria and carried her around with him everywhere. He dressed her and combed her hair and slept with her. My brothers teased him about Maria all the time. One day, Tom grabbed it and took it away from him and Nick went crying to my dad. Daddy got really mad, not at Nick for playing with dolls like you would think, but at Tom for making Nick cry. He made Tom give the doll back and apologize. I remember Nicky sitting on Dad's lap combing Maria's hair and Dad with a funny look on his face like a light had just gone on in his head. That's when I think Dad knew."

"Nick was only four, how could he know?"

Isabel raised an eyebrow. "Nick wasn't rough and loud like the rest of us kids. He's always been sensitive and gentle. Dad was thoughtful, he knew who we were and he wanted us to be ourselves, not like Mom, who wanted us to be like everyone else in the neighborhood. Like when I said I wanted to go to college? Mom said it was a waste because I'd end up getting married anyway but Dad said, no, I was the smartest and I was going to get an education. When it looked like Tom was going to get drafted, and he was so scared of going to Vietnam, Mom said it was no big deal because her brother had been in Korea. Dad told her he would send Tommy to Mexico to live with his relatives before he would let the government take his son. Good thing for Tommy he got a medical deferment. Nick never told Dad he was gay because Dad died before Nick told anyone, but Dad knew and he didn't care. He loved his little man."

Oscillating between joy and fear – the joy of loving Nick, the fear of losing him – exhausted Bill emotionally and physically, but he concealed his feelings from Nick. He was, after all, the grownup in their relationship and Bill feared Nick would think less of him if Bill revealed his insecurities. Instead, he took them to Waldo who had talked him back from the edge of an emotional trauma so many times before.

"Uh-huh," Waldo said, his mouth full of noodles. They were eating at a shabby diner near Civic Center called the Gold Mountain Café that Waldo favored. The old couple who ran it didn't bother giving Waldo a menu but brought him a Coke and a plate of greasy beef lo mien, the same meal he always ate. Bill kept to the sandwiches on the American side of the menu.

"I mean," Bill continued. "What if something happened between us?"

"You mean," Waldo said, washing down the noodles with a swig of Coke, "he meets another boy he likes better than you."

The grilled cheese sandwich turned to ash in his mouth. This was exactly what Bill feared, so much so that he was unable even to say it aloud.

"I'm his first," he mumbled. He swallowed the bread and cheese with difficulty. "This city's a candy shop."

Waldo shrugged. "So, he fucks other boys, so what? We're not like the straights, Billy. Monogamy and fidelity, they aren't the same thing. If you love him and he loves you, he'll come back to you." He crooked an admonitory finger at Bill. "Listen to me, hon, don't hold on too tight. Nick's a kid. Of course, he'll want to sample the other chocolates. You gotta let him because it ain't like the Carly Simon song. He don't belong to you."

Bill frowned at his plate of greasy fries and half-eaten sandwich. This was not the advice he had wanted to hear. "I don't know if I can do that. I'm not like the other queens in this city. I want to settle down with one guy, and one guy only."

"Then maybe you shouldn't have picked a boy who barely shaves," he replied tartly.

"He picked me."

"That's right," Waldo said, slurping another forkful of noodles. "He picked you. Listen to me. That boy has stars in his eyes for you."

At that moment, the teenage grandson of the owners whizzed by, stopped and grinned. "Hey Waldo! Hi Bill."

"Adam," Waldo said, "my hunkette. Just getting out of school."

"Yeah. Came over to give my grandma and grandpa a hand. You got everything you need?"

"You come back and ask me that question when you're eighteen," Waldo replied.

Adam laughed. "Unless you grow tits, you still won't be my type."

"We're good," Bill said. "Nice to see you, Adam."

"Bye guys," the boy said, disappearing into the kitchen.

"You should watch what you say to that kid," Bill scolded. "He's like, fourteen."

"He knows I'm playing with him," Waldo said. "And anyway, don't change the subject. Did you hear what I said about Nick? You're not just his boyfriend, you're his teacher, like I was your teacher when you first landed here. You gotta let him have his freedom, make his mistakes and be there to kiss his owies when he comes back home."

At that moment, terror bubbled up in Bill, and he blurted out, "I'm scared, Waldo."

Waldo looked at him with worried eyes. "What are you scared of, Billy?"

"I... don't know. I love Nick but, sometimes, I'm... I think of losing him and there's this fear that crawls into my gut. I thought—when I met someone, when I fell in love, you know, everything would be all right. But... I worry all the time that this isn't real, that he's gonna leave me. Jesus, Waldo, I feel like I'm going crazy. What's wrong with me?"

Waldo laid a hand over Bill's hand and gripped it. "You're an amazing man, Billy Ryan. You done so much since you got here. Made friends, got an education, built a successful business, found Nick. But there's still that boy inside you your daddy beat up and threw away. You still blame yourself for what happened back there. You're still that boy who believes that loving another boy was wrong and he deserved to be punished for it. Now you love Nick. Your daddy's not here to punish you for it. Don't punish yourself. Don't run Nick away because somewhere in your head there's that little voice telling you it's wrong to love him, that loving him is sick or a sin. That voice that says, queers deserve to be alone and miserable. Don't listen to that voice."

"I'm afraid of losing him, not running him away."

"There's different ways we punish ourselves for being queer," Waldo said. "Most of us, the way we do it, is we never let ourselves fall in love because, we tell ourselves, no guy is ever good enough. There's a better one just around the corner. The other way is to hold on to someone so tight he can't breathe and has to break away. That's what your head is telling you to do with Nick. That voice isn't love, Billy, it's hate—the hate you still have for yourself for being queer. We all got that voice in our heads, hon. Don't listen to it." He gripped Bill's hand. "If you keep Nick on a tight leash, he'll chew it off and run away. Let him have his freedom when he needs it. That's love."

"I'll lose him," Bill groaned.

"If he loves you, and I know he does, he'll come back to you."

"Okay, Waldo, I'll try. I'll really try."

Bill remembered his conversation with Waldo when, a couple of weeks later, he came home and heard Nick on the phone making plans with someone to go to a movie Bill had not wanted to see. He went into the kitchen, poured himself a drink and came out into the living room just as Nick's conversation was ending.

"Okay, great," Nick said. "Pick me up here at seven, okay? Bye Jeff." He hung up, hopped from the couch and hugged Bill. "Hi, how was your day?"

Bill untangled himself. "It was okay. Who were you talking to?"

"Oh, Jeff? I know him from school. We're going to go see *Cat People*." He took the glass of J&B from Bill, sipped it and made a face. "I don't know how you can drink this stuff. It's tastes like turpentine. Not," he added, smiling, "that I've ever drunk turpentine, but if I had, I'm pretty sure it would taste like this."

"Is Jeff gay?" Bill asked, attempting and failing to keep the question light.

"All my school friends are either gay or girls. What are we going to do about dinner? Or should I get a bite with Jeff?"

"Do whatever you want," Bill said and went into the kitchen where he opened the refrigerator and pretended to look through the cartons of takeout.

He heard Nick's footsteps and then felt his hands tentatively touch his shoulders. "Um, is everything all right, Billy?"

Bill shrugged off his lover's hands. "Yeah, I'm looking for something to eat. One of us needs to learn to cook. Takeout for two every night is expensive."

He regretted the words even as if they left his mouth because just that morning Nick had again expressed his discomfort about Bill's habit of paying for everything. "I should get a job," he had said, "and I could help out with the food and bills." Bill has assured him it wasn't necessary. "You concentrate on school," he had told him. "I can support us."

He heard Nick slip out of the room. A moment later, he followed him into the living room, where he again found him on the phone.

"Hey, Jeff? I can't make it after all," he was saying. "No, I forgot, I had plans with Bill. Sorry! This weekend? I'll have to let you know."

He put the receiver down and looked at Bill.

"You didn't have to cancel your plans," Bill said, lamely.

"You didn't want me to go."

"I didn't say that."

"You didn't have to," Nick snapped. "That stuff about money, you want to make me feel bad."

"Nick, no, I—"

"Am I supposed to ask your permission to go out with my friends?" Nick demanded.

Bill hesitated. "No," he said, but it was a beat too late to be convincing.

Nick's expression was angry but also confused as if he wasn't sure he didn't have to ask Bill's permission to go out.

"I'm going downstairs to visit Mrs. D.," he said, adding caustically, "or do I need your permission to do that too?"

"Nick, listen—" Bill took a step toward him, but Nick was on his feet and running down the steps before Bill reached him. He slammed the front door behind him.

Bill picked up his glass, drained his drink, and muttered, "Fuck."

He was in bed when Nick returned from Mrs. Donohue's apartment. He came unsmiling into the bedroom and disappeared into the bathroom where Bill heard him piss and brush his teeth. He returned to the bedroom, undressed and slipped into bed, keeping to his side.

Bill said, "I'm sorry."

"If you didn't want me to go to the movie, why didn't you say so? You didn't have to say that thing about money."

"It's not that I didn't want you to go to the movie," Bill replied, unconvincingly.

Nick turned his head and glared at him. "Yes, it was. Is it because Jeff is gay? Are you jealous? He's just a friend, Bill."

Bill looked away, took a deep breath and said, "All this is new for me too."

"What is?"

"Living with someone," he said. "And you're so much younger."

"I wish you would shut up about that," Nick said, irritably.

"I'm your first, Nick, you've said so yourself. Just your first. Maybe you'll want other guys someday."

Nick closed the distance between them so that

their bodies touched beneath the sheets. "You're wrong. I love you. I don't want anyone but you."

Bill pulled him into his arms. They nestled, not speaking, breathing in each other's breath, the hairs of their bodies grazing each other's flesh, conscious of the beating of each other's heart. Bill's thoughts took a strange but consoling turn. He imagined that primeval humans must have similarly huddled together in their dark, cold caves seeking the same animal warmth and comfort. When he and Nick were together like this, he felt a certitude beyond words, beyond thought, even beyond ordinary emotions, that they were meant for each other, now and forever. He silently resolved to stop being possessive and jealous. He swore to himself he would vanquish his fears and insecurities and be the kind of understanding boyfriend to Nick that Nick needed.

His resolution lasted a month. One night, Nick didn't return home from school until after dark because he had gone out to dinner with friends without telling Bill and Bill picked another fight. His "You should have called me," was countered by "You don't call me when you're working late," which was met with "That's different. I have to make a living." That led to another slammed front door and Bill sitting alone in the dark drinking and wondering if Nick was going to come home.

When he did, he slept in the guest room. The next morning, Bill apologized profusely.

"You have to trust me," Nick said. "I'm not going anywhere."

"I trust you," Bill said. "But sometimes I worry anyway."

Nick got up from the table, came up behind Bill and put his arms around him. "I'll never give you a reason to worry."

"I know, baby," Bill said, closing his eyes against tears he could not account for.

The next time, Nick said, "I'm going out with my friends after school. I'll be home late," Bill forced himself to say, "Okay, have fun."

He wandered through the apartment, tried to distract himself with TV and then a book before breaking down and pouring a half tumbler of scotch. He sat at the kitchen table staring at his plate of Thai takeout, remembering Nick's remark that all his friends were either girls or gay. He imagined Nick naked in another boy's bed, pushed the food away and poured another drink. Nick found him passed out on the couch. When he awakened him, Bill grabbed him and mumbled, "Don't leave me."

Bill hoped his terror would diminish with the passing of time as familiarity created trust, but this did not happen. The fear was like the summer fog that rolled into the city, sometimes in wisps, sometimes in cold, obscuring clouds, but always present. He could not see past his own thoughts which spun and spun in anxious circles whenever Nick was away. Where was he? Who was he with? What was he doing? Had he met someone else? Was he, at this very moment, having sex with this other man? Was it just one man, or were there others? How many...? And on and on. Bill's fears and fantasies were exhausting enough but trying to conceal them from Nick added another layer of anxiety and when he broke down, questioning Nick, accusing him, the arguments were poisonous. Now, Bill left the apartment as often as Nick following one of these fights, and when Bill left, he headed to a bathhouse or a backroom or someone's dungeon where Bad Bill emerged for a few hours of obliterating, dark, drug-charged sex.

I've gone home.

Bill stared at the slip of paper, turned it over looking for a further message but there were only those three words in Nick's distinctive scrawl. *I've gone home.* The bouquet of roses in his hand released its heavy fragrance into the still air. Autumn twilight darkened the room. Nick's half-eaten bowl of cereal and cold mug of coffee were on the counter beside the sink where he had left them after their fight that morning. The answering machine blinked—three messages.

Bill played them. They were the three calls he had made during the day apologizing to Nick for shoving him. Begging forgiveness. Nick must have left right after Bill had gone to the office. He grabbed a glass from the cupboard and went out into the dining room where he poured himself a scotch and swallowed it in a single gulp as if it were medicine. He poured another.

At breakfast, Nick announced he was dropping out of school and getting a job. *That's stupid, why would you do that? Because I'm sick and tired of hearing you bitch about how you pay for everything. I don't do that. Yes, you do, whenever you're pissed off at me. That's not true. Fuck you, Bill, don't you ever listen to yourself?* And it had escalated to that moment when Nick pushed his chair back and got into Bill's face and Bill instinctively shoved him against the sink. Nick's eyes went dark with rage and for a moment Bill thought he was going to take a swing at him. Instead, he ran out of the apartment. Bill's heart was pumping and his hands were shaking. He couldn't believe he had laid hands on Nick. His remorse was immediate and all-consuming. He had sat down at the kitchen table and wept.

He poured a third drink. *I've gone home.* Bill picked up the phone and dialed Mrs. Trejo's number.

"*Hola*," came her familiar voice.

He took a deep breath. "Dolly, it's Bill. Is Nick there?"

There was a heavy pause and she replied, with sadness rather than anger, "Yeah, Bill, he's here, but I don't think he wants to talk to you right now."

"Please," Bill said, his voice nearly breaking. "Please. I need to talk to him. I need to tell him I love him and that I'm sorry."

Another hesitation and then a sigh. "Okay, let me talk to him."

A moment later, Nick said, in his most sullen adolescent tone, "What."

"Nicky, I'm so sorry. I'm so, so sorry. Please come home."

"I am home," Nick said flatly.

"To our home."

"You mean your home," he replied bitterly. "That place and everything in it belongs to you. When I'm there, you treat me like I belong to you too. But I don't. I don't belong to you, Bill. I'm not," and here he spat out the words, "your boy."

"I know that. God, I swear I know that. Look, what can I do to make this right? We could start over. Move out of here and find a place together."

"That you would pay for."

Bill had no answer to that.

After a moment's silence, Nick said, "See what I mean? We're not equals as long as I'm a student and you're paying all the bills. That's why I want to drop out and get a job. I need to pay my own way."

"Do you really want to leave school?"

Michael Nava

"No," Nick admitted, adding in a voice full of confusion, "but I don't know what else to do to make you happy."

"You do make me happy, happier than I've ever been in my life."

"Then how come we fight all the time?"

"Couples fight, Nick, and then they work it out."

"Do they push each other around like you did this morning?" The bitterness was back.

"You were crowding me, I pushed you away without thinking. I'm so sorry. It will never, ever happen again."

"I'm tired of fighting with you," Nick said, and Bill heard the despair. "Maybe we should—"

"Don't leave me." Bill blurted out. "I'd die without you."

The despairing voice replied, "Oh, Bill."

"Come home. I promise it'll be different."

"My mom's putting dinner on the table," he said. "I have to go."

"Nick, please come home."

He sighed. "I'll come home in the morning. Goodnight, Bill."

Two drinks later, Bill changed from his suit into Levi's and a black T-shirt. A drink after that, he had made up his mind. He went out and drove to a private sex south of Market. He entered an unmarked door, checked his clothes, snorted a line of coke in the bathroom that a stranger

246

offered him. Then he wandered into back room, where, in an old claw foot bathtub, he lay naked as men came over and soaked him with streams of beer-scented piss or shoved their cocks into his mouth and poured come down his throat. In his scrambled mind, he thought, if Nick could see him now, he'd know how sorry Bill was for hurting him.

But the next time their fight turned physical, he gave Nick a black eye. Nick hit back and they ended up grappling on the kitchen floor, swinging and grabbing, both of them with tears in their eyes. Nick went limp beneath him. Bill sat back on his haunches. The fight was about their diminishing sex life. Nick had told him he was sick of Bill coming to bed smelling like a bar and blaming his limp dick on too much to drink. That's when Bill hit him. Now, he released Nick, stood up, went to the sink and washed his face, drying it on a kitchen towel. He heard Nick pull himself off the floor and pick up the chair they had kicked over.

"Are you leaving?" Bill asked in a flat voice.

"You want me to leave?"

He turned around. Nick's eye was already bruising. "Your eye."

Nick touched it gingerly and flinched.

"I'm sorry."

"Do you want me to leave?" Nick asked.

"I don't know what I want anymore. I'm so tired."

Nick said, "I'm going to bed." He paused at the doorway, looked at Bill and asked, "What happened to us?"

Bill would think about that question for weeks after the fight but he could never come up with a different answer than the one he gave Nick that night.

"I don't know. Maybe love is not enough."

And Nick said, "You call this love?"

He thought Nick would leave him after that fight and, truthfully, he knew it would be better for both of them if he had, but Nick stayed. He had changed. Seemed older, sadder, defeated. Bill knew he was to blame for the slump in Nick's shoulders, the frown lines that had appeared across his forehead and around his mouth. He hated himself for having put them there, just as he hated himself when Nick dropped out of State and took a job as a clerk at a bookstore. But he felt powerless to help Nick or to change the course of the life together. It felt as if they were imprisoned by Bill's fears and Nick's resignation with no way out.

A piñata swayed from the branches of the walnut tree in the backyard of Mrs. Trejo's modest house; it was in the shape of a donkey, covered with blue and yellow and pink crepe paper. A gaggle of six-year-olds, led by Nick's niece, Lila, whose birthday party this was, tore through the yard laughing and screaming. The air smelled of roses and barbecue. The kitchen table, carried out for the party, was laden with food—pots of beans and rice, platters of enchiladas, stacks of tortillas, bowls of salads and salsa, hamburger buns and condiments. Nick's older brothers, Tom and Sal with beers in hand, barbecued steaks, chicken and hamburgers on a huge, ancient, oil drum grill. Nick's sister, Isabel, sidled up to Bill who was watching Nick spin his niece in circles by her arms while the other kids impatiently awaited their turns.

"I'm glad you boys came," she said. "We haven't seen much of you lately."

"We both been busy," Bill mumbled.

She gave him a disbelieving look. "Everything all right with you guys?"

"Yeah, we're good. How's law school?"

"Tough," she replied, "but I'm tougher. You're not drinking."

Bill glanced self-consciously at the can of Coke in his hand. "I'm driving," he said. "Anyway, I'm trying to cut down."

"Why?"

"Nick thinks I drink too much."

That, of course, was only the tip of the iceberg but he hoped it would be enough to satisfy her. He wasn't about to reveal that he and Nick fought over his drinking, nor that he had gone to AA meetings but stopped because of all the talk of God. Now he tried to keep off the booze on his own but it was hard because, sober, he was filled with anxiety.

"Do you think you drink too much?"

He shrugged. "Cutting down won't hurt me."

"Hey, Billy, come over here," Tom yelled across the yard. "We need another hand at the grill. Sal's too drunk."

Bill excused himself, grateful to get away from Izzy's questions. Tom and Sal, well into their second six-pack, had reached the stage of goofy intoxication where everything seemed funny. They laughed and jostled each other while the steaks and chicken burned. Mrs. Trejo came up at the same time Bill reached the grill. She grabbed the spatula from Tom.

"*Payasos!*" she exclaimed. "You're burning the meat." She gave the spatula to Bill. "You take over. You two," she said to her sons, "get away from here before you set yourselves on fire."

"Aw, Ma," Sal said, "lighten up. We're just having fun."

Bill removed the cooked meat and put it on a brightly decorated platter while Mrs. Trejo lay corn on the grill. Nick had finished swinging the kids, and seeing Bill, smiled at him. It was his old smile, the big grin that reached into his eyes and it broke Bill's heart now because it had been such a long time since he had seen this smile.

He waved at Nick with his free hand. Nick's niece tugged his shirt and led him away to another kid's game.

He's happy here, Bill thought. *Not like when he's with me.*

He remembered their conversation after another fight when Bill had again asked, *Are you leaving me? To which Nick had replied, Where would I go? Home to my mom? When I told her we fight, she said, you made your bed, now lie in it. As far as she's concerned, we're married and married people don't get divorced. They stick it out.*

"As soon as the corn is done, we'll eat," Mrs. Trejo said, taking the platter of meat to the table.

Nudging Bill as he put the last of the burgers on the grill, Tom said, "Guess Ma has a new favorite brother-in-law."

"Hey," Sal said, "you wanna beer, Billy?"

"No, I'm good."

"Beautiful day, huh?" Tom said. "Good to see you and Nicky."

"Yeah," Sal said. "Been awhile."

"We oughta go to a game," Tom said. "Giants playing the Dodgers next weekend. I can get some good seats."

"That would be great," Bill said, "but you know how baseball bores Nick."

"Leave him at home," Sal said.

Bill nodded ambiguously.

"Speaking of the game, man," Tom said. "It's

251

about to start. Come on, Sal, we can get in a few minutes before we have to eat. You hold down the fort here, okay Bill? And if Ma asks don't tell her we're watching TV."

"Will do," Bill said, his eyes seeking Nick who was now engaged in a fierce game of kick the can.

As soon as Nick was in the car, Bill clicked the lock on his door.

"I can lock my own door," Nick said, petulantly.

"You never remember to."

He started the car and they drove off from Mrs. Trejo's house, waving goodbye to the assorted relatives in the front yard who had gathered to see them off.

"It was good to see Mom and everyone else," Nick said. "I could see them more often if you'd let me use your car."

"You're not insured on my policy."

"You could add me."

Bill turned on to the on-ramp to the 880. "I'll look into it."

"You've said that before," Nick muttered and subsided to a sulk that lasted until they pulled into a parking space in front of their house. Nick slammed the door when he got out and began walking down Diamond Street.

"Nick," Bill shouted. "Where are you going?"

"I'm going for a walk," he snapped without looking back.

Mrs. Donohue, who had been sweeping the

porch, saw it all. Bill came up the steps with a smile and a shrug.

"You boys have a fight?" she asked.

"No, Nick's just in a mood."

"He's been in a lot of those," she observed quietly.

"Yeah, I hadn't noticed," Bill said, anxious to end the conversation.

Mrs. Donohue made a skeptical noise at the back of her throat.

"You can't keep him locked up. He'll fly away."

Bill flushed. "No one's **going** anywhere, Mrs. D. We're fine."

He hurried into his apartment before she could respond. He dug out the bottle of Jameson he kept hidden beneath the sink and poured half a tumbler. No telling when Nick would come home. No telling how whether the night would end in fucking or in a fight. He might as well get drunk while he waited.

12.

I DROPPED IN TO THE DINER as usual for the next couple of weeks. Adam and I had our usual conversations but he didn't bring up getting together again. As I was unfamiliar with the etiquette of hooking up with a straight guy, I was reluctant to suggest it myself. Then, one morning, after he delivered my Denver omelet with extra toast, he asked in an overly casual voice, "You busy tonight?"

I had an AA meeting at seven but what I told him was, "I'll be free after eight. My place? Eight-thirty?"

He grinned. "Yeah." He tore off a sheet from his order pad and said, "Write down your address."

I carefully wrote out my address. "Don't expect much from my apartment."

"Does it have a bedroom?"

"It has a bed."

"Good enough." He tucked the paper into his pants pocket. "See you tonight, stud."

As the winter darkness fell, I sat at my desk

rereading the same paragraph in a search and seizure opinion over and over. I blamed my inability to concentrate on everything but the elation that flushed my chest when I thought of seeing Adam. I was reluctant to look too closely at what lay beneath my excitement because I knew it was more than the prospect of getting laid. Until I'd met Hugh Paris, sex had been little more than an appetite I fed when it began to distract me from what I believed was the only part of my life that mattered—getting justice for my clients. Then Hugh had come along, the beautiful, damaged man I had fallen in love with. Together he and I discovered that the heat of passion could cauterize the old wounds inflicted on men like us from the time we became aware of being different. He told me that the first time we made love, he had looked into my eyes and felt forgiven. I knew what he meant because I felt forgiven, too—forgiven for loving him, for the times I had hated myself, and for ever having believed I was defective. In that naked tangle of breath and bodies, a healing flowed.

Adam, I reminded myself, wasn't Hugh. He wasn't gay. All he wanted and all he was offering was companionable sex. If, when we were together, I felt a flush of what I'd felt with Hugh that was—what? My imagination? My problem? I shoved the thought aside. The sex had been good, and I liked Adam. That had to be enough.

At six-thirty, I closed my books and headed to

Blessed Savior for the seven o'clock AA meeting. Like most meetings it had been nicknamed by its attendees and it was called, waggishly, It's Come to This. Outside the parish hall, huddled like a band of aging juvenile delinquents, were the smokers still grumbling about the group's decision to make It's Come to This a non-smoking meeting. Scarves and leather jackets warded off the winter chill and out of the knot of men I heard someone call my name.

"Hello, Simon," I said, approaching a small, thin, snowy-haired man in a shearling coat and paisley silk scarf smoking a black, gold-tipped Sobranie. He favored me with his elfin grin and pale eyes. He was a retired psychiatrist, almost seventy, who had stopped drinking on his sixtieth birthday because, he said, "I'd been everything but ordinary and I wanted to know what that felt like before they dump me into the grave."

"Young Henry," he said. "You have a spring in your step. Could it be love?"

Simon, I now recalled, combined perspicuity with a sharp tongue.

"No, I'm just happy to see you."

He narrowed his eyes. "You're deflecting," he remarked. "I gather your sponsor doesn't enforce the policy of no relationships in the first year of sobriety." When I didn't immediately respond, he said, "Oh. I see. You haven't told him."

"I'm not in love with anyone," I said. "So, there's nothing to tell."

"A very lawyerly answer," he replied. "Well, if you want to keep things from your sponsor that's between you and him." He tapped ash from his cigarette. "Are you working on any interesting cases?"

"I'm doing an insurance investigation," I said, relieved to be let off the hook. "A death claim. Local guy named Bill Ryan."

He was suddenly very attentive. "Bill Ryan? I knew him."

"You did? From where?"

He waved his Sobranie in the direction of the parish hall. "From here. From meetings."

"Bill Ryan was a member of AA?" I asked, surprised.

Simon raised a doubtful eyebrow. "A member? No. An auditor. Wandered in now and then and you could practically see the little black cloud above his head. But whenever the talk turned to God, he'd bolt. I stopped him once and told him I was an atheist but AA worked for me and it could work for him. We had coffee a couple of times after that but in the end..." Simon shrugged. "Well, as the cliché goes, it's not a program for people who need it, it's a program for people who want it."

"What was he like?"

Simon dropped his cigarette to the ground and crushed it with the tip of his handmade Italian loafer. "The clinical term is decompensating."

"I beg your pardon?"

"Falling apart. His personality, I mean. That was my professional assessment."

"The booze?"

"That was a symptom, not the cause. Frankly, I never got enough of his story out of him to understand what the pressures were but, whatever they were, they were pulling him apart with centrifugal force." A bell tinkled from within the parish hall. "The meeting's starting. Shall we go in?"

"Did Bill ever talk to you about his boyfriend?"

"If he did, I've forgotten." He smiled his fey smile. "Boyfriend woes are the stock in trade around here and after a while they all sound alike. I wonder," he added, "if yours will be any different."

I found Adam looking confused on the sidewalk in front of the grand three-story Victorian where I lived. It was not an uncommon response. The address of the house was 143; my address was 143 ¼.

"You live here?" he asked when he saw me.

"In the basement," I explained.

I led him through the yard, around the side of the house, and down a flight of steps to a battered door and into my basement studio which even in the brightest light of day was funereally dark. What could I say? My landlords, the prosperous lesbian couple who lived in the mansion, only charged me a hundred and fifty in rent and had furnished the place with their castoffs. It was what I could afford.

I switched on a lamp. Adam took in the main room with its mismatched furnishings and the one sooty window through which I could see a flowerbed filled with weeds. His eye fell on my framed law degree, propped against the wall on the top of the dresser.

"You went to Linden?" he said, referring to the great university thirty miles south of San Francisco; its law school ranked, with Yale and Harvard, as one of the three best in the country.

"Yes."

"What are you doing living here?" he asked with genuine curiosity.

"Starting over."

I gave him an abbreviated version of my drinking and rehabilitation, watching his expression for judgment, but all I saw was sympathetic interest.

"So, you like, don't drink at all?"

"No."

"I don't drink much myself. It's bad for training plus I get that alcohol flush reaction where my face turns red and my heart speeds up. So," he continued, with a grin, "I don't see a bed."

"The couch pulls out," I said.

"What are we waiting for?"

"You want something to drink? A Coke or—"

He crushed me against his big chest and kissed me.

"No," he said, biting my earlobe. "I don't want anything to drink."

As I made up the bed, Adam picked through the orange crate that held my LPs. He pulled out an Ella Fitzgerald album—the Johnny Mercer songbook—and inspected it with a skeptically cocked eyebrow.

"What is this shit?"

"It's a great American singer singing the work of a great American songwriter."

"If you say so."

"Give me that."

I slipped the LP out of its jacket, put it on the turntable and skipped to the second cut, my favorite.

"Sit, listen, learn."

He flopped into the bed where I joined him as Ella began *Early Autumn*. When she sang the lyric—*There's a dance pavilion in the rain, All shuttered down*—I was seized by an unexpected grief, thinking of all the dancing boys now dying in little rooms like this all across the city. I got up and moved the needle to the next track.

"You don't like that song?" Adam asked.

"Not my favorite." I climbed back on the bed and composed myself. Adam leaned against me and muttered something about "old geezer music," but as Ella sang on, his silence became intent, his breathing deeper, and when I glanced over his eyes were closed. By the time she sang *Skylark*, he was squeezing my hand. For a moment, when the album ended, neither of us said anything but strained to hear the fading notes of *When A Woman Loves A Man*.

"Wow," he said. "Play that again."

I started the record over and when I turned back to him, he'd kicked off his shoes, pulled off his T-shirt and was unbuttoning his pants.

"This is great make-out music," he said. "Let's not waste it."

I stripped to my briefs and joined him.

You see things in another guy's eyes when you're having sex with him that he ordinarily veils, a submissiveness men are not supposed to expose to anyone, much less another man. Not the forced submission of the weak to the strong, but a relaxation into the care of another, a letting go. The little boy curling into his daddy's arms, blissfully unaware that soon the arms of other men would be forbidden. I thought I saw that in Adam's eyes when I entered him, slowly. His lips parted and his eyelids fluttered and then he looked steadily at me as I began to fuck him; his eyes filled not simply with pleasure but trust. He drew his fingertips across my lips. I kissed them. *It's just sex*, I thought, *just sex*.

When I called Larry the next morning, I could still smell Adam on my sheets, on my skin. Larry and I talked about Thanksgiving, which I was spending at his house in L.A., about work and my fourth step inventory and we again sparred over whether the belief in the existence of God was necessary for recovery. I said nothing about Adam.

Between visits to him in Los Angeles, I'd forget Larry was rich, but then I'd make my way up narrow roads into the hills and canyons above Franklin Boulevard where he lived in a neighborhood of grand old mansions that had been the original movie star colony in the 1920s and '30s. Larry's house was modest by the standards of the surrounding French chateaux, Mexican haciendas and Tudor manors but the views from his deck were equally stunning.. He overlooked a steep, wooded canyon that was home to deer and coyotes, a stucco and copper Lloyd Wright fabrication— "the son, not the father," Larry had informed me—built for a silent movie star, and, at the horizon, the tinselly towers of downtown L.A

The day after Thanksgiving, Larry and I were at a table on the deck going over my fourth step: *Made a searching and fearless inventory of ourselves*. Winter had evidently forgotten about L.A. because it was a warm and clear day, so unlike the gray, rainy city I had left two days earlier. I sipped coffee while Larry pored over my inventory as if it were one of his movie star client's contracts.

Larry's voice broke into my reverie. "Where's your father on this list?"

"What?"

"Your dad. Where's his name?"

Larry leaned forward across the wrought-iron table, one long finger tapping the yellow legal pad where I had written my inventory. Out of his bespoke suits, he preferred Bermuda shorts and Brooks Brothers polo shirts which exposed his long, pale and rather hairless limbs and conferred on him a stork-like appearance.

"My father? I thought I was writing about people I've wronged."

"No. The inventory is about the people, places and things you resent or fear. Your baggage. We'll get to the people you wronged in step nine. Anyway, what makes you think you didn't wrong your father?"

I glared at him. "Are you kidding, Larry? You know my story. The guy tormented me for being gay even before I knew it myself. When I was twelve, he sent me to the hospital with a dislocated shoulder."

"Yes," Larry said gently. "I know your story and as long as that's the story you keep telling yourself, you'll never get past hating him." He looked at me thoughtfully. "He wasn't the father you wanted, Henry, but have you considered that you weren't the son he wanted, either?"

"That was obvious," I snapped. "But how is that my fault?"

"We're not talking about fault here, we're talking about perspective. It's easier to stay a child and nurse your wrongs than to grow up and let go of them because you can't let go of them until you're able to see the other side. His side, Henry. You were his only son. Can you try to understand his disappointment from his perspective? You're a criminal defense lawyer. You defend people who've done much worse to their victims than your father did to you. How do you do that?"

"What they did, they did to someone else, not me."

"Oh, come off it. You couldn't represent your clients if you didn't feel at least a little empathy for them. If you can put yourself in the shoes of a murderer, you can put yourself in your father's."

I refused to grant the point, valid though it was.

"What does any of this have to do with drinking? You're the one who told me I can't my blame my drinking on other people."

He smiled. "That's true, Henry. You're not a drunk because your dad beat you up or because your boyfriend was murdered or your career tanked. You're a drunk because you drink. So, step one, stop drinking. You stopped. Kudos. Now we're working on how to keep you from picking up the bottle again. That means eliminating every reason that a drink might seem like a good idea to you. Anger and resentment are the big ones. All of us drunks like to drink at the people we hate."

"But my father," I said softly.

"I know. He hurt you very deeply. I won't force you to add his name but think about what I said."

"Okay, I'll think about it." I took the pad from him. "I've always assumed it was because of his Mexican machismo that my dad treated me the way he did, and that all Mexican men are like him, so I go on red alert when I have to deal with one of them. Even when they're my clients, I keep a distance. More than the usual professional distance, I mean." I sighed. "I'm afraid of them, the same way I was afraid of him. Now I have to wonder if that fear affected the way I represented them."

"I think the more interesting question is why you chose work that you must have known would force you to defend guys who reminded you of your dad."

"I don't know the answer to that."

"I do," he said. "It was your way of facing that fear, of trying to overcome it. The other side of fear is courage. You're a brave man."

"I don't know about that."

"I do. Alcoholism is a disease of self-perception. We see other people clearly, but we have a blind spot when it comes to ourselves." He tapped the pad. "This list is about all the things that conceal the truth from you about who you really are. The purpose is to clear them away so you can really see yourself, maybe for the first time in your life. Your strengths as well as your limitations.

Right now, all you see are your limitations, your fears, your worries, the mistakes you've made in life. You have to figure out and embrace your strengths. The courage, the honesty, the integrity that I see in you."

"Patting myself on my back for being a good guy seems kind of self-centered."

"I'm not flattering you. I'm giving you practical advice."

"Which is?"

"You can't continue to live in regret and shame and expect to stay sober."

"I don't really understand this, Larry."

"You don't have to." He tapped the pad. "Just do the work."

I nodded. "Okay. I can do that. You know, I met this kid the other day, a Chicano like me, from a working-class family. They didn't seem to have any problem with his being gay. I was envious."

"If we could choose our families, I wouldn't have picked a bunch of tight-assed Scotch Presbyterians who taught me to stuff my feelings so deep I couldn't find them until I was in my fifties." He turned his coffee mug in his hands. "Fortunately, we get to choose our friends and they become our real family. This Chicano boy have anything to do with the case you're investigating for Myles's company?"

"The boyfriend of the decedent." I filled him

in on my investigation and on my suspicion that Nick Trejo was sitting on secrets.

"Do you really think the kid killed his lover with a gas leak?"

"Does sound improbable when you say it aloud. But if Ryan was abusing Nick, it could be like the burning bed case they made a TV movie about."

"The one with Farrah Fawcett? I missed it. What was it about?"

"An abused woman who finally had enough and killed her husband by setting him on fire after he got drunk and raped her and passed out on their bed."

"She wasn't in the bed with him when she set him on fire. Your kid was. The gas leak could have killed him too."

"Yes, well, there's that. On the other hand, his family was awfully eager to shut down my investigation. They're protecting him from something."

"More likely they object to a nosy insurance investigator poking around in something they would like to put behind them. I mean, what do you really have? An old lady telling you Ryan gave Nick a black eye and Nick denying it."

"I know. It's thin."

"It's transparent."

"But something's not right," I said. "I feel it."

"Okay, well, you've good instincts, kiddo, so if you think there's something there, you should follow up on it." He uncurled his long body from his chair. "I have to go into the office. I'll be back by five and we'll hit a meeting and go out to sushi. I've had enough turkey to last me to next Thanksgiving."

"Sounds good."

"What are you going to do?"

"Go for a run and work on this," I said, lifting a corner of the pad.

"If you run through Griffith Park, watch out for coyotes and rattlesnakes and the undercover vice cops cruising the bushes. I don't want to go looking for you in the morgue or bailing you out of jail."

"I'll stick to the path."

He clamped my shoulder. "Always a good idea, Henry." He stopped at the door, turned and asked, "By the way, what happened between you and the guy you liked? Alan? The one who used the f-word."

"Adam," I said. I shrugged. "We talked and cleared it up."

"All good then?"

"Yep," I said. "All good."

I returned from my run unscathed, took a shower, threw on some clothes, made a turkey sandwich, poured a Coke, and carried them into the living room where I settled into an armchair that faced the deck and the view beyond. Larry's house was on a single level down from the street and hidden behind a boxwood hedge. The interior decorator who furnished the place had evidently taken Larry's measure and concluded "butch," because the furniture was clean, dark and simple. There was that side of Larry, of course, but that was mostly the mask he wore to meet the world. Off-duty he was kind and dryly funny and kind of campy. Lonely, too, I'd often thought, having picked up a scent from him I knew so well in myself. As far as I knew, he had never had a boyfriend. Lots of friends. They'd crowded his house on Thanksgiving, guys in cashmere sweaters and guys in leather vests, lipstick lesbians and tatted up, pierced riot girls. He seemed to love them, one and all, and they reciprocated, but there was no one special. When I'd asked him about that once, he'd said, too old and too busy and too set in my ways. I didn't push. As kind as he was, there was a line you didn't cross with Larry about his private life, a WASP opacity that deflected unwelcome questions with a look that could freeze water.

Adam's phone number was burning a hole in my wallet, so I took it out, looked at it again and again debated whether to give him a call. I'd called the day before, reached his machine, wished him a happy Thanksgiving, and left him Larry's number. For the rest of the afternoon, whenever the phone rang, I must have perked up like Pavlov's dog because Larry eventually asked me if I was expecting a call. I lied and he gave me the look I got when he knew I was lying. Ordinarily, he would have pressed me until I broke down, but he was distracted by his other guests and the next time the phone rang, I feigned indifference. Still, I was disappointed Adam hadn't called and then annoyed with myself for being disappointed.

I stared at his number, my chest thick with emotions that seemed disproportionate to whatever this thing was that Adam and I were doing. When had I turned into a teenage girl sitting by her phone waiting for an invitation to the prom? Because this welter of feeling churning in my chest definitely seemed like a regression into my adolescence, to the overpowering loneliness I'd felt when I believed I must be the only queer boy in the world. In this scenario, Adam stood in for all the straight boys on whom I nursed fierce but covert crushes. Only, unlike those boys, he had reciprocated. But reciprocated what? That was the nagging question. What did any of this mean to him? I could hear Larry's voice—"Wrong question. The question is what does it mean to you?" More than just sex and that was the problem. When I had looked into Adam's eyes as I fucked him and saw the trust, the tenderness, the mirroring back of my own face, I started to fall in love with him. But afterwards, when he'd slapped me on the butt gleefully, as if I'd scored the winning run in a baseball game, I realized Adam was not falling in love with me. This was sport to him, no-strings-attached fun. I'd felt as lonely as I had with those high school crushes, as filled with the words I was afraid to speak. I knew I had to speak them to someone if not Adam himself. Larry, for instance, but Larry would have advised me to end it with Adam and that was advice I wasn't ready to hear. I slipped his phone number back into my wallet and went off to distract myself with work.

I retrieved the Ryan file from my carry-on and spread it out on the kitchen table. It took a couple of minutes of reading the same paragraph over and over before I could set aside thoughts of Adam and focus. When I did, intriguing questions began to form themselves: Was Bill Ryan's death something other than an accident? Did Nick kill him? If so, why would he choose such a bizarre and dangerous method? What was his motive?

I started with the last question first. I reviewed my interview notes. Peg Donohue was the only person who alleged that Bill had hit Nick, but Michael Lauro and Randy Gifford corroborated her observation that Ryan's personality went south after his friend Waldo's death from AIDS, and he became withdrawn, angry and terrified. I had no trouble empathizing with him on that score. I could understand why his best friend's horrifying death could have sent Ryan into a downward spiral. Had he taken Nick with him? Nick was young and impressionable. Ryan was his first lover, a driven and dominant man. I could imagine that what had begun as a relationship might have turned into a hostage situation. Maybe Nick had seen no other way out. Still, the young man I'd met hardly seemed self-assured enough to have planned a killing, much less be psychologically capable of killing his lover as he slept beside him.

Which brought me back to the question of method. Homicide by gas leak? Nick would not only have risked killing himself but blowing up the building, killing Peg Donahue, and torching the neighboring houses. I found PG&E's incident report and reread it, looking for anything out of the ordinary. I found it at the bottom of the page where, beneath an illegibly scrawled signature, was the typed name of the inspector: Sal Trejo. Nick's brother.

"Do you buy the official line?" I asked.

Pat Durand pushed the utility company report across his desk with a shrug.

"Well," he allowed, "it could have happened that way. The gas line could have corroded and leaked or been knocked loose if the stove had been moved. But the occupants would have noticed the smell."

Durand was an accident reconstruction expert recommended by a fellow lawyer who specialized in personal injuries cases. I was in his office in San Mateo, a big, bright room filled with charts, graphs, photographs and models, all of them illustrating the many ways in which humans meet with accidental misfortune. Duran was comfortably padded—the extra weight gave him gravity—and spoke with an easy authority that doubtless went over well with jurors.

"Isn't gas odorless?"

"In the olden days," he said. "Now gas companies treat it with a sulfur compound called mercaptan that smells like rotten eggs to alert people to a leak."

"So, these men would have known there was a leak before it became fatal."

"You're more likely to die from a fall from your bed than a gas leak. It's just not that common anymore."

"The report says the leak was going on for some time. Could that mean weeks? Days?"

He shook his head. "Not if it was strong enough to kill someone like it did in your case. A minor leak where there's good ventilation might not have any effect on you at all. More serious leaks and you'd have headaches or feel nauseous or dizzy. Might affect your breathing. To kill you? We're talking about a flood of natural gas sucking up oxygen and causing carbon monoxide poisoning."

"So, the leak had to have happened that night?"

"Or gotten much worse for some reason."

"Let me ask you this. If someone wanted to

kill himself with gas, what would be the most efficient way?"

He thought about it. "Close all the windows, blow out the pilot lights on your stove and oven and turn up the burners. That would do it."

"But not a minor leak from a corroded gas line?"

"No, like I said, if it happened the way the report says, there would have been a flood of gas."

Salvador Trejo glared at me from across the table in the conference room at the gas company office. He wore a gray shirt with his name stitched in red over the right pocket. The second Trejo brother was stocky but solid, round-faced and handsome. Frank Fernandez, a company lawyer, sat at the head of the table between us.

"I have a few questions about your report," I said, after introductions had been made.

"Why are you still asking?" Salvador asked, sullenly. "Nick don't want the money."

"Bill Ryan's estate does. That means I still have to complete my investigation before the claim can be paid. I understand from the company you're assigned to the Oakland office, not San Francisco. How did you come to be the investigator on this case?"

"It was my brother, man. I wanted to know what happened. I asked the company to let me take the case."

I glanced at Fernandez. "Wouldn't there have

been a conflict of interest if a family member was involved?"

"A gas leak is a gas leak, Henry," Fernandez replied. "What happened is a mechanical issue and the analysis would be the same whoever was involved."

"You wouldn't be concerned that if Nick had decided to sue the company Sal might have to be a witness?"

"Nick's not gonna sue anyone," Sal interjected. "All you lawyers think about is money."

Fernandez shrugged. "I guess that's a possibility but like Sal said, he wanted to see what had happened to his brother. I suppose his supervisor decided that outweighed any potential conflict."

"Did you know that Nick called Sal and it was Sal who called nine one one?" I asked Fernandez. "Isn't that right, Sal?"

"So what?" Sal said curtly.

Fernandez shifted uncomfortably in his chair. "I was not aware of that."

"Nick told me he roused himself, smelled gas and called you, Sal. You told him to get out of the apartment. Nick said he told you he hadn't been able to wake Bill Ryan but you again told Nick to get out of the apartment and that you would call nine one one. Is that right?"

"Yeah, he called me."

"And did you tell him to get out the apartment and leave Bill Ryan there?"

His face tightened. "I was worried about my brother."

I looked at Fernandez. "Can you see the problem now, Frank? If Bill was still alive when Sal told Nick to get out of the apartment..."

"He was already dead," Sal said angrily. "Nick got out just in time."

"You know that because you turned up, right? Peg Donohue said she saw you in the ambulance with Nick."

"Yeah, I was there," he said, more subdued.

"You live in Oakland. How did you get into the city so quickly?"

"I was at my girlfriend's place. She lives in the Mission."

"How did Nick know to call you there?"

"He called my pager. I—"

Fernandez, alarmed now, said, "Okay, Henry, I don't think I want Sal to answer any more questions about what happened that night or his part in it. Let's focus on his investigation. That's what you said you were interested in."

"Sure. Your report says the leak was caused by a corroded gas line into the stove. Did you take pictures of it?"

He shook his head. "I didn't have to. I tested it and saw the leak."

"You also said in your report the leak had been there for some time. How long?"

"I can't say."

"Days?"

"Yeah."

"Weeks?"

"Maybe."

"Months?"

"It was an old line. I don't think it was ever replaced after the stove was hooked up way back when."

"So," I said, "you're certain that the leak didn't start within twenty-four hours of Bill Ryan's death?"

Fernandez intervened. "Is there a reason you're asking this question?"

"I've talked to an accident reconstruction expert who told me the quantity of gas that would have caused Ryan's death couldn't have been produced by a slow leak. A leak would have been detected by its smell or having caused some non-lethal symptoms of gas poisoning long before that night. He says there had to have been a sudden flood of gas that caused Ryan to suffocate."

Fernandez mulled it over, smiled tightly, and said, "I'm going to cut this short. I think the company's going to want to conduct its own investigation before Sal answers any more questions."

I glanced at Sal. "Sure, as long as you know that I know it didn't happen the way you said it did."

He started to speak, thought better of it, and folded his arms defensively across his chest.

When I returned to my office, there were two message slips from Ruth Fleming. I settled in at my desk and called her. I had no sooner identified myself when she said irritably, "I got a voice mail from a lawyer who wants to know why you're harassing her family after she told you her brother doesn't want the death benefit. Who is she and what's going on here?"

"Isabel Trejo is Nick's sister. She called me after I interviewed Nick and said Nick didn't want the money so I could close my investigation."

"If that's true, then why haven't you?"

"Ryan's estate is going to claim the benefit."

There was a pause. "Who's representing the estate?"

"A lawyer named Randy Gifford."

"Yeah, he called too. Didn't say why. I still don't understand why you haven't closed the case. Do you have any evidence that Ryan's death wasn't an accident?"

"Nothing that would hold up in court."

"What does that mean?" she demanded.

I filled her in on everything I had learned.

"Are you saying that Nick Trejo killed his boyfriend?"

"I'm saying the circumstances of Bill Ryan's death are more complicated than they first appeared."

"Too complicated for us," she said. "If you really think there was a crime, we need to disclose to the police and let them take over. I don't want you opening us up to a lawsuit from Trejo and his family for defamation or whatever other cause of action some lawyer can come up with. Let the police do the heavy lifting and we can hold back payment of the benefit until they figure out what happened. I want your report ASAP. And stay away from the Trejo family. You understand?"

"Perfectly," I replied.

I was thinking this over when the phone rang. The receptionist had gone for the day, so I picked it up and said, "Law offices."

There was a tentative, "Hi, I'm calling for Henry Rios."

"Adam? This is Henry."

"Hey Henry. I didn't recognize your voice at first. Working late?"

"Something like that. How are you?"

"I'm okay. How was L.A.?"

"It was a lot of fun, actually. Beautiful weather, great people."

"When are you moving?"

I laughed. "I'm not, though there are worse places to live. How was your Thanksgiving?"

"Family and then more family. And then too much food. And then more family." After a moment, he said, "Too bad you weren't here. I could have used a break from all those Chinese people."

"I'm here now."

Another pause. "You want to come over later?"

I looked out the window at the darkening sky, my stomach a knot of feelings, trying to find the will to say no.

"What time?"

"I just got home from work," he said. "I need to clean up and eat something—hey, if you want to come over now, I'll make you dinner."

"That sounds... nice."

"Are you okay? You sound a little funny."

"I'm good. Let me just finish up here and I'll be over. Half hour?"

"Cool. See you then."

Adam's tiny kitchen could scarcely fit the two of us, him cooking and me standing over his shoulder, watching. The walls had once been blue but were smeared with grease stains and the cabinets and shelves were encrusted with generations of paint. The room smelled of olive oil and garlic with an undertone of Raid. Adam removed a Tupperware container from his vintage '50s refrigerator, uncovered it, and forked a couple of chicken breasts into the pan of sizzling oil. He seared them, removed them to a plate, added a nob of butter to the pan, turned down the burner and tossed in a big fistful of shitake mushrooms.

"Don't you get enough of cooking at the diner?" I asked him.

"I like to cook and here I can make what I want, not that slop we feed to the customers."

"What do you do, spit in the soup?"

"Only yours. And it's not spit."

"That's gross."

"I didn't hear you complaining the last time you gave me a blowjob," he replied with a smile in his voice. "Too busy swallowing."

I swatted his butt. "Fuck you."

"Later. Right now, I'm cooking and you're in the way. Go put on some music."

"Any special requests?"

He filled a pot with water, dumped salt into it, and slid it onto a burner. "Surprise me."

I watched him move between sink and stove, open a packet of spaghetti, and throw me a smiling glance over his shoulder. The simple domesticity of the moment twisted my heart. I embraced him from behind, wrapped my arms around his big chest and held him tight. He turned his head to the side for a sloppy kiss. When I pulled away, he was smiling but his eyes were thoughtful.

"You sure you're okay?" he asked.

"Yeah, why do you ask?"

"Just getting a vibe."

"I'm fine."

"Okay. Put on some tunes. I'll call you when dinner's ready."

In the living room, I went through his albums and picked the Eurhythmics, a group he had introduced me to. I slipped the record onto the turntable and Annie Lennox's voice filled the room: Her*e comes the rain again.* I couldn't sit still. I studied the Angel Island photos on the wall, ran my hand across the spines of the books on his bookshelf, picked up the framed picture of Adam and his college girlfriend. Candace, not Candy. I hadn't really looked at her closely but now I did, as if she hid some secret about Adam. She had a determined intelligence about her and the kind of strong-featured face that time would settle into a mature beauty. I imagined a brisk personality—definitely not a Candy—but her eyes were sympathetic. Perfect combination for a physician. Adam had chosen a strong woman, someone for the long haul.

"Hey, dinner's ready," he said, behind me, and then he was beside me. He took the picture from me. "I talked to her on Thanksgiving." He set the picture on the bookshelf. "Come and eat."

We squeezed into the little kitchen table. He'd made a dish of chicken and mushrooms over pasta; my stomach growled at the scent of garlic and lemon and olive oil but although I was hungry, I had no appetite.

"You talked to Candace on Thanksgiving?" I asked, as he served me.

"Yeah. She's coming home for Christmas." He dug into his food, glanced at me. "Eat."

I took a bite, tasting nothing. "I guess you'll see her."

Still eating, he said, casually, "We talked about getting back together."

I feigned equal casualness, asking, "What about the long-distance issue?"

"I'm going to look at some biz schools on the east coast, see if I can get in, and she's ready to come back to California after med school, so..." He looked at me. "You're not eating. You all right?"

"I'm fine," I said, digging into the food. "This is really good. You should put it on the menu at the diner."

I was crawling inside my skin. I got through dinner and the dishwashing, but I knew I couldn't stay. The obliviousness with which he'd talk about his girlfriend forced me to see what I hadn't wanted to see—that whatever my feelings were for Adam, he did not return them. Of course, he didn't. He wasn't gay. He had told me that at the beginning and if I was blinded, it was only by the intensity of my feelings, not by anything he had said or done. I felt like a fool.

As I dried the last of the dishes, he came up from behind and wrapped his arms around me.

"It's good to see you," he said.

"Good to see you too, Adam."

"Can you spend the night?"

"I'd really like to but I have a court appearance at eight thirty and I have to meet my client at seven to prepare."

He dropped his arms. "Okay, but you can stay for a little while, can't you?"

I put the dish in the dish rack, folded the

towel and laid in on the counter. "Not tonight, Adam. I really need to put in a couple more hours at the office."

He stepped away from me. "Oh, okay," he said, but I could tell he wasn't buying it. "You sure everything's all right?"

"Yeah. Everything's fine."

13.

H IS PAGER WENT OFF. WALDO, again. Three calls in twenty minutes so it had to be more than that he was bored at work and wanted to gossip. The house was vacant and there was no way he could return the call until after the walk-through. As for the house itself, an 80-year-old, three-story Victorian, though it needed a lot of work, it had good bones and matchless views of downtown and the bay from the top floor.

"What do you think?" the real estate agent asked as they stood on the sidewalk.

"I'm definitely interested," Bill replied. "You say it's a probate sale?"

"Yeah, two gay guys bought it and meant to fix it up but one of them got sick and died suddenly and the job's too big for his partner. Just between you and me, he's looking to unload it cheap."

"Good to know. I'll be in touch."

When he got back to his office, Doris handed him a sheaf of message slips and said irritably,

"Waldo's been calling all morning. He wouldn't tell me why, just said he had to talk to you."

"I know, I've had three pages."

Once settled behind his desk, he picked up the phone and called Waldo's work number. Kelly, his assistant answered.

"Hey, it's Bill. Let me talk to Waldo."

"Waldo's not here, Bill," she said, her voice worried. "He's at the hospital with Eddie."

"What happened?" Bill asked, all attention now.

"All I know is that's Eddie's sick."

"Do you know which hospital?"

"The emergency room at General."

As she spoke, Bill scanned the messages from Waldo and noted the unfamiliar number from which he had called. He said goodbye to Kelly and rang the number.

"Bill?" Waldo said in a frantic voice. Bill heard crowd noises behind him.

"Hey, I was looking at a house. What's going on?"

"Eddie's real sick."

"You're at General?"

"Yeah, in the ER." His voice was one breath short of hysteria.

"Hold tight, Waldo. I'm on my way."

He found Waldo at the nurse's station screaming at a blank-faced nurse. "You bitch, I am his family!"

Bill came up, touched his arm and said, "Waldo."

He spun around to Bill, his pale face streaked with tears. "This bitch won't let me in to see Eddie because she's says it's family only." He turned back to her and said, "Let me see my lover before I tear your fucking throat out."

She glanced at Bill and said, nervously, "It's hospital rules. Family only."

Bill led Waldo through the crowded waiting room to an empty seat. "Wait here, Waldo, while I talk to her."

"I am his family," Waldo said brokenly. "Billy, tell her."

He returned to the nurse who looked warily at him. "I'm sorry about my friend. He's really upset, that's all. Can you tell me what's happening with Eddie Goodman?"

"Are you related to Mr. Goodman?"

"I'm his friend and I just want to know how he's doing."

"I'm sorry, I can't give out that information unless you're related."

"All we want to know is what's wrong with him."

"I can't help you. I'm sorry."

A harried, white-coated man emerged from the suite of rooms behind her, glanced at Bill and smiled.

"Bill?" he said approaching him. "What are you doing here?"

A year earlier he had sold John Owen and his lover a beautifully restored Queen Anne cottage on Eureka Street.

"Hey, Doc. My friend Eddie Goodman is back there and I was trying to get some information from this lady, but she says she can't tell me anything because I'm not family."

"It's hospital rules, Doctor."

Owen said, "Sometimes we bend the rules, Nurse." He said to Bill, "Goodman? Is that the name?"

"Yes," Bill said. "See the redhead over there? Waldo is Eddie's lover. He called me and said Eddie was really sick but that's all I know."

"Wait here," the doctor said.

A few minutes later, Owen returned. "Eddie Goodman, yeah, we're going to admit him, Bill. Not sure what's going on with him but it could be meningitis."

"Can Waldo see him?"

"He's about to be moved up to a ward. You can see him after that. Don't worry," he said, glancing at the nurse. "You won't have any more problems. I'll personally take you to him."

"So," Bill asked, after he had explained Eddie's status to Waldo, "what happened?"

The cardboard cup shook in Waldo's hand, spilling coffee on his lap. He didn't notice. "Eddie's had a bad headache for a couple of days. Bad enough so he called in sick. He never does that.

I told him, go see the doctor, but he says, no it's just a headache and all he needs is aspirin. Then yesterday, he gets a fever and starts throwing up. I thought it was flu but he wakes me up in the middle of the night talking crazy. He didn't know where he was or who I was. That's when I called the ambulance and we came here." He managed to take a sip of coffee. "Meningitis? I don't even know what that is."

"Me, either, Waldo, but you know they got a cure for everything now. Eddie's going to be okay."

Waldo spent the night with Bill and Nick. In the morning they and Mrs. Donohue drove him to the hospital. When they arrived, Eddie's ex-wife, Tamara, and their two daughters were in the hall outside the ward where Eddie had been taken the day before. They were holding each other and crying. Yvette, the oldest girl, raised her tear-streaked face and shrieked at Waldo, "Daddy's dead!"

Nick gasped, Mrs. Donohue crossed herself, and Waldo stumbled, braced himself against a snot-green wall and howled. Bill froze in disbelief. He had seen Eddie last weekend and he had seemed the same as always. How could he be dead?

Tamara ran to Waldo and clawed his chest and face. "You did this!" she screamed. "You and your faggot ways. You killed my Eddie!"

Waldo cowered under the blows. Bill pulled

her off him. Nick and Mrs. Donohue dragged Waldo down the hall to the elevators. Bill released Tamara and ran down the hall, arriving just as the elevator doors slid open. They pushed Waldo into the car and went down to the lobby, Waldo muttering, "It wasn't my fault, it wasn't my fault, it wasn't my fault..."

The morning of Eddie's funeral, Bill met Waldo for breakfast at Church Street Station. The restaurant was packed with Castro clones and drag queens hunched over massive plates of grease and carbs, hangover food to absorb the effects of the previous night's bar hopping. The place smelled and sounded like a bar, smoky and loud and dark. Bill, who had arrived early, watched a waiter sling a tray of Bloody Marys to a boisterous table of six men, all in plaid shirts and Levi button-fly jeans. He could have used a drink himself, but he was trying to get sober again after yet another bad episode with Nick who had gone back home to his mother.

"Your table's ready," the host said. He led Bill to a small table with a view of the MUNI stop. A lanky guy waiting for the train, a yellow handkerchief hanging out his rear pocket, glanced at Bill and smiled. Bill opened his menu, pretending to read. Being cruised by a stranger into watersports was more than he could handle at the moment.

The waiter came by and asked him if wanted

anything to drink. It took all his strength to say, "Just coffee."

Waldo pushed through the restaurant door, stopped and looked around. Bill waved him over. Ordinarily, Waldo would have fluttered across the room, but today he stumbled over, unseeing and clearly miserable. Tamara had phoned Waldo and said if he showed up at Eddie's funeral, her father and brothers would kick his ass.

"You know I should go," he had told Bill defiantly, "just to show her what's what, but the girls will be there and I don't want to make a scene in front of them." He broke down and stuttered through his tears, "I love them like they were my own and I'll probably never see them again."

"Hi, Billy," he muttered now that he had reached the table and dropped into a chair. "You order yet?"

"Coffee. I was waiting for you."

"I ain't hungry."

Always pale and slim, Waldo appeared almost transparent and so skinny his skull seemed to float just beneath his skin.

"You have to eat. You don't look good."

"Like you look any better. Another fight with Nick?"

Bill shrugged. "The usual."

"Don't fuck it up, Bill, because when they're gone, they're gone." He blinked away tears. "And that's when you start to miss them."

The waiter came by. "You boys ready to order?"

"The eye-opener," Bill said. "Eggs over easy, wheat toast and bacon."

"I'll have what she's having," Waldo said. When the waiter departed, Waldo continued. "I can't get it out of my head, the thing that bitch said at the hospital. That I killed Eddie. Me and my faggot ways."

"You didn't kill him."

"What about that gay cancer that's going around?"

Bill remembered the posters that had appeared in the windows of the Castro Walgreen's depicting a back and a torso sprinkled with purple blisters, signs of a skin cancer called Kaposi's Sarcoma.

"Eddie didn't have cancer. He had meningitis. Anyway, didn't you tell me the gay cancer's just a couple of drama queens trying to get attention?"

"Yeah. Probably." He raised his head and looked at Bill, not bothering to restrain his tears. "I can't believe he's gone, Billy."

Bill put his hand on Waldo's. "Me either. God takes the good ones first."

Waldo managed a skeptical snort. "When did you start believing in God?" He tightened his grasp of Bill's hand. "But thank you, baby." He sighed. "Well, at least we still got each other. Someday we'll be two old queens sitting on the porch of the nursing home cruising the orderlies and all this," he concluded wistfully, "will seem very far away."

After breakfast, Bill went to his office. He was in the process of converting the business from real estate sales to property management because, working alone, he was less and less able to compete with the big realty companies setting up shop in the Castro. Of course, he could have gone to work for one of them, they'd all been around sniffing him out, but Bill didn't want a boss. Unable to fight them and unwilling to join them, he decided to take the expertise and contacts he had accumulated over a decade of rehabilitating old houses and contract himself out as a property manager. He was negotiating with half-a-dozen owners of apartment buildings to take over the day-to-day responsibilities of being a landlord. The conversion was complicated but today he was grateful that the work kept his mind occupied and away from Nick.

When he had done all he could do, it was dark outside. He sat at his desk for a few minutes sorting through his options: home to an empty apartment, a solitary meal in a restaurant, the bars or a backroom somewhere. Another alternative occurred to him and fifteen minutes later he was sitting on a folding chair in the basement of Blessed Savior at an AA meeting. He had come in late and as quietly as he could, but a few men glanced over at him when his chair squeaked as he pulled it out to sit. Just like a gay bar, he thought disdainfully, everyone checking out the fresh meat. But even as the thought passed through his head, he knew the comparison was false. The eyes that met his were not predatory but friendly, even kind, and they did not linger, but quickly returned to the front of the room where two men sat at a table; the secretary of the meeting and the speaker.

The secretary was saying, "We ask that all newcomers raise their hands to identify themselves. A newcomer is someone in his or her first thirty days of sobriety. We ask this not to embarrass you but so that we may get to know you at the end of the meeting."

Bill flushed. He had hoped to miss this announcement. Two other men raised their hands, one saying, "Hi, I'm Bryan and I'm an alcoholic with four days." The other said, "I'm Les, and I have twenty-two days today." They were greeted and applauded. Bill kept his hand down as he always did when he went to a meeting, out of pride or shame—he was uncertain which.

The secretary got through the further preliminaries and someone read the AA preamble which included the twelve steps of AA. As always, the references to God grated on him and there had been other times when, at this point, he would leave but tonight, with nowhere else to go, he stayed put. The secretary introduced the speaker as Teddy, a nondescript white guy in his thirties, and clearly though not floridly gay. He spoke in a low monotone that Bill had trouble hearing. He was relieved when someone asked, politely, but firmly, "Could you speak up a little?"

Teddy smiled and said more loudly, "Sorry. I mumble when I tell the truth, that way I can claim I told it even if no one heard it." When the laughter subsided, he continued. "What I was saying is that the hardest and truest words I've ever heard to describe alcoholism are where the book says it's a disease of loneliness."

Bill was about to make his escape as soon as the meeting ended, but he'd been spotted by Simon, a small, slender man who reminded him of the elf in the story of the *The Elf and the Shoemaker* that his grandmother liked to read to him from a big, illustrated book of the Grimm Brothers' fairytales. The resemblance ended, however, when Simon opened his mouth. He was sharp-tongued and gimlet-eyed.

He greeted Bill with, "The prodigal son returns. You auditing or are you joining this time?"

Bill shrugged, "My partner thinks I drink too much."

"What do you think?" the little man pressed.

"Maybe sometimes I overdo it, but I don't think I'm an alcoholic."

"This is the fourth or fifth time I've seen you at a meeting," Simon replied. "You must think there's something here for you."

The unexpected softness in his voice moved Bill to the verge of tears. He blinked them back and composed himself. Simon was right, there was something at these meetings that appealed to Bill but he had never articulated it, even to himself. There was, he thought, a spirit in these rooms that had echoes of a church service and yet was far different from its enforced pieties, a calm that was communal and profound and grateful as if the men who gathered here had survived the same catastrophe. As his own life seemed increasingly consumed by a chaos compounded of fear, insecurity and booze, he longed for that calm, but it required a step he could not take, a belief that was beyond him.

"I don't believe in God," he blurted out.

Simon looked appraisingly at him for a long moment before he said, "Don't believe in God or believe that God has rejected you because you're homosexual?"

"What's the difference?" he asked bitterly.

"There's a considerable difference. You can be an atheist and still get sober. I'm an atheist myself. It's a harder road if you believe there is a God and that he's already condemned you because first you have to give up that belief. Whether or not you can depends on how brainwashed you've been by conventional religion. And psychologically," he continued, "it would mean you have to stop hating yourself for being gay."

"I don't hate myself for that."

"Oh, honey, of course you do. All of us do. How could we not? We've been taught to hate ourselves by our gay-hating culture. Taught in a thousand ways that we are abnormal and defective. It's hard enough to expel that poison even if you don't believe that some ancient bearded man sitting on a throne in the sky has already drawn a black line through your name in his book of judgment." His tone was sharp, but his gaze was sympathetic. "There's no such man, Bill. That God was a lie you were told to keep you in line. A lie."

"How can you be so sure?"

"Use your brain. Don't you think the master of the universe, if there is such a thing, would have other things on his mind than who you fuck? Here," he continued, digging into his coat pocket. "Here's my card. Call me and we'll talk about this."

Bill took the card with a mumbled thanks. On his way home, he tossed it into a trashcan.

The flat was loud with Nick's absence. Bill poured himself a glass of wine and ruminated over the phrase the AA speaker had used, "a disease of loneliness." Whether or not it accurately described alcoholism, Bill thought it certainly applied to being gay. For him, two facts had emerged as being incontrovertibly true: one, he was homosexual and, two, it was a terrible life. Not day-to-day terrible because the days could be and were filled with obligations and distractions but all that was tap-dancing at the edge of an abyss which, when he stopped long enough to look into it, was bottomless and dark. Simon was wrong. This wasn't about self-hatred or condemnation by God. It was simply the truth.

Waldo could yammer about making a family from his friends but what kind of family was it where you could be banned from the funeral of the person you loved most in the world? And friends? What kind of family was that? People drifting in and out of your life with no real obligation to you or you to them and no bond of blood or the intimacy of having grown up in the same household. That was real family. This gay community was nothing more than a bunch of outcasts who pretended to have chosen their status when everyone knew, really, there was no choice.

He finished the bottle. He was so lonely. He could go the baths and look for distraction but when that was over, he would feel even lonelier. He could drink himself to sleep but he would wake with a hangover and loneliness. He would do neither. He would go to bed now and maybe tomorrow Nick would return home. Despite everything, Nick was all he had.

"Pete's got it," Waldo confided as he broke off a chunk of apple fritter. In the six months since Eddie's death, Waldo, who had always been stick thin, had gained at least fifty pounds. His belly sagged over his belt, his face was rounded and jowly, and soft man breasts pressed against his shirt. It was as if he had cushioned himself against a coming blow. When Bill asked him about it, he'd shrugged and said, "If Miss Elizabeth Taylor can be fat and still beautiful, so can I."

An autumn shower flicked itself against the windows of the doughnut shop in the Tenderloin. At a corner table a young, bearded man dropped his head to his chest and then jerked it up repeatedly.

"He's just on the nod," Waldo said dismissively when Bill suggested he might be ill. "All the junkies come here for their sugar high after they shoot up."

"Pete has what?" Bill asked. He took a sip of the bitter, dregs-of-the-coffee-pot brew cooling in his Styrofoam cup.

"The gay cancer. The KS. He's at General right now looking like a Dalmatian with all those purple spots."

Bill hadn't seen Pete in a couple of years and as far as he knew Pete was still working as a bouncer in The Hide 'n' Seek and seducing whatever fresh meat wandered into the place.

"He always was a big whore," Waldo continued, "and crazy for poppers. That's what they say causes it, poppers. Thank God, I always hated them. Smell like dirty socks and give me a headache. Anyway, I'm going to visit him tomorrow and I want you to come with me."

"I don't know. I'm pretty busy."

Waldo broke off another piece of fritter and said, "I don't want to go either but he's our friend." He plopped the pastry into his mouth. "Plus, I'm so over the gay cancer hysteria. All these queens dragging themselves around the Castro like they're Camille. It's a plot, you know."

"A plot?"

Waldo nodded. "A new way for straight people to shame us for fucking each other. Gay cancer my ass." He sipped his coffee. "Meet me in the lobby at General tomorrow at seven."

"Should I bring anything?" Bill asked. "Flowers?"

"A blond eighteen-year-old with a bubble butt," Waldo said. "But no flowers."

When Bill arrived at the hospital the next evening, Waldo was arguing with a nurse who wanted him to wear a gown, gloves and a mask before she would allow him to visit Pete. His thick neck was as red as his hair and in a voice quivering with rage, he said, "I'm not going see my sick friend dressed like he was a fucking space alien!"

"Those are the rules," she replied curtly. "He may be infectious."

Bill came to the desk. "He has cancer," he said calmly. "Since when is cancer infectious?"

She turned her attention to him. "The KS is a symptom of a problem with his immune system and we don't know what caused it or how it's spread."

"His immune system? What is that?"

"When we start to get sick, the body uses its natural defenses to fight off the sickness, whether it's a virus or bacteria or a parasite. That's the immune system. Your friend caught something that knocked his out. If you catch whatever it is, the same thing could happen to you and you'd get all kinds of sick." She turned to Waldo. "That's why you have to protect yourself."

"Come on, Waldo. I'm sure Pete wouldn't want us to catch it."

Waldo hissed, "Traitor," but he put on the gear.

The tip of Pete's nose was covered with a round purple blister, like a rubber clown's nose, and might have been comic except that the left side of his face was nearly obliterated by other puffy purple welts. Looking at him, it was all Bill could do not to run into the bathroom and throw up. Pete's loose hospital gown showed smaller welts descending from his neck to his breastbone. He gripped the hospital bed railings with shrunken arms and his legs stuck out from beneath the thin hospital sheet like matchsticks. He looked half the man he had been when Bill had last seen him sauntering down the dim corridors of the Club Baths, a skimpy towel tied around his waist.

"Hey, boys." His weak smile revealed prominent gums, also marked with lesions. "Thanks for coming to see me."

Waldo pulled a chair up to the side of the bed, removed his gloves, lowered the face mask and laced his fingers into Pete's.

"I gotta be honest, girl," he said. "You ain't looking your best."

Pete's laugh ended in a spittle-flinging coughing jag. Bill recoiled and watched fearfully as Waldo wiped Pete's spit from his face.

"Yeah, I seen better days," Pete said, when the coughing ended.

"What do the doctors say?" Bill asked, still standing well away from the bed.

"They say I'm sick, baby, and then they scratch their heads."

"But they're giving you medicine or something, aren't they?"

"Yeah, they tried chemo and some other stuff," he said vaguely. "But the lesions keep spreading. Got some in my stomach now. That's why I'm so skinny. Nothing stays down." He grinned. "When I think how I used to worry about my spare tire. Shit, I'd pay to have it back."

"But they can cure you, can't they?" Bill asked.

"Sure, Billy," Pete replied. "Don't stress, baby. I'll be good as new in no time." He smirked at Waldo. "There's this orderly here, some Chicano kid. His ass? One of the seven wonders of the world."

"He give you a sponge bath?"

"I wish. You know what I miss most in here? Cigarettes and sex."

"Well, I ain't got any cigs on me but I can give you a hand job?" Waldo said.

"Seriously?" Pete said, smiling. "Not even sure I can get it up."

"Honey, I can get a dead man hard," Waldo said. He turned to Bill. "Go stand by the door. If anyone tries to come in, block it."

"Waldo, you're not gonna..."

"Go watch the goddamn door," he snapped. Then he turned to Pete, slipped his hand beneath the sheet, fumbled and said, "Now what's this orderly's name?"

"Luis," Pete murmured, and closed his eyes.

Taped to the door of The Hide 'n' Seek was a homemade sign that read, *Closed for a private event*. Inside, the place was as packed and noisy as ever. In the center of the bar was a framed photograph of Pete, a vase of roses and the bronze urn that contained a handful of his ashes. The day before, a group of his friends, including Waldo, had carried out Pete's wish and scattered most of his ashes at his favorite cruising spots, Land's End and Buena Vista Park. Those that remained in the urn were mixed with glitter and at the stroke of midnight would be tossed like confetti over the revelers at the bar.

Bill stood in a corner, his arm around Nick, as the crowd grew drunker and louder. Sylvester's *Mighty Real* blasted from the jukebox and men rubbed against each other to the beat in what was more simulated sex than dancing. Someone fired up a joint, adding to the stink of cigarette smoke, beer and cologne. Bill was sober—a glass of Perrier sat within his reach—and the smell and noise distressed him. He pulled Nick closer.

"I've had enough. Let's go," he said.

"Isn't someone going to say something about Pete?" Nick asked.

"Like what? Pete was a slut, he caught something and he died. End of story."

Nick looked at him. "Pete was your friend."

"That was a long time ago."

Waldo elbowed his way through the crowd to them.

"We're leaving," Bill said.

"Before they toss his ashes?"

"Yeah, that's disgusting."

"Pete wanted to party one last time," Waldo said. He looked around. "It's like nothing's changed."

"Nothing has. Still the same shallow fags dancing and groping each other."

Waldo shook his head at him. "What's up your ass, Bill."

"Pete's dead," he said. "But the party goes on."

Waldo, still studying the crowd, said, "Not for long, Billy. Not for long."

14.

N THE DAYS THAT FOLLOWED my last encounter with Adam, I found myself thinking about lies. In my experience, lies tend to metastasize and this is as true of lies of omission and lies of commission. Whether the lie is a deliberate falsehood or a withheld truth, it expands until it taints everything. I had told Adam everything was fine instead of being truthful and now I wasn't able to face him. For the same reason, I could scarcely bring myself to make my morning phone call to Larry and pretend everything was all right. Everything was not all right. I had fallen half in love with a straight guy who did not, could not, reciprocate. The situation churned up feelings I thought I had left behind as a lonely teenager with a terrible secret. They surfaced into my consciousness like bloated bodies emerging from the bottom of a lake, a toxic and decomposing mix of fear and loneliness and self-loathing that drove me into myself.

One night, I passed the bar at the corner of Castro and Market where groups of men sat drinking behind plate-glass windows beneath dim, forgiving lights and a drink seemed like a wonderful idea. Just a couple of shots to warm up my insides and calm down my mind. My hand was on the door when I heard a familiar and, at that moment, unwelcome voice.

"Do you really think that's going to make it better, young Henry?"

Simon stood behind me, the black cigarette burning between his fingers, his expression unreadable.

"As a matter of fact, I do," I said.

"Then you're an idiot." He pulled his scarf tighter around his neck and approached me. "Because you can drink yourself into a stupor, but whatever you're running from will be waiting for you when you sober up and it won't be happy. Or don't you remember that dance? I mean, it hasn't been that long for you, has it?"

"Go away, Simon."

"I'm on my way to a meeting," he replied. "Come with me."

I glanced at the bar, the seductive lights, the laughing men lifting bottles and glasses, the handsome bartender mixing a drink behind the long, curved bar and then I thought about a group of men sitting on hard, folding chairs in a church basement drinking coffee out of Styrofoam cups. I heard Larry telling me, when I had asked him at the beginning of our work together, "It's simple,

Henry. If you want to stay sober, all you have to change is everything."

A third man came up behind me and snapped, "Are you going in or not?"

I released the door handle. "No. Let's go, Simon."

He smiled. "Perhaps you're not such an idiot after all."

When I got home, I dialed Larry's number. He picked it up on the first ring with, "Henry?"

"How did you know?"

"The only calls I get after ten are from people I sponsor, and I've already talked to the other two. What's going on?"

"I've been keeping something from you."

He laughed. "Of course, you have! I'm your sponsor. Everyone in AA keeps secrets from their sponsors until they get so miserable it's either confess or drink. You didn't drink, did you?"

"No," I protested. "But I came close tonight."

"Why don't you tell me about it."

I carried the phone to the couch, lay down and told him about Adam. He listened, making only noncommittal noises now and then to reassure me he was still on the line. When I was done, he said, simply, "You know what you have to do, don't you?"

"Would I have called you if I did?"

He chuckled. "You didn't call me for advice. You called me so you could think aloud."

"Let's pretend," I said a little annoyed, "that I did call you for advice. What would you advise?"

"Stop seeing him."

"I'd have to tell him why."

"And that's a problem because?"

"Because I feel like a fool," I said. "Falling for a straight guy. It's a fucking cliché."

"Really, Henry? All you feel is foolish? Is that why you were about to throw away your sobriety?"

"No," I admitted. "This situation with Adam took me down a black hole where every negative feeling I ever had about being gay was waiting for me. I needed that drink to shut those voices up."

"Yeah, been there," Larry replied. "There's good news and bad news. What do you want first?"

"Give me the bad news."

"The bad news is those feelings, those voices, they never go away. We all got the poison early on and we got a steady diet of it. You know what I mean. The world we grew up in told us queers are sick or sinful or criminal. Those were our choices. We metabolized that message. That self-hatred is part of us and like you said, it's waiting for us, waiting to exploit those moments of weakness or doubt when it tells us the world was right after all. Tells us we're defective, abnormal, broken. That voice is what drives our compulsions—for booze or drugs or sex—anything to drown it out, to distract ourselves or it takes us to that place where self-destruction seems like the only option."

"Yes," I said. "That's what was happening." I sighed. "So, what's the good news."

"The good news is that you know that voice is a lie. You know who you are and you know you're not any of those things the world says about you. You're not sick, you're not immoral and you're not a criminal. You know it about yourself and you know it about other gay people. That's our truth and the truth will prevail but it won't happen by itself. It's up to us to shout down the lie with our truth and it's going to take all of us, an army of us. But first, you have to confront the lie in yourself, see it for what it is, and reject it whenever it rears its ugly head. You can't do that if you're drunk."

"Do you ever wonder what life would be like without this struggle?"

He laughed. "Everyone has a struggle. This just happens to be ours."

"You know what I mean," I said. "To walk the street without having to look over your shoulder. To not have to calculate, every time you meet someone, whether to come out. To love freely."

"You'll have all that when you decide to give it to yourself."

"What do you mean?"

"Being comfortable in your own skin happens when you really and truly accept who you are. When you love yourself."

"Ugh, I hate that new age bullshit."

"Okay, let's try it this way. Think of someone you really love. Think of all the good things in life you want for that person. Think of how you accept that person's flaws. Think of the happiness that the mere fact of that person's existence brings you. Think of how grateful you are to have that person in your life. Got all that in your head?"

Of course, I was thinking of him. "Yes."

"Then imagine that person is you."

My startled "Oh!" drew a laugh from him.

"I see we still have a lot of work to do," he said. "Goodnight, kiddo, call me in the morning."

"Goodnight, Larry. Thank you."

"I love you, Henry."

The rain obscured my view of the Trejo residence but my more immediate problem was that I really needed to take a leak. I'd been sitting there for over an hour. I cast a grim glance at the oversized, now empty coffee cup in the cup holder and wondered what cops did for toilet breaks when they were on stakeouts. I got out of the car and discreetly pissed into a hedge. A half dozen houses down the block, Nick Trejo finally came out of the front door with his mother in tow. I could almost hear his eyes roll as she gesticulated and talked to his back. I ducked into my car.

Ruth Fleming had instructed me to back off the Trejos for fear of a lawsuit but, like most laypeople, her fear of litigation was exaggerated. Lawsuits are complicated, costly to bring and can drag on for years. They also tend to expose secrets in the discovery process. The Trejo family didn't seem the suing types, even with a lawyer in the family, and they were clearly hiding something about Bill Ryan's death.

But what? There was really only one person who could tell me what had really happened that night. Nick. My interest in the case had taken on a life of its own unrelated to my employer's. I could care less whether Western States paid out the claim. I needed to know how Bill Ryan had died, and Nick was the only witness to that event. Unexpectedly, I had come to care for them. They were part of my tribe, apples who'd fallen, not just far from the tree but rolled into another orchard. I didn't want what I suspected had happened that night to be true. I didn't want Nick to have killed Bill. But even if he had, there are many degrees of culpability and not all of them warrant the same punishment. I had to find out where Nick fell on that spectrum. What would I do then? I didn't know yet.

Nick drove across the Bay Bridge and onto the 280 and exited at Ocean. When he took a left on Junipero Serra, then a right on Holloway, I realized he was heading to San Francisco State University where he had been a student when he met Bill Ryan. By now the rain had abated. I parked a couple of cars behind him and waited a moment before following him onto campus.

The sprawling, factory-like campus with its concrete buildings and cemented quadrangles looked particularly naked in the gray winter light. Only a few students picked their way along the leaf-strewn paths. Nick went into the administration building. When he emerged sometime later, he was tucking a sheaf of papers into the inside pocket of his raincoat. I followed him into the student union where I found him drinking a cup of coffee and eating a Danish. His long dark hair was brushed into wings around his face which seemed even younger to me than the first time I had seen him.

"Hi, Nick," I said, pulling a chair from the table and seating myself.

Panic flashed in his eyes but he managed a stuttered, "Hi."

"I'm not here to hurt you, but I have some questions that only you can answer."

"I don't want Bill's money."

"This isn't about Bill's money anymore. I think you're in trouble and I want to help you."

"What do you mean? You work for the insurance company."

"Only part-time. I'm actually a criminal defense lawyer." I let that sink in. "I discovered things about Bill's death that don't add up to an accident. If I found them, so will the police. Do you understand what I'm telling you?"

He was so still, it was as if he had turned to stone.

I continued, "You lived with Bill for what, four years? You must have cared for him."

"I loved him," he said carefully. "He loved me too."

I prodded him with a gentle, "What happened?"

He took a deep, shuddering breath and then the dam burst.

"I couldn't believe he liked me," he said. "I'm just a skinny kid with a big nose. Bill was so handsome and successful. When I moved in with him, I didn't know what to expect or what to do. I had never had a boyfriend before. Bill said since he worked, it was only fair that I take care of the apartment and the shopping and stuff. It was fun for a while, like playing house. I was still going to school but Bill wanted me home when he got done with work. I lost touch with the friends I'd made here. I stopped taking as many classes, and then I dropped out to work because I didn't want him to support me. I wanted to pay my own way. Pretty soon the only people I saw were Bill's friends and it was obvious that they just thought of me as Bill's little twink. Except for Peg. She was my friend."

"What about your family?"

"I didn't have a car so it was hard for me to get out there to see them during the week. I wanted to go on weekends, but Bill always seemed to have other plans for us. I talked with my mom almost every day, but I didn't see much of my sister or my brothers."

"Sounds like you were pretty isolated."

"Yeah, it was like I woke up one day and realized I didn't have a life anymore except for Bill and his friends. I loved Bill, but I couldn't breathe. I tried to talk to him about it, but he would accuse me of wanting to break up with him. Then he would either get angry or sad and start drinking."

"When did he start hitting you?"

A look of dismay passed across his young face. "It was only the one time and he didn't mean to. He felt terrible afterwards."

"In my experience as a lawyer, if someone's partner hits him once, he will hit him again."

He blushed and looked away from me. "The drinking made him mean," he said, "and I think he was using drugs too." He played with his cup. "I found a little bottle of white powder in his pants pocket when I was going through them before I put them in the washing machine."

"Cocaine?"

"I didn't ask. I washed his pants and put the bottle back in his pocket."

"Why didn't you leave him?"

His gaze seemed to go inward and after long pause, he said, "I thought that's how things were supposed to be. Fight, make up, fight some more." His face, when he looked at me, was pleading.

"You're gay. Isn't that what it's like when you live with another guy?"

He was so young and he'd been even younger when Bill Ryan had taken him hostage in the name of love. It was a scenario I had seen before, usually with women abused and manipulated by their husbands or boyfriends until their emotions were so twisted, and their wills so broken, they saw no way out. Except, sometimes, by killing their abuser.

"You didn't think there was a way out, did you?"

"I was afraid he would kill himself if I left him."

"Did he tell you that?"

He nodded and then added, quietly, "I loved him. You have to believe me."

"I do."

"Everything got worse after Waldo died. It was like he couldn't let me out of his sight, even for an hour."

"Why?"

"AIDS," he said. "He told me he had to protect us from getting sick."

"By keeping you locked up?"

"He wasn't making a lot of sense by then."

"What happened the night he died?"

He froze. "I can't talk about that with you."

"I told you, Nick, I'm a criminal defense lawyer. I can help you."

"It's private."

"But your family knows."

He looked startled. "That's my family. You're a stranger. I shouldn't have talked to you at all."

"But you did," I said. "I can tell you want to get this off your chest. It's eating away at you."

He gazed at me, understanding dawning in his dark, luminous eyes. He said, incredulously, "You think I killed him."

"Did you?"

He bolted from his chair, knocking the coffee cup over and spilling the last of his coffee on the table.

"Nick," I called to his back as he fled into the rain.

Driving back to my office, I was convinced Nick was implicated in Bill's death but I no longer suspected he had killed him. From Nick's description of their relationship it was clear that Nick was Bill's hostage, emotionally manipulated to remain with him. In that state, even if Nick had reached a breaking point and decided his only way out was to kill Bill, he would have lashed out at him impulsively in a sudden fury. He would not have concocted an elaborate and premeditated plan involving carbon monoxide poisoning.

I considered another scenario. Maybe the gas leak *was* accidental and when Nick woke up and smelled the gas, Bill was unconscious in the bed beside him. Nick panicked and called his brother. Sal told him to get out of the apartment. Instead, Nick returned to the bedroom and saw Bill was still breathing. In that moment, he had a choice: try again to rouse Bill and drag him out of the apartment or leave him there. By now, Nick would have been disoriented, struggling to breathe and unable to think clearly. In that confused state, he left Bill behind. It would be easy for Nick to now blame himself for Bill's death because it had liberated him from Bill. But had he killed him? Under the circumstances, he might have died himself had he tried to rescue Bill. Whatever had been in his mind in those moments, the law would not have held him responsible for Bill Ryan's death. Which is not to say he wouldn't still feel guilty. He might even believe he did have some criminal as well as moral liability. That would explain why he refused to talk to me about what had happened that night.

Where did this leave me? I still had a report to write. I needed someone in that family to answer my questions.

Isabel Trejo's office was in an old building on Montgomery Street that featured a grand marble lobby at street level and sepulchrally austere corridors on the upper floors. Her name was written in gilt on the frosted windowpane of an oak door. I entered a small anteroom furnished in the usual heavy, dark, lawyer office furniture. Behind sliding glass windows, a middle-aged woman glanced up at me, slid back the glass and said, "Can I help you?"

"I have an appointment with Ms. Trejo. I'm Henry Rios."

She glanced down at a sheet of paper. "I'll let her know you're here."

I sat down and thumbed through a two-month old issue of the *ABA Journal*. After a couple of minutes, the door to the inner office opened and a tall, dark-eyed woman in the standard navy-blue suit favored by women lawyers strode into the anteroom. "Mr. Rios?"

I stood up. "Ms. Trejo?"

She looked me up and down, frowned briefly as if she'd come to a not entirely favorable conclusion, and said, "Come in."

I followed her down a short corridor to a large but windowless office where, to my surprise, Mrs. Trejo was seated at a small conference table. She glanced at me warily. She had dressed up for this encounter and looked uncomfortable out of her apron and sack dress.

"You know my mother," Isabel Trejo said. "Please sit down."

I sat and she took the chair across from me, beside her mother. Isabel Trejo had the strong features of her brothers but what was handsome in them was intimidatingly stern in her. This was not going to be an easy conversation.

"Okay, Mr. Rios," she said, almost indifferently. "It's your meeting."

"I have to submit a report to Western States about Bill Ryan's death."

"I told you Nick doesn't want the money," she said flatly.

"In that case, the policy becomes an asset of the estate and estate plans to file a claim. I still have to write the report."

She frowned. "So what? Write your report. Bill's death was an accident."

"There's some room for doubt."

Mrs. Trejo shifted in her chair but said nothing. It was her daughter who spoke, "What doubt?"

"It's obvious to me that Nick feels guilty about whatever happened that night and it's also clear your family is protecting him. I've uncovered enough questionable circumstances around Ryan's death to raise the possibility it wasn't an accident. If I file that report, the company will refer it to the police and the cops will open an investigation. I'm giving your family one last chance to tell your side of the story before I do that."

Mrs. Trejo gasped. Her daughter touched her arm as if to silence her and asked, "What questionable circumstances?"

I laid it all out for them: what I knew about the relationship between Bill and Nick, Bill's apparent paranoia that Nick might leave him that culminated in his hitting Nick, Nick's desire to get out of the relationship, the inconsistencies between Sal's report and my expert's opinion about the gas leak, Nick's behavior that night, and Ryan's will naming Nick as his heir.

"You're a lawyer, Ms. Trejo," I concluded. "I'm sure you know enough criminal law to see what this could add up to if the cops and the DA get their hands on it. Motive and opportunity for murder."

Mrs. Trejo spoke tremulously, "My boy did not kill Bill."

"Mom, let me do the talking." She tapped her fingers on the gleaming surface of the table. "You're right that it wasn't an accident, but you're wrong if you think Nick was responsible for Bill's death. Give me the letter, Mom."

Mrs. Trejo grabbed her big black purse from the floor, unclasped it, fished around in its contents, and pulled out an envelope she handed to her daughter. Isabel removed a single handwritten sheet of paper from it and slid it across the table.

"What is this?" I asked.

"Read it," she said.

I glanced at the salutation. "Dear Dolly?"

"That's me," Mrs. Trejo said. "My name is Dolores but everyone calls me Dolly."

"Who wrote this?" I asked.

Mrs. Trejo said, "Bill."

15.

Dear Dolly, I know how sad you must be that Nick is gone because he was your baby but I had to take him with me because he was going to suffer so bad if I left him behind. I have AIDS, Dolly. I found a spot on my leg and I went to my doctor and he told me it was what they call a Kaposi's sarcoma lesion and it's the first sign of AIDS. If I have it then Nick has it too, because I've infected him. I didn't do it on purpose and I hate myself for having given it to him because it means Nick will die a horrible death. There's no treatment, there's no cure, just suffering and more suffering and then a miserable death. I couldn't let that happen to my Nick. Forgive me, Dolly. Try to believe that I did this out of love. Bill Ryan

I read it twice before the monstrousness of the note fully registered. "Bill Ryan killed himself?"

Isabel Trejo nodded. "Yeah, and he tried to kill Nick."

Mrs. Trejo pulled a tissue from her purse and dabbed the tears from her eyes.

"Where did you find this note?"

Her daughter responded, "Bill mailed it the morning before he died. My mom got it the day after."

She handed me the envelope; the postmark confirmed that the letter had been mailed from San Francisco the day before Bill Ryan died.

I turned the envelope over in my hand and looked at the two women. Isabel Trejo's blunt features were expressionless. A tear trickled down her mother's cheek, making a furrow in her face powder. She clutched the used tissue in her fingers. A working woman's rough fingers, a mother's fingers.

"Mrs. Trejo, why didn't you tell me about this when I first spoke to you and Nick?"

She glared at me, "Because it was none of your damn business."

Isabel Trejo directed a silencing hand at her mother. "When my mom got the letter, we figured that was the end of the story. We didn't know about the insurance policy. You caught us off guard."

"But still. This note exonerates Nick."

"Exonerates him?" Isabel Trejo said, angrily. "Nick didn't do anything wrong. We thought you'd see that and go away but you couldn't stop digging. You figured out that Sal lied about the gas leak."

"Why did he do that? Why not tell the truth from the beginning?"

Isabel Trejo shook her head. "You're a smart man, Mr. Rios, can't you figure out why we would want to keep this in the family?"

Before I could answer, her mother said, "No one needs to know my boy has AIDS."

So that was it. I was right all along. Nick's family was protecting him, but I was wrong about what they were protecting him from.

"Has he been sick?"

Isabel Trejo shook her head. "No, no symptoms, not," and here she paused, glanced at her mother, and said, quietly, "yet."

"Not everyone gets sick," Mrs. Trejo said to her. "Not everyone dies."

"But if he does get sick," Isabel Trejo said evenly, "we'll take care of him. His family. We won't let anyone hurt him."

"I need to tell the company about this to close the investigation."

"Absolutely not," Isabel Trejo said.

"Ms. Trejo, be reasonable. I promise you no one will know except me and my supervisor."

She shook her head. "I don't want any record out there about Nick being exposed to AIDS. It would ruin his life."

I couldn't argue the point.

"We figured when we told you Nick didn't want

the money, you would drop the case. I didn't consider Bill's estate might want it."

I thought about it a moment. "The estate's the only other possible claimant," I said. "There's Bill's family but none of them know about the policy and Bill's lawyer is fighting them to keep them from getting anything, so he's not going to tell them. If the estate drops the claim, the investigation becomes moot. Bill's lawyer is gay and a decent guy. I think he would understand if you at least let me tell him the real story."

"What if Bill's family finds out about the policy somewhere down the line?" Isabel Trejo asked.

"I suppose that's a risk you'll have to take to protect Nick. Will you let me talk to Bill's lawyer? Between the two of us, we can make it all go away."

Daughter and mother exchanged glances.

"Okay," Isabel Trejo said grudgingly. "But only to him."

"I need to show him the letter. A copy anyway."

"You'll destroy it after he reads it?"

"I promise. I don't want to hurt Nick either."

Isabel got up and went into the corridor where I heard a copying machine running. Mrs. Trejo and I were left alone.

"I'm sorry about Nick."

"Do you think they'll find a cure?"

"I hope so," I equivocated, not wanting to tell her what I really thought which was that the government seemed perfectly content to let us all die. I added, "He's a lucky boy to have such a loving family."

She looked at me, puzzled. "Why wouldn't we love him? That's what families do."

One morning on the phone, Larry cut short my complaints about writing a fourth step inventory saying, I'm going to read you something Bill Wilson wrote. Listen carefully. "Fear is an evil, corroding thread; the fabric of our lives is shot through with it. Fear is surely a bar to reason, and to love, and of course it invariably powers anger, vainglory and aggression." Vainglory? He was a terrible writer. His prose is not the point, Henry. You don't want to write an account of your life because you're afraid of what you might find there but putting it off only feeds the fear. So, let me help you here and tell you what you're going to find when you look at yourself. You'll find you're a garden-variety neurotic like all the rest of us, Henry. You're not special. Is that supposed to make me feel better? Yes. Strangely, it did.

I remembered that conversation with Larry as I lay in bed that night and thought about Nick and Bill. There was a third party in their relationship from the beginning; there was Nick, Bill and Bill's fear. I knew the fear I'd been struggling with myself, that terrible, profound ache of loneliness you feel when you know you are different and conclude that no one else in the world is like you. I woke to that fear every morning when I was a boy before I escaped my father's house and discovered there were other boys like me. By then, however, as Larry had told me, the poison had done its work, mutating from *you'll always be alone* to *no one will ever love you* to *you'll never be good enough to be loved*. That last fear was the worst because no amount of achievement or good works could change it. It was a done deal, it was fate.

That must have been what Bill Ryan felt, and when his mother drove him to the bus station and told him not to come back, it would only have confirmed his belief he was irreparably defective. Then he got here and he met Waldo and later Nick and for a while the fear subsided. But something triggered it and to judge from what Nick had told me about Bill's possessiveness, that something was likely love itself. The more Bill loved, the less worthy he felt of love, and the tighter he had held on to Nick. This set up the cycle: Nick squirming to escape, Bill using everything at his disposal to keep Nick with him, including threats of suicide. Then the AIDS tsunami touched down, swept Waldo away and, for Bill, added to his old fears, the terror of dying a ghastly death. The terror swamped him so that when he discovered the lesion on his leg, there seemed one way out for him and for Nick.

As I lay there in the dark, my thoughts turned

to my situation with Adam. I was still avoiding him, still putting off the inevitable conversation and still, I realized, holding out hope that, somehow, I could make him feel for me what I felt for him. How different was I from Bill, thinking of ways to manipulate another guy's emotions so as to bind him to me and avoid the fear of being alone and unloved? I was shamed but also grateful for the insight. As soon as I finished this case, I would do the right thing with Adam.

Randy Gifford read Bill Ryan's suicide note and then slowly massaged his temples as if trying to expel its content from his mind.

"I knew he was obsessed with getting sick, but God Almighty." He looked at me wearily. "You know, there will be other stories like this. Men killing themselves when they get the diagnosis. Abandoning sick partners. Getting thrown out by their families."

"Not everyone will cut and run. The Trejos aren't abandoning Nick. You and I both know men whose friends have taken care of them as they were dying. We both know men who are sick and fighting it."

He allowed himself a small smile. "You keep being the voice of hope. We'll need it."

"It's not hope," I said, thinking about how Larry Ross had extended himself unselfishly to me. "It's experience."

He tapped the note. "You want me to send a

letter to Western States disclaiming any interest by Bill's estate in the policy?"

"Yes. Isabel Trejo's already sent a letter on Nick's behalf. I realize it's a little more complicated for you to renounce a potential asset because Bill's family is trying to get their hands on the estate."

"I don't represent his family," Randy said. "I represent Bill and his wishes. Nick's his heir and if Nick doesn't want the insurance money for whatever reason, I don't feel compelled to go after it for the estate. There's plenty without it."

"If Bill's family litigates the will, won't you have to disclose the existence of the policy?"

He sighed. "They won't sue. I'm settling with them."

"Last time we talked it sounded like you were going to go the mat."

"Yeah, well, I calculated what it would cost to fight them and decided it was cheaper to buy them off. They'll take fifty thousand to go away and renounce any further claims to Bill's estate. They'll never find out about the policy." He grinned. "So Western States gets a windfall. Won't that raise eyebrows over there?"

"I'm counting on their greed outweighing their curiosity."

"Good luck, Henry," he said. "It was a pleasure doing business with you."

Back at my office, I spread out the contents of

Bill Ryan's case file on my desk. I pondered how to explain to Ruth Fleming why, after implying that Nick had murdered Ryan, the renunciation of the death benefit by Ryan's estate—of which Nick was sole heir—wasn't simply further evidence of Nick's guilt. That's how it would've looked to me. As I'd told Randy Gifford. my best hope was that whatever questions she might continue to harbor about the circumstances of Ryan's death, the bottom line would win out. That depended on how scrupulous she was. Even if Western States was off the hook for having to pay out the benefit, she might still insist the police should be informed that a potential crime had been committed to make sure she was in the clear. A crime had been committed, but not the one I had imagined. Nick hadn't murdered Ryan; Ryan had attempted to murder Nick, but Bill Ryan couldn't be prosecuted so it was all a wash. Life would be easier if I could tell her that, but my hands were tied by my promise to Isabel Trejo.

I picked up the suicide note. *Dear Dolly.* The Trejos had taken Ryan into their family and yet he felt enough of an outsider to have signed his full name to his suicide note as if they might not know who had written it had he simply signed it Bill. Something drew my attention to the insurance policy which was open to the signature page. I looked at it, then back at the note, then back at the policy. I put the note side by side with the policy and compared the signatures. They were completely and dramatically different.

Ruth Fleming compared the signature on the policy to Ryan's signature on the last page of his will that I had obtained from Randy Gifford.

"You'll see the signature on the will doesn't remotely match the signature on the policy," I said.

Without looking up, she asked, "Did he authorize someone else to sign the policy on his behalf?"

"Brendan Scott specifically told me that Ryan signed the policy in Scott's office and in his presence."

She looked at me, troubled. "Have you asked Brendan about this?"

"I wanted to talk to you first. You told me the first time we talked that you bought this policy from Scott. Have you bought others?"

"Yes," she said, drawing out the word. "We buy a lot of policies from Confederation, not just in San Francisco, but nationally." She frowned. "Are you implying that Brendan forged Ryan's signature?"

"Does Western States independently verify that these are legitimate policies?"

"Of course not," she snapped. "Confederation Insurance is an established company that writes thousands of policies a year. We trust them implicitly. Besides, what would be the point of Scott fabricating policies?"

"You told me he sells them at a profit to you. Isn't that motive enough?"

She thought about it. "That's true but—it's like this. He brings us a policy with a thousand dollar premium and we buy it for fifteen hundred, so he makes five hundred the first year. But in the second year, he has to forward the premium to us, minus ten percent for his administrative costs."

"So, in year two, he has to come up with nine hundred dollars to pay the premium on the policy he sold you the year before for fifteen hundred."

"Exactly," she said. "That year and every other year as long as the policy is in force, he owes us nine hundred dollars. If he had to pay it out of his own pocket because a policy's fake, where's his profit? It doesn't make sense."

"Unless, of course," I ventured, "he sold you five other fake policies and made twenty-five hundred on them. He could pay the premium on the first policy with your own money and still make a profit."

"You're describing a Ponzi scheme. I've known Brendan for years. That's not something he would do. There has to be a simple explanation for why Ryan didn't sign the policy. Go talk to Brendan."

"Before I do that, why don't you let me see the last twenty or thirty policies you bought from him. If they all check out, then clearly, you're right and there's an innocent explanation but if not—"

She picked up her phone and instructed her assistant to pull the last thirty policies from Brendan Scott. "You're not going to find anything amiss," she said.

I tapped Ryan's policy and said, "I already have."

I sat at the top of Dolores Park, the cityscape unfolding in the clear, bright air. I felt a hand on my shoulder, looked up, and Adam smiled at me.

"Gorgeous day, isn't it?" I said. "Pull up a seat."

He sat down beside me. "How you been?"

"I'm sorry I haven't returned your calls."

"I figured you were busy with, you know, lawyer stuff."

"There was that," I said, "but I also needed to say something to you and I didn't know how to say it."

"Maybe you should just say it."

Words raced through my head, but I couldn't find the right ones, so, after a couple of minutes, I blurted out, "You know, we gotta stop."

"Stop..." he repeated uncertainly.

"Stop dating or fucking or whatever it is we're doing," I said, not looking at him.

He was quiet for a long time and I was about to say something else when he said, "I figured it was something like that. Can you tell me why?"

"It turns out I can't do 'just sex,' Adam. I thought I could, but I was wrong. I'm sorry."

"You know it wasn't just sex," he replied. "I like you."

"Yeah, I like you too, but you're not gay. There's no future in this and I want a future. With someone. Like you want with Candace. Can you understand that?"

"Yeah. Of course." He sighed. "You know, Henry, if I was gay, I'd be all over you like white on rice."

I laughed. "Thanks."

"The funny thing is," he continued, "that being with you, liking you so much, really, really made me think about whether or not I could be with another guy. I mean, you're the best there is and if I could be with anyone, it would be you, but I can't. I'm just not that guy."

"Life lessons," I said.

"Yeah, they kinda suck. So," he said, after a moment, "can we at least be friends?"

"Yes, eventually. I need a little more time away from you to let my feelings settle down. I hope you understand."

"Break-ups are hard," he said. He leaned over and kissed me. "You know where to find me, when you're ready." He got up and dusted off his pants. "Don't be a stranger."

"I won't. Goodbye, Adam. Thank you for everything."

"Goodbye, Henry."

I sat there for a moment after he left, looking at the city, as a future that might have been slowly dissolved in the autumn brightness and what I felt, along with sadness, was relief. Breaking up *was* hard, but in exchange for the sharp sting of heartbreak, I had avoided a lot of unnecessary suffering trying to make something work that was doomed from the start and which also could have made me so miserable that a drink would have sounded like a solution. I got up and went off to call Larry.

16.

RANDY STOPPED BILL WHEN HE entered the ward and pulled him aside.

"I wanted to warn you he's been raving," the nurse said.

"What do you mean by raving?"

"You know he's got toxo and his brain is, well, scrambled. We call it AIDS-related dementia. He's not in his right mind and he's saying things he wouldn't say if he was. So, don't take them all that seriously, okay?"

Another patient—Ted something, Bill remembered—approached them, his IV trailing behind him. Ted had once told him he had been a runner who had run a half-dozen marathons. Now he walked slow laps around the cheerfully painted ward. He nodded as he passed, leaving in his wake the sour whiff of disease, like spoiled meat, a smell that permeated the ward. From the dozen rooms, televisions blared soap operas and movie dialogue, punctuated by commercials loudly advertising items for which these men would never again have any use. There were cut flowers everywhere, in vases and bowls. Glittering streamers hung from the ceiling of the common room where one of the patients had, the previous day, celebrated his last birthday.

"Like what?" Bill pressed. "What is he saying?"

Randy was a big, gentle man whose habitual expression was a smile but now he frowned. "You'll see. Just don't let get it to you, okay?"

"Sure," Bill said. "I better go in."

Randy touched his arm. "Also, he might not recognize you."

"Yeah, that's happened before, but there's usually a minute or two when he knows who I am."

"Call me if you need anything."

As he did every time he visited, Bill paused at the doorway to prepare himself before he stepped into the room that Waldo, when he was still himself, had christened "the honeymoon suite." That seemed like a long time ago, when Waldo could still walk and joke and insist, "Honey, what does the Grim Reaper want with a fat old queen like me? I'm gonna beat this thing, you'll see," and Bill had believed him because Waldo was, above all else, a survivor. That was what? Eight, nine hospitalizations ago. With each one, Waldo's jokes became more brittle until they stopped altogether. The last time, he'd been wheeled into the room in a wheelchair, looked around and said, "Where am I?"

His hair had fallen out during his last chemo treatment and had regrown in straggling clumps like a clown wig. His arms and legs were sticks, skin stretched over tendon, muscle and bone without any cushioning, and his hands were bent into claws, an effect accentuated by his long, yellow fingernails which he refused to allow anyone to cut. He was covered with bruises. The first time Bill saw them he had screamed at Randy that someone was hurting Waldo. Randy explained that Waldo's body had stopped making the cells that helped his blood clot, so that the slightest bang or bump left a dark mark. The condition had inflamed his abdominal organs and doctors had had to remove his spleen and parts of his stomach and liver. Now he was retaining fluids and his belly was distended and bloated. His eyes had been attacked by a virus called cytomegalovirus leaving him nearly blind. He had survived two rounds of pneumocystis pneumonia, the infection that had killed Pete, and he was attached to an oxygen tube as well as a morphine drip and another drip that fed him now that he could no longer digest solid food. A catheter carried off his piss. His face could have been that of a mummy unwrapped after centuries in the crypt, dark and skeletal and alien.

"Waldo? It's Bill."

The cadaverous head turned an inch toward him and made a croaking noise.

Bill bent over the bed, holding his breath against the stink, and said, "What did you say?"

He made the same croak but in three distinct phrases. "They... were... right."

Bill sat down. In the corner of the room, Jeopardy played on the TV. The smiling host interviewed the nervous contestants. The sounds of the street, faint but lively, filtered through the heavy windows. Sunlight poured into the room. On the bed stand was a vase filled with sunflowers and irises that Mrs. Donohue had left on her last visit. She and Bill were Waldo's most faithful visitors; other friends came or didn't come as time and temperament allowed. An orderly pushed a trolley past the door. The world proceeded apace, which for Bill seemed the most unbelievable part of this horror, because inside his head, he was screaming.

"They were right about what?"

Waldo closed his eyes and was still for such a long time Bill thought he had drifted off but then he grabbed Bill's wrist with a claw-like hand.

"About... us... Us fags... God... hates... us." He released Bill's wrist and turned his head to him. "Look... at... me... You're... next... God... hates us."

Twenty-two minutes later, he was dead.

The boat drifted beneath the Golden Gate into the mist of the open sea. Bill looked up at the massive girders with a chill that had nothing to do with the weather. He remembered—now so long ago—the first time he had seen it, when it had seemed like a graceful gesture welcoming those who sailed beneath it into the magical city it enclosed. Now it seemed to him the bridge was the boundary of life while the sea represented the deep and unknown reaches beyond the living. He held in his hands the ceramic urn where Waldo's ashes were mixed with sequins, glitter, confetti and grape Kool-Aid. The last and most loyal of Waldo's friends were gathered around him, waiting for Bill to open the urn and spill the contents into the sea. Someone at yet another memorial for another friend had read a poem and now the words came back to him: *Parting is all we know of heaven, and all we need of hell.*

Waldo had wanted this party, had provided in his will the money for the charter, for food and for drink and music, but it was a miserable, gray day and the mourners, bundled in heavy clothes, had little appetite for the food and drink and the music went unplayed. Nick put his hand on Bill's shoulder.

"How far out are we going?"

"A little farther. I want to clear the bridge."

"Are you going to say anything?"

Bill shook his head.

"Someone should."

"Waldo was always the one who made the speeches," Bill said. He glanced over his shoulder at the pale faces of Waldo's other friends. "Maybe one of them will have something to say."

Bill had never revealed to Nick or to anyone else Waldo's last words to him—*were right. God hates fags. You're next.*—but he had thought of little else in the weeks since Waldo's last gasping breaths. He wanted to believe they were the ramblings of dementia but he had not detected any confusion in Waldo's staring eyes when he spoke the words. At first, he was furious at Waldo who in those few words had negated all the positive assertions he had made over the years about being gay, assertions that Bill had clung to when he struggled with his own uncertainties and shame. Waldo, he believed, had lied to him. But then he thought, no, Waldo had not lied, Waldo had believed his own claims, had had to believe them in order to get up in the morning and confront a world in which, if being gay was not at least morally neutral, he would have been a freak, a mistake, or worse. It was only on his deathbed, stricken by the horror of AIDS, that his deception was revealed to him—*They were right. God hates fags*—and faithful to their friendship to the end, he had shared the revelation with Bill.

But why? It was far too late for Bill to change, even if that were possible, which it was not. The worm had eaten into his heart, the evil flowed in his veins, circulated in his breath. No, it wasn't a warning Waldo had shared in his last coherent moments but a curse. *You're next.*

"Billy," Nick said quietly, "people are starting to get seasick."

"Yeah, okay."

He walked the few steps to the stern, turned to the shivering mourners and shouted above the clanking engine, "Does anyone want to say anything?"

When no one responded, he turned to the water, unscrewed the top of the urn and poured the contents into the chop. For a moment, they made a glittery, lavender trail before they were submerged into the gray sea.

Bill whispered, "Goodbye."

The nightmares started the day after he had scattered Waldo's ashes in the sea. In one, he was walking down the hall of Ward 5B toward the room where Waldo had died and everyone he passed, patients, nurses, orderlies, bore the stigmata of AIDS; lesions and wasting and the slow death shuffle of the terminally ill. He paused at the door and his reluctance to enter was primal because he knew what he would find there. At last, he broke through his terror and plodded into the room where, as he had expected, it was he in the bed, not Waldo. The skeletal creature in the bed raised blind eyes toward Bill and whispered, "You did this to me."

"Bill!"

He woke with a gasp, Nick shaking him.

"You were shouting in your sleep."

Bill caught his breath. "Sorry, bad dream."

"Again?" Nick asked, worried. "Was it about Waldo?"

"Yeah." He felt the damp beneath him. Sweat. "Listen, I'm sorry, baby. You go back to sleep. I'm just going to get a glass of water."

As he closed the bedroom door behind him, he heard Nick said, "Bill, you need to talk to someone."

The apartment was still and cold. He went into the kitchen and switched on the light, then carefully dug around the bottles and canisters of household cleaners in the cabinet beneath the sink for the fifth of vodka he hid there. He drank it straight from the bottle, grateful for the burn. He capped it and put it back. Did Nick know about it? Or the other bottles he had squirreled around the house? If he did, he didn't say anything. But then Nick rarely spoke unless Bill asked him a question. At first, Bill thought Nick was giving him the silent treatment for some imagined offense, but the silences deepened and lengthened until the Nick he had first known, the awkward, cheerful chatterbox with a silly streak, completely disappeared into them. This new Nick was quiet and sad and compliant. He joylessly agreed to whatever Bill suggested, whether it was a restaurant or sex or one more night at home watching TV. Guiltily, Bill plied him with gifts, clothes, books, records, even, finally, a car so he could visit his family. Nick accepted them but the clothes went unworn, the books unread, the CDs unopened, and the car gathered parking tickets on the street. A dozen times a day, Bill wanted to scream, "What's wrong with you!" but he held his tongue. He knew what was wrong with Nick. He—Bill—was what was wrong with Nick. Nick was no longer his lover, but his shield against a loneliness that grew more fearsome with each new death of a friend or acquaintance. Nick was his hostage who, overwhelmed by Bill's need, had lost the ability to walk way. Only Bill could release him, but if he did, the loneliness would eat him alive.

Bill went into the bathroom where, before a mirror that ran the length of the vanity, he inspected himself for KS lesions, felt his lymph nodes, studied his tongue for signs of thrush, drew deep breaths to assure himself his lungs were clear and strong. When he finished he studied his face. Worry and fear had etched deep lines across his forehead and along the sides of his mouth. His hair was thinning, his chest and belly had begun to sag. He was only thirty-two but he looked ten years older. Soundlessly, he wept.

"It's just a cold," he snapped at Nick.

Bill was lying in bed, the sheets damp beneath him, wheezing and coughing. Nick stood over him anxious and exasperated.

"You can hardly breathe. You've got to go to the hospital."

Bill shook his head and tried another tack. "Listen, baby, let me rest today and if I'm not better tomorrow, I'll call my doctor, okay?"

Nick pursed his lips skeptically but said, "Okay. Are you hungry? I can warm up some soup."

"No, I just need to sleep. Don't worry about me."

When he woke up, it was dark and Nick was again standing over him, his expression more terror than worry. Bill tried to speak but could not catch his breath long enough to mumble even a few words.

"You've been asleep for twelve hours," Nick said. "I couldn't wake you up." He sat at the edge of the bed. "Don't get mad, but I called an ambulance. It's on its way." He touched Bill's hand. "Your breathing scared me. I didn't know what else to do."

By now, he was conscious enough to take stock of his condition, and having assessed it, understood the terror in Nick's eyes. His body felt brittle and barely clinging to sentience. His breath was a narrow thread of air as if he were submerged in water and breathing through a reed. From the roots of his hair to the tips of his fingers, he burned with fever. He slumped into the bed and closed his eyes as the sound of a siren approached.

He had last seen Dr. Owen in the emergency room where he had intervened at Bill's request to allow Waldo to see Eddie. Now Owen stood at the foot of his bed, medical chart in hand.

"It wasn't a flu, Bill, it was pneumonia."

"But it was the regular kind, right? Not the other kind."

Owen frowned. "Your chest X-rays are consistent with PCP."

"Are you one hundred percent sure?"

"Maybe not one hundred percent," Owen replied, "but there's not too much room for doubt and you need to prepare yourself."

"Prepare myself for what?" Bill said angrily. "To die? Is that what you're saying?"

"For other infections," Owen replied mildly, "if this is what we think it is."

"What you think it is. I don't think it was anything but a bad case of the flu."

Owen looked sympathetically at him. "Well, whatever it was, you're well enough to go home and let's both hope I don't see you in here again."

"You won't. I guarantee you."

But the day came when, pulling off his socks, he saw a raised, purple squiggle on the sole of his right foot. He knew immediately it wasn't a callous or a bruise. Gingerly, he ran his finger across it. There was no discomfort or pain. There was nothing, just the lesion, dark against the soft, pale flesh of his foot, mocking him. For a wild moment he considered grabbing a razor blade and cutting it off but that would accomplish nothing, solve nothing, end nothing. Others would follow, disfiguring his body and perhaps, as they had with Waldo, scabbing his internal organs until he wasted away. He raised his head, looked around the pleasantly furnished room, heard Nick singing to himself in the kitchen where he was frying hamburgers for dinner, watched the dusk settle in the sky beyond the dust-streaked windows. The thin black sock was still in his hand. He had not yet removed his tie. Everything seemed the same as it had been the moment before he had noticed the lesion, but it was all changed, for he had crossed from the world of the living to the world of the dying. He closed his eyes, thought about Nick whom he was now certain he had infected, remembered Waldo's last, gruesome moments of life, and began to make a plan.

17.

PLASTERED ACROSS THE FRONT PAGE of the *San Francisco Chronicle* was the headline: *Confederation CEO Arrested in Insurance Scam* accompanied by a photograph of a tall, middle-aged man in a beautifully cut suit being led away from an office building in handcuffs by two plainclothes police officers. I had been expecting something like this since that afternoon, six months earlier, when I had presented Ruth Fleming with indisputable evidence that Brendan Scott had forged most of the thirty insurance policies he had sold to Western States that she had given me to investigate. Still, the scale of the fraud was breathtaking, going far beyond one corrupt agent. According to the newspaper story, the scam had been devised by Confederation's top officers who had sent out secret (but not secret enough) memos to key agents across the country that had generated thousands and thousands of fake policies that were then resold to a half dozen of the biggest insurance companies.

Their motive was simple greed, a principle

that in the age of Reagan was celebrated as a positive virtue as long as you didn't get caught. The cash generated from the sale of the bogus policies inflated Confederation's profitability which, in turn, made it attractive to investors who snapped up its shares, driving them up on the stock exchange. When the shares reached their apex, company insiders, who were compensated in part by stock, sold them and reaped millions. Now, as the dust began to settle, there were losers everywhere: the other insurance companies stuck with the fabricated policies, the investors holding Confederation's worthless stock and Confederation's legitimate policy holders who had paid their premiums for years, decades, on policies that would never pay out.

For me, however, the most gruesome aspect of the fraud was what I encountered when I began to review the policies that Ruth Fleming had given me. Brendan Scott had written more than half of them for men who had already died from AIDS, one of them my rehab mate, Tom Rustin. His forged signature appeared on a policy for life insurance issued by Confederation Insurance two weeks after he had died. It was then I remembered the gay paper on Scott's desk opened to the obituaries and realized he had been trolling for victims for his scam.

I was so incensed that without telling Fleming or seeking her approval, I marched down to

Scott's agency, past his protesting secretary and into his office.

"We need to talk," I said.

Scott was too seasoned a salesman to be more than momentarily startled by my unexpected appearance. He quickly composed himself, put a friendly grin on his face, and said, "You know, I remember you work for Western States, but sorry, I've forgotten your name."

"Henry Rios," I said.

The grin broadened. "Right, right. Henry. You were in here asking about poor Bill Ryan. What can I do you for?"

I tossed a sheaf of photocopies of obituaries across his desk. "You can explain to me how these men signed up for life insurance with you after they were dead."

He thumbed through the pages, glanced up, shrugged and said, "I don't know what you're talking about."

I tossed him the signature pages of the applications he had filled out and signed for the dead men. "Maybe these will refresh your memory. You signed them, under penalty of perjury, attesting that all the information in the applications was true. But every one of these applicants was already dead. Perjury is the least of your problems."

He wasn't grinning anymore. "Close the door and sit down."

I shut the door, sat down and watched him

examine the signature pages with a furrowed brow. When he finished, he looked up and said, "Where did you get these?"

"Ruth Fleming. We're investigating all your recent sales of life insurance policies to Western States. I've looked at thirty so far, and only five of them are legitimate. Ten people you made up, the other ten are all men who died from AIDS in the last two years."

He plucked at the yellow suspender he wore to match his yellow tie, a calculating look on his broad, affable face.

"Ruth knows about this?"

"Not yet, but she will by the end of the day."

"Does she have to?" he asked.

"What do you mean?"

"You keep this quiet and there's something in it for you."

"You're offering me a bribe?" I said, incredulous. "Are you fucking serious? These men died a hideous death and then you come along and steal their good names to make a little money for yourself? You're a graverobber!"

"Hear me out. Yeah, I wrote policies for these guys and sold them to Western but it wasn't my idea. I was ordered to."

"Ordered by who?"

He leaned back his chair and his shoulders sagged as if he was unburdening himself of a heavy load. "It came down from the top. We were given quotas of policies to write for resale. The numbers were impossible but when I complained, that's when they told me that other agents were meeting it by writing these..."

"Fake policies?"

He nodded. "The company even flew me and a bunch of other agents to company HQ in Chicago and trained us in how to do it. I didn't want to, but what was I going to do? This place is my livelihood."

"You could have ratted out your company."

"After twenty years with them? I'm no whistleblower."

"No. You're a crook."

He glanced at me with distaste. "Screw you. I'm just a guy trying to make it through the day. I've been at this long enough to know that most people are dishonest. Most of them would have done what I did. You, too if you'd been in my position."

"Most people would have drawn the line at exploiting AIDS victims."

"I wasn't exploiting them. I was trying to help them."

That took me aback. "You were what?"

"The way this... process worked is that I wrote up the policies and resold them. For it to look legit, I had to make a claim every now and then, you understand?"

"You mean that you had to file a claim on one of your fake policies, saying that the insured had died, to make it look like these policies covered real people."

"Exactly," he said. "That's why I filed the claim on Bill's policy."

"Bill wasn't dead when you forged his name on the application?"

"In the beginning," he said, "I used whoever I could think of, including Bill, but when guys starting dying, I switched."

"How is that not exploitation?"

He strummed his suspenders again. "Most of these guys died with nothing. Nothing for their lovers or their friends. Or families, if they still had them. But if I filed a claim for them, and the claim paid out, there would be insurance money for their survivors."

I looked at him and shook my head incredulously. "So, what, now you're Robin Hood, stealing from the rich insurance companies to give to the survivors of guys who died from AIDS?"

"Yeah," he said. "Something like that."

"Except you personally profited from the scam," I said.

"I told you, I had to do it."

"And I told you, you didn't." I stood up. "Here's some free legal advice. Get yourself a good criminal lawyer, go to the authorities and cut a deal in exchange for your testimony against Confederation's higher ups."

"I'll go to jail."

"Yeah, probably, but for how long is up to you."

I left him slumped back in his chair, staring at the ceiling.

I folded the *Chronicle*, set it aside and had picked up the indictment against one of my clients that had come down the day before when a young voice spoke a tentative, "Mr. Rios?"

I looked up and saw Nick Trejo standing in the doorway, a backpack slung over one shoulder, smiling.

"There wasn't anyone at the front desk," he said, apologetically, "so I came down the hall to find you. Are you busy?"

"No. Come in, Nick. It's good to see you. How have you been?"

He loped into the office, dressed for the warm spring weather in shorts and a T-shirt, the arms of a sweatshirt tied around his shoulders. He had filled out in the six months since I had last seen him and from the look of his arms and chest it appeared he had been hitting the gym. His hair was cut short and his face, no longer hidden by its wild tumble, was settling into its adult lines, strong, sensitive and as handsome as those of his older brothers. But the change in him seemed rooted in something more than the passage of time. Clear-eyed and poised, he radiated confidence and calm.

"I'm really good, Mr. Rios," he replied, sitting

down across from me. "I'm back in school and living on my own."

I smiled. "Your mom let you move out?"

He grinned. "She said she couldn't wait to get rid of me but I know it was hard for her to let me go. As she constantly reminds me, I'm her baby."

"You look pretty grown up to me."

His expression became serious. "That happens when you know you might not be around that long."

I let the words settle between us. The sun smearing my grimy window cast his face in shadow. He was so young, so full of life that I couldn't bear the implications of what he had just said.

"Have you been tested?" I asked gently.

He slowly shook his head. "No. I figure I'm positive because of Bill, but something about having that confirmed..." His voice trailed off.

"A lot of guys feel that way."

"It's not so much me, but my family. They're so happy to have me back. I want them to enjoy it without having to worry it won't last. Does that make sense?"

"I'm sorry you even have to make those calculations at your age."

He shifted a bit in his chair, looked past me and out of the window before answering. "You know the quote that goes something like, nothing focuses the mind like the prospect of being hanged?" He met my eyes. "It's true. The last few months I had to sit down with myself and figure out what was important to me and what I really wanted to accomplish while I could. My mom couldn't help me with that. My brothers or sister, either. As much as they love me, these were decisions only I could make because in the end, it's my life."

"You really have grown up. I've just got to that point and I'm ten years older than you."

He laughed, then asked, quietly, "What about you, Mr. Rios? Have you been tested?"

"A couple of weeks ago. I'm waiting for the results."

He nodded. "Why did you decide to go for it?"

"My friend Larry sort of shamed me into it when I told him I was afraid of the results."

Fear is an acronym, Henry. It can be either Fuck Everything And Run—or Face Everything And Recover. Which is it going to be?

"Everyone's afraid," Nick said. "You can feel it in the streets."

"That's what I told him. He reminded me there's no magic in the test. My status is a fact that getting tested or not getting tested won't change, so ultimately, I'm afraid of reality, and that's pointless. He also offered to take the test the same time as me."

Nick digested this and said, "Maybe I *should* get tested."

"You've got good reasons not to."

We were silent a moment, then he said, "I came by to thank you."

"Thank me? For what?"

"For screwing everything up!" He laughed. "For getting into my business and upsetting my family. For forcing me to face reality. I was in shock after Bill died."

"That's understandable."

He became somber. "No, Mr. Rios, with all due respect, you don't understand. Not everything."

I leaned toward him. "What do you mean, Nick?"

"I'm going to tell you something I haven't told anyone else," he said softly. "Not even my family. You have to promise me you won't repeat it."

"You have my word."

He took a deep breath. "I knew what Bill was going to do that night. I agreed to it."

I stared across my desk at the handsome young man who met my gaze without flinching. "Are you telling me you knew Bill wanted to kill himself and you?"

He nodded. "After he found out he had KS he told me we had AIDS. He talked about how much Waldo had suffered and that that's all we had to look forward to. He couldn't stop talking about how horrible it would be and then I'd walk down Castro and see these guys, no older than me, emaciated and covered with lesions, walking with canes or in wheelchairs. My world was so small by then. It was just Bill and me, really. I was barely talking to my family and I couldn't tell them I had AIDS. So, when Bill started talking about suicide, I couldn't come up with any good arguments against it. I know that sounds strange but like I said, I was isolated and terrified. Plus, being the youngest in my family, I always did what the grownups told me and Bill was the grownup in our relationship."

"Bill had been manipulating you for a long time. If you felt isolated and terrified, it was because that's where he wanted you. To keep you close."

He looked down. "I understand that now." He met my eyes. "I've been seeing a therapist. When I told her about my relationship with Bill, she told me he had abused me and I got really mad." He half-smiled. "Not at Bill, at her."

"Why?"

"I thought what Bill and I had was what all gay relationships were like because Bill was my first. I had nothing to compare it to and no idea of my own how things were supposed to work."

"Yeah," I said. "I can see that. We don't have roadmaps."

"Plus," Nick added, "Bill really did love me, in his own way. He wasn't a bad man."

"Nick, he tried to talk you into killing yourself."

"I know, but even then..." His voice slipped and he paused to compose himself. "He thought he was protecting me from a worse death. I'm not saying what he did was right because it wasn't.

All I'm saying is that in his mind he thought he was doing a good thing."

"But you didn't go through with it," I pointed out. "What happened?"

"I decided I wanted to live," he replied firmly. "The plan was we would take sleeping pills and he would turn on the gas and we would die in our sleep. I didn't swallow the pills he gave me and when he wasn't looking, I spat them out. We got into bed and he held me tight. He told me how much he loved me, how happy he had been with me and that soon we would be happy together forever. He drifted off to sleep. By then, the apartment was filled with gas. I forced myself out of bed and called my brother, Sal. You know the rest."

"Did you try to rouse him?"

He bit his lip and shook his head. "I went back to say goodbye." He threw me an anguished look. "He wanted to die, Mr. Rios. Should I have tried to wake him up? Did I kill him?"

This, I understood, was the reason he had told me the story.

"No, Nick," I said immediately, crisply. "You did not kill Bill Ryan. He killed himself. That's not on you. You understand?"

His eyes glistened with tears. He murmured a relieved, "Thank you, Mr. Rios."

"I mean it, Nick, it's not on you. Not legally, not morally, not in any way."

He nodded.

"You said you been thinking about what you want to do with your life," I said after a moment. "What have you decided?"

He accepted the change of subject gratefully. "Finish up at school."

"And then?"

Shyly, he said, "I've always dreamed of being a writer. Is that crazy?"

"I look forward to reading your first book."

He got up, extended his hand. "Thank you for everything, Mr. Rios."

I got up, came around my desk and pulled him into my arms. "Good luck, Nick."

He whispered back, "You too, Henry."

I never saw him again. Years later, I was walking around the National Mall in Washington where the AIDS Memorial Quilt had been unfurled, each panel bearing the name of someone who had died. I came across a sky-blue panel. Stitched across it in green lettering were the words *Nick* and beneath it *Manito*—little brother. I've often wondered if it was him.

I remember in law school having been exposed to gonorrhea and taking the train to San Francisco to get tested in one of the city's free VD clinics. The clinic was located in a blocky building constructed of unpainted concrete bricks on a side street in the Castro. While its outward appearance was grim, the waiting room inside was filled with other gay men chatting and joking and cruising as if we were in a bar rather than a medical office.

"You again," the male receptionist said to a handsome man checking in with him. "I'm beginning to think you get the clap to have a reason to come and see me."

The other guy said, "I wouldn't have to if you'd go out with me."

I had been astonished at how casually the other men regarded exposure to an STD while I, embarrassed and guilt-ridden, hid behind a magazine and waited for my fake name to be called.

"Number four twenty four."

The nurse's voice broke into my recollections, returning me to the waiting room where the half-dozen other men sat silently, each lost in his own thoughts, our eyes never meeting. The party was definitely over.

"Yes," I said, rising. "That's me."

"Come with me."

A middle-aged man lifted his head, smiled, and gave me a quick thumb's up as I passed through the door that separated the waiting room from the examination rooms. I followed the nurse to the end of a short, fluorescently lit hall where she deposited me in an office. There, a bearded man in a white coat told me to sit. No names were given by anyone, as if the entire process had to be shrouded in secrecy.

He opened a file on the desk, glanced at it, and said, "Your test is negative."

I simply stared at him.

He smiled. "Yeah, I know. You expected something else. Most men do. But it's negative. That's good news. Breathe."

I blurted out, "Why?"

"Why what?"

"Why am I negative? I took as many risks as the other guys sitting out there in your waiting room."

He studied me for a moment, his eyes unreadable. "Why? It's a statistical fact that not everyone exposed to the virus will become infected. I know that's probably not what you're asking, but I can't give you another answer. I can't give any of you another answer to that question. Now," he continued briskly, "let's talk about how you're going to stay negative, okay?"

I left the clinic and stepped out of its windowless confines into a bright spring afternoon. As I walked down 17th Street, I noticed the flowering bushes and the translucent green of new leaves of the trees above me, the stubborn blades of grass pushing their way through the cracks in the sidewalk, the spill of color from a garden, and the birdsong that persisted just beneath the rumble of traffic and human activity. Life. I noticed life. Mine had just been given back to me. Until that moment, I hadn't realized how resigned I had been to dying. But I wasn't going to die, at least not from AIDS. I wish I could say I felt unmitigated joy, but I thought of the guy in waiting room who had given me the thumb's up. He would have received his diagnosis by now. Which side of the statistics had he fallen on? How happy are you supposed to feel when you dodge a bullet only to see it splatter the head of the man next to you in the trenches? I needed an adult perspective.

I searched for a payphone to call Larry Ross. His secretary no longer asked me what I was calling for and put me through.

"I tested negative," I said, not even bothering to greet him.

There was a small pause before he said, "Thank God."

And then, in a phone booth on Market Street on a sunny spring day, I began to sob. Really sob. It was a sign of the times that no one who walked by seemed to notice.

"I don't even know why I'm crying," I stuttered.

"It's gratitude, Henry. The slate is clear now. You got sober and you tested negative. You've been given a second chance at life."

"Then why do I feel so fucking miserable?"

"Because you have a heart," he said, "and you know not everyone is going to get that second chance."

There was something in his voice, a tiny twist

of regret, and then I remembered that he would also have received his results today.

"Larry, what about you? Have you got your results?"

Calmly, he said, "I tested positive."

"Oh, no!"

"It's like I told you before," he said. "Our status was going to be what it was whether or not we took the test. The only thing that's changed is now we know for sure. It's always better for alcoholics like us to face reality than to live in the fear of the unknown."

It seemed he was trying to convince himself of this as much as me.

"What will you do?"

He managed a small laugh. "Have you learned nothing from sitting in AA meetings? One day at a time. Take it easy. Let go, let God. This too shall pass. Stuff they didn't teach at law school. It'll come in handy now. What will you do?"

I heard myself say, to my immense surprise, "I'm moving to L.A."

"You're what?"

Although the thought had just occurred to me, I knew it was what I had to do.

"There's nothing keeping me here," I said. "A basement apartment. A small practice that doesn't seem to be going anywhere. I like L.A. There'd be more opportunity for me and, honestly, San Francisco is filled with ghosts."

"Are you doing this because you have some crazy idea you can rescue me?"

"No," I replied. "Well, not entirely. I want to be near you, that's true, but that's not why. You said I have a second chance at life. I believe you. I want a fresh start. I want to see the sun rise in a different sky. Is that so hard to understand?"

"You know you can't run away from yourself."

"I'm not trying to," I said. "I'm not running away, I'm running towards."

"Towards what?"

"I won't know until I get there, will I?"

There was a long silence on his end and then he said, "In that case, Henry, welcome to L.A."

AUTHOR'S NOTE

There is no single story of how the AIDS epidemic swept through the gay male community in the 1980s and I make no claim that this novel is anything other than one, fictional version. I was born in 1954 so, of course, I lived through the era but my experience was rather different than Rios's. I lived in Los Angeles in the early '80s, not in San Francisco, and the full impact of the epidemic came a little later to L.A. than to San Francisco which truly was, along with New York, the front lines.

To reconstruct what it was like to be in San Francisco in those years—between 1981-1984—I consulted the invaluable archives at the city's GLBT Historical Society. They contain, among other material, the diaries and journals of ordinary gay men who died during the plague. Reading them brought that world back to me, and what was most interesting was how ordinary life went on despite the emergence of AIDS. There is a famous poem by W.H. Auden called *Musee des Beaux Arts* that begins:

About suffering they were never wrong,
The old Masters: how well they understood
Its human position: how it takes place
While someone else is eating or opening a
window or just walking dully along...

Those lines capture what I discovered in those journals and diaries—that life with its mundane obligations and sentiments went on in the shadow of AIDS. Thus, in an entry in one of these diaries the writer is hospitalized for what appears to be a bout of pneumocystis pneumonia, one of the harbingers of AIDS and then, a dozen pages later, out of the hospital, in another entry he moons over a cute boy he spots at the gym and berates himself for not working up the nerve to say hello. I found passages like this to be almost unbearably moving. They reminded me forcefully, viscerally, that what is now passing into history, into the official record as statistics, chronologies and judgments began in the bodies of young men who wanted for themselves what most people want and not least of all to love and to be loved.

Reading these innocent scrawls in dime store notebooks I was reminded, too, that they and I, then also young, lived in a country where such aspirations were jeered at by the majority. A recent book about the changing attitudes toward LGBTQ people notes that as late as 1987, "the General Social Survey found that 78 percent of the American public thought that same-sex relations were 'Always Wrong.'" (Garretson, *The Path to*

Gay Rights (New York University Press, 218) p. 3.) The disapproval of the majority, even before the epidemic, manifested itself in aggressions both macro and micro. At several points in this novel, I have tried to capture the attitudes toward gay men at the time which ranged from suspicion to disdain to outright hatred. Needless to say, these attitudes, coupled with the virtual invisibility of the gay and lesbian community (as it was then known) in mainstream media and the pervasive and unrelenting celebration of heterosexuality could be morally and psychologically isolating if you were gay or lesbian. It's hard for any human being to be hated for something that he or she cannot change and even those who are strong enough to resist the hatred as irrational cannot help but be damaged by it. Those who lack this strength, which is probably most of us, can be driven into the darkness of self-destructive thought and behavior out of which they may never emerge.

The onset of the epidemic only increased the burden of difference, not only for gay men but for lesbian women as well, because it empowered all the old lies that had been told about all of us from time immemorial. The modest political and social gains we had made in the late 1970s seemed on the verge of extinction. It was a desolate season, but as it turned out, it was only a season. Hopelessness gave way to anger and out of that anger a community organized itself to, in the words of the most famous of its factions, act up and fight back. That fight changed America in ways that are not yet fully appreciated because they continue to unfold. In this new dark age in which we find ourselves, let that resistance provide a template for how evil may yet be overcome.

Michael Nava

CPSIA information can be obtained
at www.ICGtesting.com
Printed in the USA
LVHW111512131119
637245LV00003B/645/P